THEY NEEDED FRESH WEAPONS FOR THE ENDLESS WAR. OF COURSE, SOME EXPERIMENTS FAILED...

Ch'en-Gordon, pain and weakness in every seam, lurches between tables, falls to macro-knees, elbows resting on the table of the two blacks. Se looks into eyes of the man, hir mouth opens and shuts trying to cry for aid. The black looks pityingly, uncomprehendingly.

Se moans, hir mouth falling open on the table, spiremes emerging, writhing, screaming mutely to be understood.

Ch'en-Gordon falls from the fakewood table, clatters onto the floor, hir seams open. Dark fluids rush out.

The black shoves his pipe into his pocket and takes his companion, her face buried in his coat, quickly from the room.

RICHARD A. LUPOFF

A DELL BOOK

Published by
Dell Publishing Co., Inc.
1 Dag Hammarskjold Plaza
New York, New York 10017

Portions of this work first appeared in
different form as follows:

"With the Bentfin Boomer Boys on Little Old New Alabama"
in AGAIN, DANGEROUS VISIONS edited by Harlan Ellison,
Doubleday & Company, Inc., 1972.
"Our Own Little Mardi Grass" in *Heavy Metal* magazine, 1977.

"After the Dreamtime" in NEW DIMENSIONS IV edited by
Robert Silverberg, New American Library, 1974.

"Sail the Tide of Mourning" in *New Dimensions 5*
edited by Robert Silverberg, Harper & Row, Publishers, Inc.,
1975.

"The Bentfin Boomer Girl Comes Through"
in *Amazing Stories* magazine, 1977.

ISBN: 0-440-16292-0

Printed in the United States of America
First printing—June 1978

SPACE WAR BLUES

Introduction

SAILING THE DARK WITH THE BENTFIN BOOMER BAPPA ZAPPA KID

It's crazy to think so, I know it's not true, but so help me God, I imagine sometimes that I've spent the entirety of my life involved with this book. Waking in the moment of shattered silver dreaming, sometime past moonlight, cold with fear and cobwebbed with free-floating guilt, I hear demon voices echoing in my head, "Where is the introduction to Lupoff's book?" And in the background, other demon voices demanding, "Where is *Again, Dangerous Visions*?" and "You screwed me out of millions at Dell!"

I rush to the bathroom, douse my face with icy water and hang tremblingly over the wash basin, trying to catch my breath, trying to flense the sounds from my brain. And not till morning, when reality rings my telephone and knocks on my door, am I free to live my life unumbilicized with this book and its editor and, most of all, its author. Oh, God, to be free of it all!

There are at least four people in the world who will attest to my decency as a human being (affidavits on file with this publisher available on request). I contribute to good causes, support my indigent friends, scratch the flea-spots behind dogs' ears, have even read a Taylor Caldwell novel without losing my lunch.

Why then, oh why, must I lurch on through life bearing the Sisyphean weight of this novel?

Clearly, somewhere along the way I have polluted the hell out of my karma.

In nowhichway did I suspect, back in 1969, when Richard Lupoff first contacted me about this story in its primal form, that I would be inheriting a dark destiny of anguish and *angst*. Had I known, I would have fled to Ultima Thule, or perhaps someplace even more desolate, like Billings, Montana.

But I was only the first person to resonate to the song this excellent novel sings. In that primacy of perception lies all the justification for the subsequent *agita*. Because *Space War Blues* (which I will *always* think of as "With the Bentfin Boomer Boys on Little Old New Alabama" no matter *how* many commercially-oriented titles are slapped on it) is an extraordinary piece of writing. It was apparent when I saw the first pages Dick Lupoff sent me for *Again, Dangerous Visions*; and it is even more apparent now, in the totality you've just bought.

But in 1969, this novel had had a very different history than the one that followed its appearance in *A,DV*.

The publishing world is filled with classic stories of fine novels that had a hard time finding homes. One can only wonder what mass lunacy prevails when James Jones's *From Here to Eternity* is rejected not once or twice, but over thirty times by different (one would assume knowledgeable) publishers. Or what is one to make of the initial rejections of Alex Haley's *Roots*, Richard Bach's *Jonathan Livingston Seagull*, or Mika Waltari's brilliant historical novel, *The Egyptian*, which (in its American translation) was rejected somewhere between twenty-eight and thirty-six times?

To say that Dick Lupoff's *Space War Blues* had a history of rejection is in no way to denigrate it. Sir Arthur Conan Doyle's finest story of Sherlock Holmes, *A Study in Scarlet,* was bounced four times before someone had the sense to buy it. Mr. James Payn of *The Cornhill* kept it a month, thought it "capital," but rejected it, as did a gentleman named Arrowsmith, who saw it next. And two more, before Doyle found a publisher whose wife read the novel and demonstrated better taste than the male editors of her time by urging her husband to buy it. Which he did: all rights, for £24. Margaret Mitchell submitted *Gone With the Wind* under its original title, *Mules in Horse's Harness,* to twenty-one prospective buyers, if legend is correct, before it was accepted by Macmillan. Thomas Wolfe, Herman Wouk and William Faulkner were all summarily turned down when they submitted their initial writings. Hemingway's *A Farewell to Arms* was rejected repeatedly. During his lifetime, Edgar Allan Poe was unable to find a single publisher who would take the risk of issuing his tales in regular volume form; and so Poe published them himself in pamphlet form, at one bit each—12½¢—and if one could lay one's hands on such a pamphlet these days, it would cost between four and five hundred dollars.

Which is not to equate any claim on posterity shared by the foregoing with *Space War Blues,* but only to lay a groundwork for the sad and sorry tale of discouragement and rejection that attended this fine book's birth.

In 1966, the late James Blish prodded Lupoff into writing his first novel, *One Million Centuries.* Lupoff's grounding in fiction, up till that time, had been in early twentieth-century fiction, the sort of novels Edgar Rice Burroughs himself would have read. But in 1967 there was an upheaval in the genre of the fantastic, and Lupoff recalls that much of the ennui and insularism generated from the reading of science fiction of the period was blown away with the shock waves produced by anthologies of experimental writing. He notes Judith Merril's *England Swings SF* and my own *Dangerous Visions* as eye-openers. I bow gratefully.

Intrigued by the intersilient portals to Wonderland this "new wave" revealed, Lupoff decided to try his hand at the game by way of getting into a second novel. And so, in 1967, he wrote the first three chapters of what was to become "With the Bentfin Boomer Boys on Little Old New Alabama."

Experimental in style, far-flung in concept, it was a vast departure for the Lupoff of that time: thirty-two years old, twelve years in the computer business, still three years away from a commitment to full-time freelance writing, married and the father of three children, Lupoff hardly seemed—to himself or to his auctorial contemporaries—a likely candidate for the position of Wildly Innovative Novelist. But he wrote the first three chapters, and he sent them off.

To his friend Terry Carr, who was, at the time, editor of the Specials series at Ace Books. A logical target for first submission: Carr and Lupoff had known each other for years and had been science fiction fans during the same period, and it was Ace that was about to publish the paperback edition of Lupoff's 1965 hagiography, *Edgar Rice Burroughs: Master of Adventure*.

Carr hated it.

Now unsure of the worth of the story, having had it

bounced by an editor who, by all counts, should have been well disposed to its innovative nature, Lupoff dropped his sights considerably and sent the section off to Lancer Books, which had just released *One Million Centuries.* Lancer was a paperback outfit with a splendid editor but run by a publisher whose business ethics had been (not to put too fine an edge to the remark) pluperfectly Watergatian. Larry Shaw, Lancer's editor, was—and is—a professional with excellent taste and a keen eye for new talent. I say this not only because Larry Shaw was the first editor to buy a story from me, but because this has been the judgment of his editing throughout the field for thirty years.

Nonetheless, Shaw hated it.

That made two rejections, neither of which had come from paperback publishers of Olympian reputation. Lupoff's reluctant conclusion: the story must stink.

Seeking vindication of the work, Lupoff sent the three chapters to his agent, Henry Morrison. Sounds of teeth chattering in the background. But surely one's own agent, heir to ten percent of one's creative life, helpmeet and friend while one toiled in the fields of literature—surely such a person would succor and assist in maintaining.

Morrison hated it. Returned the manuscript and labeled it "unmarketable." It was now 1968, and Lupoff was into other projects. He tossed the portion into a drawer and thought of it, if he thought of it at all, as a "perpetual orphan." Lupoff's phrase.

Pause for a moment.

I have no hard data to confirm this supposition, but my gut and my skin tell me that there has never been a human being since circa 3500 B.C., when the oldest known written text—pictographs of Sumerian speech, the Gilgamesh epic—was placed in the Temple of Inanna, who has not believed in his or her secret heart that he or she is a writer. The occupation looks both easy and remunerative . . . from the outside. The greener grass. Same color as fame and money.

But there isn't one of those garage mechanics, computer programmers, secretaries, plumbers, taxi drivers, law enforcement officers, airline pilots or politicians who could stand a week of the insecurity. Nine to five, steady paycheck, regular meals on the table, decent clothes for the kids . . . that's what separates free-lance writers from the rest of normal humanity. Because writers are like Willy Loman, out there on "a smile and a shoeshine." Living on ideas. Going from word to word. Nothing is ever certain, nothing is ever really firm. And every time out it's a new roll of the dice. Even the best of us, the most famous, the ones whose names alone can sell a manuscript, even they crap out from time to time.

And so writers cannibalize themselves. Not merely feeding off the experiences of their lives to inform the stories they write, but psychologically, as well: reassuring themselves that the work is solid, sustaining themselves from that inner pool of strength, reaffirming their faith in the only God they know—the validity of their talent. It is the only thing they can permit themselves to worship. Without it, the fear and the insecurity generated by being at the whim of editorial selection would kill them as dead as a manuscript in Middle English.

The days between mailing out a story and the editor's response are certainly the emotional equivalent of the terrain Dante mapped as the Eighth Circle of Hell. A constant, all-pervading sense of imbalance. A low-level trepidation. The nerve ends and the muscles fibrillate as with nicotine hunger. Rotten to those around you. Start at unexpected sounds. Pick fights. Surly, sleepless, anxious. No, the writers-who-never-write couldn't stand the gaff. They'd pack it in and rush back to their sinecures.

Because a writer is always alone with the dreams. And when the dreams are rejected, there is a time when the God is up for question. Those who see the greener grass in a writer's territory never understand that terror.

Thus: see Lupoff, 1968, trying to break in as a full-time writer, his first novel published to vast disinterest and a minimum of recompense by a borderline paperback house, his second start turned down not only by editors, but by the man who was supposed to be his good right hand. In the drawer, the beginning of a dream, now called a "perpetual orphan." The Eighth Circle of Hell.

Early in July of 1968, Richard Lupoff happened across a mention in one of the many fan-produced amateur journals of my preparations for a sequel to *Dangerous Visions*. On July 8th he wrote me, in part, "I hear you're working on another volume like *Dangerous Visions*; if that's true, I'd appreciate your reading the enclosed material. It is the first chapter of a long story I started some time ago, and if you think it suitable for your book, I'll resume work on the thing.

"Problem is, everybody likes it except the right people. Chip Delany is enthusiastic about it; Jack Gaughan thinks it's great; Bob Silverberg likes it. But of course none of them are in a position to *buy* it. And it really is a dangerous vision, as you'll see.

"Terry Carr says he likes it 'but . . .' Larry Shaw

hates it. And my agent, Henry Morrison, says, 'Why don't you write a nice comprehensible story like *One Million Centuries.*' "

I answered Richard's letter three months later. The reason for my tardiness is lost in a decade of memories, and consider his state of mind during those three months . . . waiting. But I did answer on October 9th, and told him "the story-thus-far fascinates and compels me. . . . I would be favorably disposed to buying the story."

He responded with pleasure, advised me there was some more material intended for insertion later in the story, sent me the sections, and we entered into a protracted correspondence about possible directions and expansions of the basic idea. My part in the game was one of suggester to Lupoff's suggestee. Nothing any nobler or more creative than that done by *any* conscientious editor who understands that it is the *work* that demands love and composure and attention to detail, even when the human beings involved in its creation are suffering.

But from that point on, the story and its author had a shield from the fear and trembling.

On February 9, 1969, I received the manuscript of "Bentfin Boomer Boys." There was nervousness and reserve in Richard's letter of submission. It came in at 35,000 words.

Then there was more delay on my part. I kept him waiting for a decision—unintentionally, but nonetheless unforgivably—through February, March and half of April.

The Eighth Circle revisited.

On April 15th, I received a letter, reproduced *in toto* here:

April 15, 1969

Dear Harlan,

It's reached the point where I don't know what to say any more; I feel as if I've said it all, not only that I've said it all but that I've said it all, over and over again. So what's left to do?

Shall I plead, demand, threaten, complain, bluster, curse?

Should I review the history of this thing? You know it as well as I do.

Should I remind you of all the promises and assurances you've given me, that you have then left in shreds? You know about those things too.

Should I appeal to your professional pride by pointing out how very <u>un</u>professional it is to become known for making commitments and then ignoring them? Or should I get very personal and contrast the way I went through contortions to save your place in "All in Color," with the shabby treatment I have received in return?

I'm really at my wits' end. What the hell are you trying to do to me, Harlan? If I were a little more paranoid I would think that this was some kind of subtle and elaborate plot.

Dick

PS (8:45 PM)

I wasn't kidding -- the above is only the most recent in a long series of letters variously pleading, demanding, threatening, etc. What can I say <u>now</u> -- I'm delighted that you like the story. [Like, like? He said he <u>loves</u> it!. That's something so precious that I'm scared to repeat it for fear that it will turn unreal.]

I'll hold off any polishing-type changes of my own until I get your letter; then I'll do the whole thing including the glossary.

Meanwhile -- goshwow!

Yippee!!

W-h-e-e-e-e-e-e-e!!!!!!!!!!!!

W - H - E - E - E - E - E - E - E - E - E - E ! ! ! ! ! ! !

What had happened, of course, was that I'd gotten boxed in with my own writing, personal problems, business that couldn't be shunted aside, and had let "less pressing" matters slide. But I'd called him on the very day when he'd written the letter, and had conveyed my wild enthusiasm for the story.

In an instant, just like that, how fragile writers can be, it had all gotten better. Wounds and stigmata miraculously healed; soul taken flight to soar; Daedalus, never Icarus; the God back on its throne; the talent vindicated. In a moment.

There was more interchange of correspondence, suggestions for a new chapter, acceptance of the suggestions by the author, a check sent, contracts signed, and in a June 8th letter from him, an effulgent glow of sunlight and bright hopes. He was in the clear and running. His work was being bought.

By January of 1970, Richard and his family were making ready to leave Poughkeepsie and IBM to move to the West Coast, where Richard was intending to set up shop as a full-time writer.

All through January and February Richard and I worked on polishing and expanding the story. Understand something: when I say *I* worked on "Bentfin Boomer Boys," I want you to clearly understand that it was analogous to a child in a candy store wanting a tiddle of this and a tad of that. The story was *so* good, *so* rich, *so* innovative, that I really didn't want it to end. And so I would keep suggesting scenes to Lupoff. It was obvious he loved the story, too. He kept writing the scenes. It grew in length. Our pleasure and mutual joy in it also grew.

But a worm was gnawing its way into our apple.

As a matter of course (and not coincidentally, I suspect, to imply "I told you so") Richard had sent a carbon of the story to Henry Morrison, the agent who had called "Bentfin Boomer Boys" unmarketable. You'll pardon the bemused expression on my face as I write this, but as if he had had an epiphany, Morrison now saw the story as eminently marketable. I will make no snide comments about his editorial perceptivity, nor will I comment on such interesting human character traits as venality, opportunism and cupidity. I will merely observe that Morrison immediately fired off the carbon to Gail Wendroff at Dell Books. Gail was the editor, having recently moved over from Belmont Books, a publisher of whom it can be said that trying to carry on ethical business dealings with them is like trying to run an alligator farm on the honor system.

Yet even Gail, who was generally a superlative editor, had difficulty recognizing the value of "Bentfin Boomer Boys." After reading the manuscript as submitted by Morrison, she rejected it, saying, "I don't understand why you sent this to me. Are you angry about something . . . or is this a bad joke?"

Morrison urged her to read it again, and resubmitted it.

Days passed. Then she called Morrison and said she'd been wrong, had read it too hurriedly, had been so deluged with junk manuscripts of a familiar style and content that she had not opened herself to Lupoff's unusual technique. But now, she said, "it is the best manuscript I've ever read." And she wanted to buy it, expand it by a mere five thousand words and publish it as a "slim novel."

There was only one problem. She didn't want it to appear in *Again, Dangerous Visions*. Reasoning (illogically) that a prior appearance of so much of the book's material in an anthology would cripple the sale of the paperback, she made her purchase contingent on my releasing the story. She offered very good money.

Gail's position was wrongheaded, as time has proved. At least half a dozen stories published as originals in *Dangerous Visions* and *Again, Dangerous Visions* have garnered so much praise and attention that they have been successfully expanded to full book-length, and their sale, grounded in the popularity of the *DV* books, has been uniformly good. Quite the opposite of Gail Wendroff's fear has been shown to be the reality. Rather than dulling the potential market value of a story, the *DV* books have served as widely-noted showcases, and the spectacular stories have demonstrated a viability apart from the anthologies.

(In this regard I cite, with considerable pride, Robert Silverberg's "Flies" that went through a transmogrification and became the novel *Thorns*; Ursula Le Guin's "The Word for World Is Forest" that has been published, unexpanded, as a "slim novel"; David Gerrold's "With a Finger in My I," which acquired sufficient fame to be used as the title story of his collection; and such stories as "Riders of the Purple Wage" by Philip José Farmer, "Faith of Our Fathers" by Philip K. Dick and Samuel R. Delany's ". . . Aye, and Gomorrah," which have been reprinted again and again.)

Much of this was already history when Gail Wendroff made her judgment; she should have known better. But she didn't; and so Morrison, whose voice, unlike that of the turtle's, had not been heard in the land during the year-plus that Lupoff and I breathed life into "Bentfin Boomer Boys," dangled the belated bait in front of Lupoff. Richard and his family were about to undergo a major change in their lives, were about to set forth into the no-man's-land of insecurity wherein all writers abide, and the offer from Dell looked good. Too good to resist. And so, on February 3rd, 1970, I received the telegram on page 22.

Oh my God, the moral quandary.

Locked on the horns of a situation that had no equitable solution. I had no desire to stand in the way of Richard's making his first big novel sale to a major publisher. No one knew better than I how much he had suffered with that book, how long he had waited for the big break, how tempting such an offer could look to a man about to *schlep* himself and his family and his life into the Great Unknown. If I held to the letter of our contract, it was guaranteed that Dell would pass.

But then there was *Again, Dangerous Visions* and its forty-one other authors, many of whom were unknowns breaking into print for the first time. Understand (as I tried to make Richard understand): the *DV* books are community projects. By using the lure of big names, a wider audience is drawn to the work of those who might otherwise never be noticed. It is a gestalt, every element contributing to the commonweal. Writers of the stature of Sturgeon and Blish and Bradbury and Ballard serve not only as significant contributors in their own right, but serendipitously as loss leaders to get readers to read James Hemesath and Edward Bryant and Joan Bernott and Ken McCullough.

Sturgeon had already turned down *Playboy's* two-thousand-dollar offer to publish his *DV* story in their pages before the anthology was released. Ted understood and chose to pass up desperately needed money to hold faith with the young writers whose careers were linked with *Dangerous Visions*. There were oth-

western union **Telegram**

232P PST FEB 3 70 LA313
SYA479 SY PKA165 JM LONG PDF POUGHKEEPSIE NY 3 402P EST
HARLAN ELLISON
3484 COY DR SHERMAN OAK CALIF
DEAR HARLAN I HAVE HAD A VERY HIGH OFFER FOR RIGHTS TO DO BENTFIN
BOOMERS AS A PAPERBACK ORIGINAL WITH OPTION FOR ALMOST CERTAIN
HARD COVER AND PUBLISHER INTENTION TO PROMOTE BOOK AS A MAJOR
LITERARY EVENT, OFFER IS CONDITIONAL UPON WITHDRAWAL FROM THE
AGAIN DANGEROUS VISIONS. MY REPLY YOU HAVE BOTH LEGAL AND MORAL
CLAIM TO STORY AND I WILL NOT BUDGE WITHOUT YOUR PERMISSION.
IF YOU RELEASE I WILL PROMPTLY OFFER SHORT STORY REPLACEMENT
NO OBLIGATION TO YOU. AS BOOMER BOOK WILL BE DEDICATED TO
YOU. PLEASE THINK THIS OVER FOR A COUPLE OF DAYS AND I WILL
PHONE OR IF YOU PREFER CALL ME COLLECT
DICK LUPOFF
(422).

SF-1201 (R5-69)

ers who had had similar experiences: Barry Malzberg, Tom Disch, Kurt Vonnegut. They had all responded to the lofty intent of *DV* and *A,DV*.

I spoke to Richard at length. I told him I was hamstrung, but that I could not, in good conscience, allow him to pull the story. It was, additionally, a large chunk out of the book: over forty thousand words. He was bitter about my decision. I cannot fault him for his feelings. But I promised him, I swore solemnly that I would undertake to get "Bentfin Boomer Boys" published as a book, by Dell if I could somehow finagle it.

He did not think much of my oath.

Dell withdrew its offer.

Then began a period of terrible rancor between Richard and me. Word leaked out that I had screwed him out of a fat deal at Dell, and the fan press thrust its collective snout into the already bubbling soup of discontent. Public utterances were made. Vicious letters were exchanged. *A,DV* was delayed because of its size and the complexity of the project, and Richard grew even more furious. He had been shafted, and now the story was being held back from public view a year, two years. At one point, in a letter dated just about the time Doubleday was putting *A,DV* on the presses, Richard quite correctly pointed out that my contractual hold on the story was about to expire. I wrote back in a white rage and told him that yes, the option would run out just about the time the book was printed, and he had every right, at that time, to yank the story; and if he wanted to do it, he should goddam well go ahead and do it!

He didn't. Thank God.

Again, Dangerous Visions was published in 1972 and "Bentfin Boomer Boys" drew more attention and analysis than any story in the book with the exception of Ursula's. But as dynamite as Ursula's short novel was—eventually it was a Hugo winner—the true purpose of *A,DV* in breaking editorial taboo barriers was better served by Lupoff's wonderful story. It was, for me, the essence of that book.

After *A,DV* came out, I tried to sell the story as a book. As I'd promised. But it didn't happen.

Years went by, and Richard and I did not speak.

Occasionally the background to "Bentfin Boomer Boys"' publication in *A,DV* came up in the fan press; neither of us was particularly charitable to the other in these encounters. It was animosity.

Several years ago, the anger passed into history. We got together. He did a very ethical thing when we crossed paths on a television deal. We met again. We had dinners. We talked. It was tenuous, but we could be polite to each other without stomach cramps. And the rift seems to be healed. We are friends again. I am smiling because I'm writing the introduction to this book. Can you see me smiling?

I have codified all this, of course, from my point of view. Richard's is no doubt very different. We are both correct in our views of what happened. And it doesn't matter. It doesn't even matter that a human being suffered considerably in the course of the creation of an artful object, because writers, though they share a symbiotic liaison with torment, are indeed magical creatures: they are infinitely replenishing. Until the shit kills them. What *does* matter is that the book you hold is the dream come true. It lives, it exists, it is here to sing its song for you. In 1973, after Gail Wendroff had left Dell, after Bob Abel passed through, David Harris became the science fiction editor at Dell and he read "Bentfin Boomer Boys" in

Again, Dangerous Visions, and he loved it, and he bought it, and he signed the contract for its publication. And even though David left Dell and Fred Feldman came in, and Fred left and Jim Frenkel came in; and even though each time there was a changing of the palace guard the manuscript was gone over by divers hands who saw it in a slightly different light; and even though it has gone through an unnumbered number of title changes . . . *Space War Blues* has become a reality, a decade after Richard Lupoff first rolled paper into typewriter. It is a novel of something like 80,000 words, twice the length of "Bentfin Boomer Boys," and it is a fine book. That is why I'm smiling, why Jim Frenkel is smiling, why Richard Lupoff looks on it as an artifact, an icon from a departed age. No one can sustain pain for ten years without becoming inured. Even to a *fine* book.

But for us it is new. It exists here in this space where no other artifact precisely of its kind ever existed. And you come to it open and ready. Prepared to sail the dark with Lupoff, the bentfin boomer bappa zappa kid who had the *chutzpah* to dream this dream, the stamina to stay with it even when it was relegated to the status of "perpetual orphan," and the pride in craft to set it down in just this special way.

There are moments of madness here, and moments of special calm; high points of extrapolative vision and sustained notes of pathos; characters both bizarre and engaging; ways of looking at the world that are peculiarly skewed and memorable.

Some of you may have read sections of this novel as they appeared through the years in anthologies and magazines, some of you may have seen the excerpt in *Heavy Metal* last August; but for each of you now coming to the end of these remarks, what lies just beyond is the moment of wonderful encounter that I felt swamping me as I opened that manuscript envelope in 1967 and for the first time permitted Lupoff to run through my brain with his webbed feet and vicious imagination.

I've done what has been expected of me, and if my name has any coin with you as a buyer, I have returned the loss leader favor I asked of Lupoff when he chose not to pull the story from *Dangerous Visions.* And having done so, may at last have stilled the demon voices in the night.

Where is the introduction to Lupoff's book, Frenkel?

Here is the introduction to Lupoff's book.

And now, here is Lupoff's book.

Free at last, free at last, dear God, free at last!

HARLAN ELLISON
Los Angeles
9 August 77

Preface

AND I AWOKE–WAS THIS SOME KIND OF JOKE?

When you read this thing it will be in the form of garamond eight-point extended roman (or some such typographer's gobbledegook) printed on nekoosa twelve-pound eggshell book and bound in holliston novelex blue or champion kromekote sixty or something of the sort, and it will be a book. That's what a book *is*. But right now—right now while I'm writing (more precisely, typing)—it's just a manuscript.

Manuscripts and books aren't real in the same way. And excerpts, takeouts or condensations of books aren't *real*, not the same way that a real book is real, either. So if this is a book, and you're reading it, and it's real, then I'm very happy; but right now it's only a manuscript, and as far as a *book* is concerned, I'll believe it when I see it. In fact, I think I'd better feel it and smell it too, and maybe even take a little bite off one corner and see what it says to my taste buds.

All of this sounds vaguely solipsistic. Doesn't this guy Lupoff believe in *anything*? Sure I do. But I find it hard to believe in *Space War Blues*, for reasons which Harlan has made more than amply clear. Various editors and publishers and publications have run various chunks and versions of *Space War Blues* over the years: Harlan himself in *Again, Dangerous Vi-*

sions, Bob Silverberg in *New Dimensions IV* and *New Dimensions 5,* Ted White in *Amazing Stories,* and Julie Simmons and the rest of the Twenty-First Century Communications crew in *Heavy Metal.* And the book itself (the manuscript, that is) has been in the custody of a veritable apostolic succession of Dell editors: Wendroff, Abel, Harris, Feldman, Frenkel.

A terrible amount of ill-will has been generated over the years, as well. Some of it on my part, I must say. But these days I'm trying, I'm trying *desperately,* to get *Space War Blues* behind me. Not because I'm ashamed of it, or wish to disown it, or don't want to see it published. On the contrary, I want with all my *kishkes* to see it published.

As for the cause of all the delays and setbacks, Harlan has had his say, most eloquently, in the Introduction. In passing, he delivers a couple of pokes-in-the-eye to various people, most notably my agent, Henry Morrison. Now Morrison is normally the most mild-mannered of men, a courtly, pipe-puffing, Vandyke-bearded, tweed-jacketed gentleman of the old school of literary men.

But some of the things that Harlan said about Henry, made Henry very upset. And in the interests of fair play, he has asked for the inclusion of the following statement in this book:

> Dear Dick:
>
> A feeling of déjà vu, as the curtain rises. We have been here before.
>
> But with a difference.
>
> The dispute was never about money; it was about what might best forward Dick Lupoff's career. I took exception to Harlan's attitude then, and do so now. In those wonderful days of yester-

year, Dell was offering $3500 for *Bentfin,* no fortune; but Dell was offering *book* publication. I never had an epiphany, but I saw one once (a black bird with a long tail, right?). Harlan did indeed see the potential of *Bentfin* right off, and I'm glad he did. I told Lupoff so then, and I repeat it for all the world now.

What Harlan seems to want to ignore in his own snide way is that he was very late in delivery of *Again, Dangerous Visions* to Doubleday, which kept the Lupoff story unpublished and unsung. By agreement, no author in the book could resell his or her work elsewhere until *after the publication of* A, DV *in paperback.* And paperback publication of *A, DV* was understood to not occur *for at least one full year after hardcover publication.* Dell's offer to publish *Bentfin* more quickly and with promotion would have given a great push to Lupoff's career, and to ask Harlan to release the story from an already-late anthology did not seem unreasonable. A detailed explanation and dedication of the book to Ellison would have made clear his "Founding Father" status.

What's wonderful about Harlan's version of events is that he wants to believe that publication of the Lupoff first in his book has improved *Bentfin's* value. Perhaps so. But think what might have happened if it had been published expanded and *solo,* with some drum-rolling, in 1971?

Yes sir, free at last!
Best wishes,
Henry

* * *

I for one have had my differences, Lord knows, with Harlan Ellison. And if the truth be known, I've been heard to growl about Henry Morrison on occasion. But an author and an agent, like a husband and a wife, if they truly love each other will have their spats and make up and go on through life together. And I do truly love Henry Morrison and wish to go on through life with him as my literary representative, so you can for sure bet that I'm not going to involve myself in a tiff between him and Harlan Ellison.

I wish them both well. I even wish *me* well. I just want to get this matter behind me and go on to other things.

For a while there I had this recurring experience. My phone would ring and an unfamiliar voice would speak. "Mr. Lupoff? You don't know me, sir, but I'm the new science fiction editor at Dell. I've been going through the files left behind by my predecessor and we seem to have this, ah, this *thing* here with your name on it. I was wondering, Mr. Lupoff, if you could possibly explain to me what this *thing* is."

There would follow a lengthy series of telephone conversations, correspondence, and/or meetings in New York and California. After a while we'd have the manuscript straightened out (in its umpteenth version) and placed in Dell's inventory. There, I hoped, it would make its way to the top of the heap and *actually get published*. Someday.

Then there would be another round of the familiar publishing industry game of musical desks, and in a little while my phone would ring and an unfamiliar voice would speak. "Mr. Lupoff?" the new unfamiliar voice would say, "you don't know me, sir, but. . . ."

When James Frenkel examined the files bequeathed him by Fred Feldman and found the *thing*, he sent it out to a "reader" to get a fresh perspective. I don't have a copy of that reader's report. I wish I did. But I got to see one once, briefly.

What it said, in close paraphrase—as close as I can get, from memory—was this: This *thing* is unutterable bilge. It is vile, debased, disgusting, degenerate, incomprehensible, incoherent trash. The only part of it that makes any sense whatever, that has any remote claim to readability, is the little prefatory note by the imaginary "Uncle Dudley."

Shortly after receiving the reader's report, Frenkel telephoned me. "Listen, Dick," he said. (We had progressed well beyond the "Mr. Lupoff, sir," level but had not yet reached the "You son-of-a-bitch" stage that my editors and I always come to, sooner or later.) "Listen, Dick," Frenkel said, "I really think we ought to drop the 'Uncle Dudley' thing from the beginning of the book."

"Okay, Fred," I replied.

"This is Jim," Frenkel said.

"Oh, okay, Jim. Drop it. Or David. Larry? Gail? Who's my editor at Dell this week?"

"I don't understand you," Frenkel said. "I expected a fight from you about this thing. I was willing to listen, to negotiate, maybe even to lose. And all you have to say is, 'Okay.' Don't you *care*? It's *your* book, after all!"

"You don't understand, Jim," I said, shaking my head (in case he had a spy-ray trained on my house). "I wrote this book *ten years ago.*"

"But you did write it. Don't you *care*?"

"I care about what I'm writing now. And I care about the books I hope to write in the next five to ten years. I care a lot about the book I hope to write about Shelley. I figure I'll be ready to attempt that around 1980–81. And I care a lot about the book I want to write about the turmoil in China after the death of Sun Yat-sen. That should be a project for around 1983. I should live so long.

"But in all honesty, I don't feel a hell of a lot of emotional involvement with a book that was created in 1967."

I'm afraid that I pick on Jim Frenkel sometimes. He's a good fellow and he's a good editor; it wasn't his fault that he inherited the . . . *thing*. Eventually I went to New York and Frenkel and I spent hours in his office, sorting and shuffling the manuscript of *Space War Blues*. (It was known, at the time, as *New Alabama Blues*. "Doesn't sound like sci-fi to me," a sales manager at Dell said. "Change the title!"

("What about *New Alabama Spacewar Blues*?" Frenkel said.

("Okay by me," the sales manager said.

("I'll clear it with the author," Frenkel said.

("That's okay with me," Lupoff said.

("Don't you *care*?" Frenkel complained.

(And then at the *next* meeting in the glittering tower at Number One Dag Hammarskjold Plaza [the employment test for Dell editorial employees has one question: Spell Hammarskjold] the cover designer complained. "Too long. The title's too long. We'll have to use such small type, you won't be able to read the title. Change it!"

("What about *Space War Blues*?" Frenkel said.

("Okay by me," the cover designer said.

("I'll clear it with the author," Frenkel said.

("That's okay with me," Lupoff said.

("Don't you *care*?" Frenkel complained. Etc.)

And now (in one "now") I'm sitting here pounding my Selectric, and now (in another "now") you're reading this preface in a *book* and about to read the damned *novel* itself.

I hope you enjoy it, or learn from it, or are stimulated by it, or angered by it, or any combination of these things; at least, I hope that the book *reaches* you. I wish it could have reached you in 1967. But I suppose '78 is better than never.

And as for me, if you want to talk about *Space War Blues,* try me in the stacks down at the University of California library in Berkeley. I'll be the tall, skinny guy with the bald spot and glasses. I'll be researching Shelley.

RICHARD A. LUPOFF
Berkeley, California
August 30, 1977

1. By His Own Speech

Jiritzu in his own way did not see that the membrane ships closely resembled the clippers that long ago plied the living oceans of earth, those mighty windjammers that stood so tall above the ever-moving brine, their shafty masts thrusting canvas squares high into earth's salt-tanged air. Possibly *Djanggawul's* captain, Nurundere, would have something to say on the topic; he was learned in history, law and custom. Or better yet old Wuluwaid—but no, old Wuluwaid will tell you nothing.

Wuluwaid is gone. The modern outlook will mark him simply dead. The older religious would mumble of heaven, or of reincarnation. Nurundere, *Djanggawul's* captain, might have something other to say of the fate of Wuluwaid. In the tradition of his people, he might well say that Wuluwaid had returned to the Dreamtime.

One should respect the ancient traditions. Surely Jiritzu would rather believe in the Dreamtime than in any heaven or in the workings of the great wheel of karma, but what he actually believes is very little.

"Jiritzu," old Wuluwaid used to say, "you lack all regard for your ancestry and for the traditions of our people. What will become of you and your Kunapi half Dua? For what did my Bunbulama and I raise our beautiful Miralaidj—to marry a lazy modernist who cares nothing for the Aranda, who thinks that *maraiin* are mere decorations, who can hardly read a *tjurunga*?

"She might as well marry a piece of meat!" And saying this old Wuluwaid would grimace, reminded by his own speech of the grayness of his skin. And Jiritzu, touched, would embrace him. Wuluwaid would take Jiritzu's face between his two hands, rubbing his cheeks as if some of the blackness would be absorbed into his own melanin-poor cells, then sigh and mutter "Soon I will be with my Bunbulama, and you will sail the membrane ships with my Miralaidj, and she will bear you beautiful sons and daughters to carry on the line of the Aranda and to sail the membrane ships after you."

Wuluwaid envied Jiritzu. They were the sailors of the starwinds, the Aranda and the Kunapi. The few thousands who owned a world, Yurakosi, where their old folk go to live when they become grayed-out, caring for the children too young for space. The rest of the Aranda and the Kunapi, melanin-rich skins protecting them from the hard radiations of space, were the select of all mankind.

They alone, those few thousands, can sail the membrane ships, working their decks and masts all but naked to the stars. Other humans, blasting from sun to sun sealed in iron boxes, venturing out only when clad in clumsy, clanking spacesuits—envy these sailors in trousers and sweaters, the only known beings who can survive in deep space, sustained only by a close-air generator the size of a half-liter flask strapped to one leg.

Back on the mother planet, Old Earth, their distant

ancestors had been separated by a trick of geography, cut off from human crossbreeding and left to survive beneath the burning sky of the old Australian continent. Blackfellows, the other earthers called their ancestors when they found them after an isolation of a quarter of a thousand centuries. Blackfellows, aborigines, or—confusing them with another black race of earth—bushmen.

Great Mother knows there were plenty of other blacks on Old Earth. (There, Wuluwaid would be pleased to hear one call on the Great Mother for strength even though claiming no belief in the old mythology of the Dreamtime.) There were peoples in old Africa, old Asia, with as much dark pigment in their skins as had the Aranda and the Kunapi in theirs. But among those old Australians alone was there some subtle difference, some microscopic chemical variation that was amplified by the hard radiation of space.

Other humans would sicken and die in the raw blast of the cosmos—but these folk could thrive. Only slowly, in the course of many years, does the solar wind, the cosmic radiation, break down their melanin.

Then they gray out. Then they can travel in space no longer on the decks, in the masts and the rigging of the membrane ships. Then to venture outside the protection of a passenger tank they would need to wear spacesuits as do other men. The decks are still open, but in a spacesuit one cannot work the lines properly, and even if one could—what point in thumping about like a leaden automaton in the midst of grace and freedom?

Sail in a spacesuit? No sky-hero has ever so chosen. Space is not closed even then to them. They travel if they wish—with the meat. They loll if they wish—in the comfort of the passenger tank along with the men and women who are carried like freight in the iron bellies of the membrane ships.

This they do—if they wish.

But who would travel with meat, who had ever sailed the night between the suns?

You have never sailed this night and you never shall. You cannot know one minnow's worth of the experience. You have seen representations, recreations of membrane ships, but they are feeble attempts to communicate the experience.

Start with a rod of collapsed matter, matter incredibly dense yet drawn so thin that it cannot exercise the usual property of its kind, of capturing all matter nearby and even all radiation, and crushing them to itself.

The rod that lies at the heart of each membrane ship is so thin that it is barely visible—beside it a pencil lead is incredibly fat, even a fine electronic wire is a gross and clumsy thing. A rod of collapsed matter drawn so thin that it is all but invisible—straight as a plumb line and two hundred meters long.

At each end a matter converter, a small device using the agonized-matter principle to convert a tiny chunk off the end of the rod into pure energy, enough energy to start a membrane ship on her way from port-orbit upon her interstellar journey, or at the end of that journey to brake her from interstellar speed and permit her to achieve port-orbit and dock and unload.

Around the rod place a structure of flat decking material, sixty meters in width, a hundred eighty meters in length, triangular in cross section—and around that, a cylinder of thick radiation shielding running the length of the ship. That makes the passenger tank:

three gigantic decks, flat-bottomed, mounted at vertiginous three-hundred-degree angles to one another, beneath a single, curving roof.

There the meat stays during a voyage. They may come onto the outer decks to inspect cargo if they wish—some shippers insist on riding with their cargo and inspecting it periodically throughout a voyage—but what good is that? Clad in huge and cumbersome spacesuits like the repair crews of ordinary ships, they peer at the sailors in amazement and envy.

Sailors return their stares, faces showing pity and contempt.

And then they crawl clumsily back through the airlocks into their tank.

When Jiritzu becomes grayed-out—*if* he becomes grayed-out, one should say, for it is not in the least certain that he will live that long, that he will choose to live that long—when he is grayed-out he will ration his last melanin carefully, making certain that he can sail back to Yurakosi as a man, not as a piece of meat.

He will debark at Port Bralku. He will turn, still wearing sailor's garb, and wave farewell to the Kunapi and the Aranda aboard whatever membrane ship he has last sailed. He will board a little shuttlecraft and return to the surface of Yurakosi and will find himself a little house, perhaps at Snake Bay or Blue Mud Bay, and he will build himself a sailing canoe, and he will be a water sailor when he can no longer sail in space.

He will not travel as meat.

Perhaps Jiritzu will go to visit Wuluwaid's Bunbulama if she is still alive by then. She will be very old then if she still lives. He will sit by her side holding her grayed-out hand in his own, and they will speak of her Wuluwaid and of her beautiful Miralaidj, and they will weep together.

Perhaps Jiritzu's Kunapi half Dua will be with them.

Bunbulama will say, "Ah, Jiritzu, now we are alone. Now whom have we to love?"

Childlessness is unusual among Yurakosians. There is a rivalry between the Aranda and the Kunapi to grow more numerous but there is no serious wishing of ill between the tribes. There is need for them all: no other race of mankind can sail the membrane ships.

Without them there would be only the huge clumsy sealed ships that other men can manage, ships constructed all of sealed and shielded tanks where men travel between the stars like bits of canned dingo-meal.

Bunbulama does not know that she is alone. She thinks that her man and her daughter are sailing *Djanggawul* on the great path from Yurakosi to N'Jaja to pick up meat, passengers—thence by way of Yirrkalla to make the great tack at the place of the triple suns, from there to N'Ala to deposit her burden of meat, and onward by way of Old Earth before returning to Yurakosi.

Djanggawul will brake as she approaches Yurakosi's sun, will swing into docking orbit at Port Bralku, sailors will make planetfall along with a cargo of trade goods, families will be reunited. Bunbulama will await sight of Wuluwaid her man and Miralaidj her child but they are in the Dreamtime and she will not see them again on Yurakosi.

Should Jiritzu return to Yurakosi he will bear her word of what took place on this voyage. Otherwise the duty will fall to Dua, Kunapi, Jiritzu's friend and half. That would not be an enviable task.

Jiritzu will not flee, will not transfer to another ship or make planetfall at any world other than Yurakosi. Not even at Old Earth, although he might wish to set foot on the soil of old Australia, sail a ship on an ocean of Old Earth. But he will bear news to Bunbulama if he is not himself by then in the Dreamtime. If he is, Dua will carry word to Bunbulama on Yurakosi.

Djanggawul's journey started well enough. On their little mudballs the meat were warring again. Old Earth remained aloof, her concern turned inward as it had been since the fast ships had first permitted the escape of her children to the stars, to find new planets of their own on which to plant their banners of nationhood or religious tyranny or ideological orthodoxy.

The great nations of Old Earth had been dismembered, their petty successors had seen opportunity for new glory out among the suns. Whole worlds had beckoned, an infinity of them among which to choose. No matter that on nearly all the climate was too cold or too hot, the atmosphere poisonous or nonexistent, the land too dry or too rocky or the sea too great and too deep.

Move on, seek another world, seek another star. Great Mother had made enough worlds in the Dreamtime; man could now seek and find as many homes as he wished.

But where men went, except for the Aranda and the Kunapi, they went as meat only.

Old Earth grew more and more deserted save for those few tribes whose tradition made them love the land itself. These stragglers spread from their ancient homes and covered the globe. Their interests were inward. They set a satellite dock above their world, called it Port Hussein, and did trade with the daughter worlds.

As they still do.

But their interest is in the earth, the Old Earth.

And *Djanggawul* like the other membrane ships that ply between the stars carries meat, carries freight, faster and cheaper than the clumsy sealed ships of ordinary men.

If the meat on their little mudballs go to war, it is of small concern to Yurakosi. The ships of the Aranda and the Kunapi trade with the meat, carry the meat about as they wish.

The money of the meat is good, with it the sailors obtain the trade goods that make life on Yurakosi comfortable for the old people who spend their grayed-out years there—and for the children whose early days are passed also on the planet, while they husband their precious melanin against the day when they might sail the membrane ships.

Djanggawul braked to docking-orbit at Port Upatoi, the satellite of N'Jaja. The port workers were of course meat, tending to their tasks as best they could within the sheltering walls of their artificial moonlet, venturing out from those walls into the vacuum and radiation of space only when they must, only when clad in the clumsy sealed suits that meat must always wear in space.

The sailors of *Djanggawul* scurried about on the masts and spars of their ship, glorying in the beauties of space. The sails were furled—no need for membrane when the braking power of agonized matter is used, any more than there was when that same power was used to break orbit and commence an interstellar journey.

And of course the delicacy of the membrane is such that sky heroes would hesitate to leave it unfurled during docking and undocking maneuvers. It is only when the journey is under way that the matter converter is switched off—the use of the converter is little more than an auxiliary in any case—and the sails are unfurled.

Tall and thin the masts rise from the passenger tank, standing far above the body of the membrane ship. This is what makes some antiquarians compare the craft to the clippers of Old Earth's seas. But while they rested atop their watery medium, their masts rising only upward from the sea, these new ships are immersed in their medium of nothingness, their sailors free to build their masts out in all directions.

The masts of the membrane ships rise, ringing the passenger tank like spokes from a hub, and from the masts there spring spars, and from the spars are spread the membranes which catch the starwinds and drive the ships between the suns.

Sailors the Aranda and the Kunapi are, sailors and sky heroes of their people's tradition. Still they affect the scarification of their skin in the traditional *maraiin,* the sacred patterns of the Great Desert of Arnhem Land whence their ancestors came to space. And still they retain the garb of Old Earth's sailors though a few think this vain affectation.

Old Wuluwaid clung to the old ways and was pleased that Jiritzu showed willingness to wear the woolen cap, the heavy sweater and white duck trousers of tradition.

When *Djanggawul* made dock at Port Upatoi orbiting N'Jaja, Jiritzu was off watch. He climbed a tall mast and sat on a spar, careful of the furled membrane even in its protective case. Membrane sails are expensive as well as fragile. Jiritzu's sweetheart Miralaidj was beside him: she too was off watch.

The light upon Miralaidj's face was the reflected

glow of dayside N'Jaja, a world of mottled green forestations, red earth, and blue oceans. Jiritzu sat beside Miralaidj on the spar, hundreds of meters above the membrane ship's sealed hull. The face of Miralaidj was the blackest of blacks, rich with the generous melanin of youth. Her hair, long and glossy, hung in braids that would not handicap work or play. Her body filled her thick-knit sweater and tight trousers, every graceful line filling Jiritzu with love for her, eagerness for their wedding and the days of the birth of their children.

Jiritzu placed his hand on the face of his sweetheart Miralaidj, his fingertips tracing the *maraiin* raised there in her infancy, its swirls and symbolic patterns bearing their secret meaning known only to her parents, to herself, and to her Kunapi half, different from those of any other person. When they were married, she would tell Jiritzu the meaning of her *maraiin* and he would tell her the meaning of his.

Both had turned off their radios—they were out of touch with the rest of the crew of *Djanggawul* and out of communication with the net that by now linked their ship with Port Upatoi. They could speak with each other only by leaning close so that their close-air envelopes mingled, carrying ordinary sound waves between them.

Jiritzu examined the dial on the close-air generator on his leg. The miniature digital clock-face indicated that there was an ample supply of close-air. Miralaidj smiled as he leaned over her own generator, checking the security of its straps, the indicator on the face of the machine, to see that she too had a safe margin of air with her.

She placed her cheek beside his, her mouth close to his ear, and said, "You take good care of me, Jiritzu.

Without you I would surely forget my air!" There was irony in her voice, but a sweet warmth as well. She drew back laughing, the sound that carried through the air envelopes to his ears disappearing as they separated.

He seized her hands for a moment, a trace of the laughter returning as the sound was carried into his air envelope at the hands. "I will always take care of you," he said, knowing that his words would reach her only faintly, traveling through the close-air, down his arms and up hers.

"If harm befell you," he went on, "I would have to contend with the vengeance of Wuluwaid!" As if it were her father whose favor mattered to him and not his sweetheart's own. It was a lasting joke between them.

"You know old Wuluwaid," Miralaidj responded. "He is so caught up in duty and tradition, he cares more for the meat than he does for the Aranda."

"I know," Jiritzu said—and there was truth in that. Wuluwaid often said that the care of passengers was a sacred trust, that it was a charge to the Aranda and the Kunapi from the Great Mother herself, to transport those less fortunate than themselves safely from one little mudball to another little mudball. Only Yurakosians could know the joy of sailing space—let the little crawlers have their safety and their wars.

"Look," Miralaidj cried, holding her hand to Jiritzu's ear to conduct the sound, "look, the shuttle!"

There beneath *Djanggawul* a triangular craft had made its appearance. How long it had been climbing through the atmosphere of N'Jaja was of no concern: now it had burst from the air envelope of the planet, achieved orbit, was itself approaching Port Upatoi to dock.

The shuttle's thick body, its carefully faired edges, its airfoil design all spoke of the clumsy hybrid duty which it served, rising through the atmosphere of a planet, entering orbit, carrying passengers or trade goods to the orbiting port—then dropping away, falling back into atmosphere, skipping across the top of the globe's air cover constantly losing speed until it could fully reenter the atmosphere and glide to its landing.

Neither true aircraft nor true spacecraft, the shuttle served as both, served clumsily but performed its task.

And now, where Miralaidj pointed her slender black finger, Jiritzu could see the shuttle from the surface of N'Jaja approaching Port Upatoi. Behind the shuttle sputtered a tiny trail of reaction stuff—not even agonized matter for these little trips—and from time to time there would be a tinier spurt of vernier engines to make a minor course adjustment.

Wuluwaid, as his daughter had said, was down in the passenger tank, awaiting the arrival of the meat. He would know, as did all of the crew, that the meat would be dressed in their heavy spacesuits, that they would clump through the airlocks and corridors of Port Upatoi and make their way to the airlock and the passenger tank of the ship *Djanggawul*. Normally this would be a slow process with halts and delays and the filling out of forms and stamping of documents.

But not this time.

This was an assemblage of diplomats from scattered worlds, ambassadors plenipotentiary and their staffs and flunkies who would attend some sort of war conference with many more of their ilk at the next planet-of-call, N'Ala.

Little concern to sailors. Let the planet-squirmers have their squabbles and fight their wars.

Miralaidj tapped Jiritzu and pointed down the mast they had both climbed. Scrambling up its meager handholds he saw the form of little Bidjiwara, Miralaidj's Kunapi half, her closest friend, a girl just making her first sail. It was unusual to permit halving by two persons so disparate in age, Miralaidj a grown woman nearing her marriage, Bidjiwara a slip of a child five years her junior.

But as a young girl Miralaidj had astounded her family and friends in their town of Kaitjouga by declining to select a half from among Kunapi her own age. She was a child of five, long since talking and reading, learning now her simple sums in school, when she saw the newborn Kunapi Bidjiwara. "There is my half," Miralaidj had said, and that was the settling of the question.

She had helped in the raising of her little half, an unknown thing among a people where halves were expected to be of an age. When Miralaidj's parents Wuluwaid and Bunbulama had sent for her to be taken into space aboard *Djanggawul*, Bidjiwara had remained behind on Yurakosi, in Kaitjouga. For five years the halves had lived apart, Miralaidj sailing *Djanggawul*, Bidjiwara in school in Kaitjouga.

But now Bidjiwara too was sailing *Djanggawul*, the halves were reunited, and Jiritzu found himself occasionally burdened, more often delighted, with the presence of little Bidjiwara.

2. Beneath the Pelican Banner

Leon and Sophie sat in the little bar near Bourbon Street, listening to the revelers on the wider thoroughfare, the shouts, the laughter and mock-screaming, the strains of old-fashioned digzeland music drifting through the warm spring night. Leon reached across the small wooden-topped table and took Sophie's hand, smiling as he did so.

"I never thought we'd make it," he said.

"Nor I," she laughed. "How many years has it been? You're always away on business, or attending an urgent meeting at the department. This is the first Mardi Gras I've been able to attend since I was a little child."

Leon waved a hand at the bartender, a hand speckled with years and darkened by exposure to the rays of N'Loozy's sun, Lafitte 519. The bartender brought the bottle from behind the polished, darkened wood. He excused himself from the few customers drinking quietly on their barstools, approached the wooden table across the room.

"I think you can just leave it, Jacques," said Leon.

"Surely, Mr. Pineda. You folks going to make an evening of it here? Not going to look at the costumes and such?"

"Maybe later on. They keep at it pretty late, don't they?"

Jacques nodded in agreement. In the heat of the evening his perspiration gleamed against the black of his skin and soaked into the white of his bartender's apron.

"Glad to have you spend some time in the place for a change," the bartender added. "We don't get to see you and missus as much as we'd like."

Leon exchanged a knowing glance with Sophie. Then he said "Business, Jacques. Have to give the taxpayers their due, you know."

They all laughed at that. Leon delivered a friendly pat to Jacques' casually-clad shoulder and watched the barman return to his post behind the bar. It *was* good, very good, to be able to spend a little time with his wife, to relax and watch the Mardi Gras almost as if they were tourists.

"How do you feel about it, dear?" Leon said.

Sophie said "About what?"

"About the rest of the evening. And the next few days. Until I have to report back to the department."

"It's been so long since we had any real time to ourselves. I think—let's not do anything tonight. Tomorrow we can stroll in the morning, and for the rest of the day, D'Arcy called earlier—did I tell you? No? Well, she and Randolph have asked us to join them for the remainder of the day."

"Ah."

"I think they have news for us."

"News?" Leon was unused to hearing much news from his daughter and son-in-law. He got along well enough with Randolph but he was busy at the department, and Randolph had his own career with the babbage manufactory. The closeness of the family, such as it was, derived mainly from the exchange of womanly confidences between Sophie and her daughter D'Arcy.

"Yes," Sophie was saying, "she was so coy on the phone, I think she must be . . ."

"Be what?"

"Ah, Leon, you men are so dense at times. Pregnant."

Leon put down his glass with a small thump. "Pregnant!"

"Why yes. Don't you relish the idea of being a grandfather? It was always such fun when D'Arcy was a baby. Wouldn't you love to play with a darling little girl or boy again? *Grand-père* Leon! How does it sound to you?"

He rolled the term on his tongue for a while, decided that it was a pleasant one to think of. "Yes," he said, nodding happily, "and *Grand-mère* Sophie!

They laughed together, then Leon wanted to summon their old friend Jacques to hear the happy news but Sophie refused to permit it before their daughter had made the announcement officially. "It's her secret, Leon, her news to give when she is ready. It was wrong of me even to tell you. Now you hush. Come, let's drink up and be on our way home. Leave the late reveling to the youngsters and the tourists."

They settled with Jacques and made for the doorway. As they passed through the arch and into the street, Leon threw his arms around Sophie and held her to him. "So old, Sophie! Are we so old? Grandparents! I cannot believe it!" He squeezed her once, feeling the pointed edge of his pocket summoning-device through the cloth of his shirt.

"Ah, not so old, you rascal," his wife told him.

"Come on home and we'll see who is an old man, an old woman."

They found an empty conveyance, rarity of rarities in Mardi Gras, and returned to their apartment. Soon, inside their home, Sophie pushed Leon into his favorite chair and went to the kitchen. For years, while D'Arcy was growing up, they had lived in a house in the suburbs. Now that she was a married woman they had moved back into the city, to this apartment. Despite Leon's good salary and government perquisites, Sophie preferred to keep her own home, and these smaller quarters were easier for her as well.

From the kitchen Leon could hear Sophie working, the crack and rattle of ice as she filled a bucket. Ah, then, she was preparing to ice glasses and to bring a cold bottle that she had prepared earlier. Champagne! He smiled happily in anticipation, rose and crossed the room to the small sound panel, mused over a selection of romantic music.

Not too old, he thought, not too old to appreciate an evening alone together, a bottle of champagne, some quiet music—ah, not so different from the first years of their marriage, when he was a petty clerk at the department, she a secretary. Then they had lived on dreams and love, and now they could recapture the days of so long ago, could pretend, for a few hours, that they were young and poor and so happy once again!

He started the music, stood for a moment wondering whether to enter the kitchen, approach Sophie and put his arms around her, or to return to his chair and wait for her to make an entrance. He held her briefly in his mind's eye, seeing her as she had been as his bride, so many years before, the beauty and joy of her body revealed to his eyes, and as she was today, not so very different, really, from the girl she had been.

He started to cross the room, heard the low, insistent signal of the pocket summons. He halted, stood unmoving, wishing that he was mistaken, that the device had not summoned him. But again it gave its low signal, and again. Leon knew that it would not stop until he had contacted the department.

He sighed and walked quietly to the bedroom which he and Sophie had shared since moving to the apartment. Quietly he closed the door, lifted the telephone, tapped the direct-line button which connected him with the department. He looked at the tiny screen and saw the eye beside it wink on as the connection was completed. The picture of the secretary himself sprang from the gray of the screen.

"Pineda," the secretary said. "I'm very glad you called in. A matter of uttermost urgency."

Leon wondered for a moment at his appearance. He had not expected to talk with the secretary himself. But. . . .

"You'll need me in the morning, sir? I had promised Sophie and our daughter, it is Mardi Gras . . ."

"Not in the morning, Leon. You are needed immediately."

"Immediately? At–," he looked at his watch. But before he could mention the time, the secretary continued.

"Immediately, yes!" He was nodding vigorously.

"At the department?" Leon sighed.

"No. At the Presidential Palace."

Involuntarily, Leon gasped. "The Palace! Then–is the President involved personally? A matter of such urgency?" Even as he spoke, Leon was rising to his feet, moving to take off his casual clothing and dress for an audience with the President himself and the secretary.

"Don't change," the secretary said, anticipating Leon's moves. "Just get down there as quickly as you can. There is a limo on its way to your building now. It will be there by the time you can get downstairs."

Leon ran a hand nervously through his graying, thinning hair.

"And, Pineda—"

"Yes, Mr. Secretary?"

"You have some materials at home with you on the situation involving N'Alabama and N'Haiti."

"Yes, sir."

"Bring along whatever you have." The light winked out and the screen returned to its neutral gray.

Wearily, Leon gathered up his briefcase and opened the door to the living room. Sophie was awaiting him. She had rearranged her hair and somehow changed her dress without entering the bedroom while Leon was there. On a low table stood a frosted silver bucket of ice cubes, a tall green bottle poking its mouth from among them, a glass to either side.

The music which Leon had selected was playing softly, drifting from the sound panel.

Sophie lifted her hands, smiling, as Leon stepped through the doorway. Then, as she saw the briefcase in his hand and the expression on his face, she dropped her hands. Her face seemed to grow gray, almost like the vision screen. Her body sagged, the concealed years suddenly descending.

"Business?" she asked dully.

Leon nodded his affirmation, started toward her.

She turned her back and walked away from him, back toward the kitchen.

"Sophie?"

She did not speak, continued from the room.

He stood for a moment, confused. "The Presidential Palace," he said. "I have to—I'll be back as quickly as I can. I—"

The kitchen door slid closed on its rollers. Leon was not sure whether he heard sounds from the other side of the door.

Briefcase in hand, Leon made his way to the lobby of the building, then into the street beyond. The department limousine was waiting as promised, uniformed driver waiting beside the car. He offered an almost-military salute, said simply "Mr. Pineda?"

Leon advanced to the limousine. The driver opened the passenger door and Leon began to climb in. He recognized the driver and said "Sorry you have to miss the festivities, Johnson."

Johnson said it was simply his duty. "Besides, double premium for holiday work and graveyard shift, Mr. Pineda, I don't really mind at all. Kids in college, you know, sir."

Leon grunted his agreement. "The secretary gave you your instructions, Johnson?"

The car moved off smoothly from before the apartment building. As the limousine penetrated the warm air, the darkened residential street away from the noisy, glittering celebrants, Leon twisted around in his seat to get a look from the rear window. He could see a lighted rectangle on a high floor of the building, he could calculate the distance from street level to the lighted window, could identify it as the kitchen where Sophie would be dumping ice cubes into the sink.

The limousine climbed a ramp and sped down a nearly vacant highway, leaving behind the downtown area of the city. Soon Johnson pulled the car off the highway again. Leon looked up at the sky. The air was fairly clear for so warm a night, the glow of the downtown lights illuminated one horizon, but in the other direction Leon could see the swarming stars and N'Loozy's binary moons circling each other slowly as they crept across the sky of the planet.

Johnson drove through the open gateway and toward the small business entrance of the Presidential Palace. As the car began its roll up the long, gravel-covered path a light flicked on at the side of the passenger compartment. Leon lifted a handset from its covered cradle and held it to his ear.

"Pineda," the secretary's voice came, "gatehouse just blipped you through. You're cleared straight through. There'a a tin soldier waiting for you at the door. You have the file?"

"Yes, Mr. Secretary," Leon replied.

The light flicked off.

The car rolled smoothly to a stop and Johnson was opening the passenger door before Leon had even gathered his briefcase. He thanked the driver, hopped up the steps to the business door of the Palace. It was opened by a man in the scarlet tunic and golden frogging of the Planetary Guard of the Republic of New Louisiana. His shoulder boards carried the glittering stripes and stylized ballistic capsules of a brigadier. Leon was startled at the man's apparent youth.

"If you'll come with me, sir—," the officer began.

"Thank you, young man," Leon replied, falling into stride at the officer's side.

"—the President and the secretary are waiting," the guardsman finished. He escorted Leon into a modest meeting room, not as large, Leon noted, as the one his son-in-law used for getting out his paperwork at the babbage manufactory. The room contained only a large, plain table with scarred wooden work spaces, and a half-dozen straight-backed chairs.

The President, stubble on his cheeks and styrofoam coffee cup in hand, looked up. "Here's your man, Walther," he said to the man at his side, Leon's superior. Then, "Glad you're here, Pineda, hope we didn't interrupt your Mardi Gras."

Leon advanced to the table, lowered his briefcase. The only people in the room beside the President and the secretary were a handful of petty functionaries and clerks, and himself.

"If I can be of service, sir," Leon said.

The President nodded to Walther. The secretary motioned Leon to a seat. The President said, "We're in trouble, Leon. We need your know-how and we need your skills."

"Is it the war? Secretary Walther asked me to bring my notes."

Walther said, "Precisely. They're going at each other hot and heavy, Pineda."

Leon looked from the secretary to the President and back. He said nothing.

"Thing is, Leon," the President said, "Youngerman on New Alabama is trying to get up a consortium against the N'Haitians. Wants to pull together the old racist parties of O'Earth. He's called a meeting in Letohatchie and we're committed to attend."

Leon said, "Hmmph."

Secretary Walther said, "The President agrees that you should be the man to represent our government. We need a good man there who can make all the right noises, not commit us to anything. We want to send someone with enough rank and clout that Youngerman won't get his snout out of joint, but we don't want to overdo."

"And I'm your man," Leon gritted unhappily.

"That's right. And since Youngerman will want to make a military alliance, we're sending a military aide with you. All right to take that tin soldier who ushered you in here? He cuts a very impressive figure. Should look good coming down the ramp at your elbow, Leon."

"Uh. You mean that grand admiral fellow?"

"Brigadier Guardsman Foch-Giraud. Most distinguished military man. Impeccable record. Magnificent bearing. Excellent family background. Constantly in demand. Dull as a man can be."

Leon nodded ironically. "Fine. I accept him."

"And when you reach N'Ala . . ." the secretary said.

"Of course we don't want any part of Youngerman's lunacy. Polite expressions of support, et cetera."

"One other thing," the President injected.

"Ah, yes," Secretary Walther said. "Some of our other friends and commercial partners may not understand just what's going on. In particular—"

"Accra!"

"Exactly. We don't want to cross N'Ghana. If we should come into the war on the side of N'Alabama, Moshi-Nzima will feel called on to send the N'Ghana Regiments in to help N'Haiti. We don't want that, and even more we don't want any disruption to the trade between N'Loozy and N'Ghana."

"But we have no intention of coming into the war on anybody's side."

"That's what you have to make Moshi-Nzima understand—then go make Youngerman and whatever lunatics he convinces to join him, think that we're on their side. I suppose old Moshi will make grouchy noises then. Well, he'd have to or the New Togoland Congress will be up in arms and then he'll have to call a new election. Why did I ever get into politics, Walther?"

"Spirit of public service, Mr. President."

"Um. Thanks for the reminder. Have someone write that down."

3. Call It Yurakosi

Leon left the Presidential office after a handshake from the President and one from Secretary Walther. He found Brigadier Guardsman Foch-Giraud waiting for him in an anteroom. The officer had been notified by a functionary of the trip and was ready to depart, an orderly bearing his official-issue uniform case with spare service, dress, semidress, fatigue, formal, and informal uniforms.

"Shall I summon military transport, sir?" the brigadier asked.

"No," Leon said, "I have a car and driver. Is there a phone around, son?"

The brigadier flushed at the last word. "In the alcove, sir."

Leon lifted the handset and signaled a call to his home. Sophie answered and he explained, briefly, his travel plans. She said she would join D'Arcy and Randolph for the rest of Mardi Gras. D'Arcy would withhold her announcement until Leon returned.

Sophie sounded resigned. Leon was unable to tell whether she was sublimating hostility or truly sympathetic toward his duty and his job. He promised her he would retire from the department as soon as he was eligible, in less than two years. She expressed her love and ended the conversation.

He stood for a moment, handset upheld, then placed it back in its cradle, drew a breath and took Brigadier Guardsman Foch-Giraud by the elbow and headed for the doorway that would lead them to their car. Foch-Giraud looked down at the short, squatty Pineda and seemed to decide that the elderly man was wordlessly asking for his support, rather than patronizing him.

They reached the car and climbed in. Johnson had received his instructions and he headed for the shuttleport without questioning the passengers.

They rode in silence, Leon alternating parting glimpses of the night city with sidelong glances at Foch-Giraud, attempting to size up the military man. The unofficial evaluation he had received seemed entirely accurate. A perfect piece of window dressing. And, heaven be praised, the brigadier seemed to know how to keep quiet. Maybe it was simply a lack of thoughts that could be spoken, but it was still a blessing for their journey, and it would be invaluable once they reached Youngerman's conference.

The journey was a quick and relatively pleasant one, save for Leon's recurring nausea. He had been into space—he had lost count of the number of times. A few times, as a young man, on pleasure trips, until he had learned once and for all that the sensations of being off-planet were simply not attuned to his own constitution. Since then, only as his duties required, but for any man to rise in the department, a good deal of travel to other planets was mandatory, and Leon each time swallowed his medication and suffered through the journey.

At least it was good for a spreading waistline, he

thought grimly. Sophie always welcomed him home from official travels with bright comments on his slim appearance.

He sighed.

They shuttled from the surface of the planet to its orbiting transfer station, Port Andjack. The fastest means of travel in space was a sky heroes' membrane ship, and standing schedules called for the membrane ship *Makarata* to call at N'Loozy, to unload passengers and freight, and pick up a fresh load, and continue on her star-spanning path.

Leon and Foch-Giraud paid their courtesy call on the commandant of Port Andjack, saw their baggage carried to the station's prestige guest suites. *Makarata* was due within one N'Loozy day, would remain in port a mere matter of hours. The membrane ships did not stay long in port: they seemed to yearn for the solar winds, to strain at tether any time they came to halt within the grip of an orbiting station. Assembled in space, they spent their lives in space, never touching down on any planet, for their delicate structure would never survive the stress of a planetary landing, much less a lift-off.

As Leon relaxed in his suite he thought of the past hours. It was not yet morning at home, although Port Andjack rode high in the morning sunlight of Lafitte 519. Sophie would be in bed in their apartment. Their daughter would be in bed with her husband in their own home, the new life within her a tiny slumbering speck.

Leon found himself strangely stirred by the thought of the child quickening within D'Arcy's womb. When he and Sophie had been young they had hoped and dreamed of children, and when the passing years of their marriage brought none had grown gradually reconciled to a childless life; then the miracle had occurred and Sophie had conceived.

A hard pregnancy, bleeding and the threat of miscarriage, but they had persisted, the child had been born, a perfect, tiny girl. And now, the years of childhood behind her, the joys of her presence gone from the lives of her parents, she was to bear a child of her own.

Sophie would be asleep at home, and Leon sat in a comfortable chair, held in it by the pseudogravity of Port Andjack's rotation, savoring the moments ahead: the swelling of D'Arcy's belly, the excitement as her time grew near, the nervous pacing he would do during her labor, the joy of hearing his grandchild's first cry of life!

He could not sit quietly, no less think of going to bed. He changed to fresh clothing and left the guest suite, made his way to an observation lounge and stood before a panoramic port. So far, no nausea had struck and Leon stood, dazzled by the sight of *Makarata's* approach and docking with Port Andjack.

The membrane ship caught Lafitte's rays. It glinted with a brilliance and a beauty that took away Leon's breath. He watched the ship sliding gracefully into the tethers extended by Port Andjack, the N'Loozian space crews black specks in their heavy radiation-shielded space gear, the membrane ship's Yurakosian crewmen scurrying about, their white duck trousers turning golden in the rays of Lafitte, their figures making tiny, perfect human silhouettes as their work placed them directly between his own eyes and the distant sun.

Leon laughed briefly. Am I becoming an aesthete, he wondered, a poet at my time of life? Can a grizzled hack bureaucrat turn into a sensitive artist overnight?

He decided it was a chemical imbalance caused by the excitement of impending grandpaternity.

He checked a wall-clock to see what hour it was by standard Port Andjack time, was pleased to find it was the hour for breakfast. Aboard this orbiting station, with men and women arriving with subjective times of their own, it was possible to obtain any meal, any standard service, round the clock.

Still, Leon felt cheered at the prospect of breakfasting when the port crew did, of being attuned to his hosts and to his surroundings. A missed night's sleep could be done without. A diplomat became accustomed to planet lag, not merely losing or gaining hours as he might by traveling across the meridians of a world, or reversing the seasons as he might by changing hemispheres, but shifting his time-sense on a planet of longer or shorter day, adjusting to altered weight in accord with local gravity, and to subtly differing air chemistry, lighting conditions based on local suns, the gamut of adjustments he must learn to take in stride.

He made his way to the shippers' dining room, found it full of off-duty crewmen. Foch-Giraud was nowhere to be seen—either sleeping in, Pineda thought, or lording it in a VIP area in his splendid uniform. Leon shook his head, sighed, found a seat near a small viewport and watched N'Loozy spinning below Port Andjack.

A storm system had formed near the central continent, over open sea. Leon could see the area near his home, still clear of the moiling clouds. He flashed a wish downward, that the storm would hold off, permit Sophie her day with D'Arcy and Randolph before the rain arrived.

He returned to his guest suite, checked on the status of *Makarata* and found the ship ready to receive passengers. He contacted Foch-Giraud—in the VIP lounge of the port, of course—and arranged to meet and transfer to the membrane ship together. The transfer was through sealed umbilicals, Leon gave thanks, permitting them to enter *Makarata* without heavy space gear.

They were greeted by an officer of *Makarata*—not the captain, in keeping with the calculated key of their mission—and shown to the passenger deck of the ship.

The deck seemed to tilt and dip beneath his feet as the Yurakosian ship swung at tether. Leon felt a twinge in his stomach and clutched at his midriff with both hands.

"Are you unwell, sir?" the ship's officer asked.

Leon explained his problem.

The officer clucked his tongue in sympathy, offered to send the ship's doctor to Leon's cabin. Leon explained that it was a hopeless case. When they reached his cabin he shook hands with the officer, shut the door and lay down on his bed.

He lay on his back, gazing at the ceiling overhead, thinking of the Yurakosian sailors above, scrambling through lines and working the deck of the ship like water-sailors, free of the encumbrance of space armor. He started to shake his head at the phenomenon, wondering at the quirk of genetics that made one strain of man immune to radiations that would kill any other. Although he had traveled by membrane ship repeatedly, Leon was still impressed and mildly envious of the sailors each time he came aboard.

He felt *Makarata* cast off her tethers and begin to move away from Port Andjack under temporary power of her auxiliary drive; soon the ship's sails would be unfurled and she would pick up the solar wind, accelerating to incredible speeds. For now, every jolt, every dip, every quiver of the lightly constructed craft threw his intestines into worse turmoil.

Leon lay back, moaning, thinking that he might better have resigned from the government and forfeited his pension than ride again between the stars.

By dinner time he was sufficiently recovered to take a slice of dried toast and a half-cup of tea in his cabin.

Afterwards Foch-Giraud dropped in to visit.

Leon ordered cordials for them and sat up in his bunk, discussing the mission with Foch-Giraud. "Your main task," he began, "your main task, Brigadier, is to listen attentively—or seem to listen attentively. That is your own choice to make.

"I can tell you that at diplomatic conferences very little of importance is said in formal session. A quiet discussion in one corner, a few words exchanged over a drink—I can tell you that more diplomatic business is conducted in bars than in conference rooms by a factor of a hundred to one."

Foch-Giraud, splendid as ever in his Guardsman Brigadier's uniform, was striding up and down the small cabin, hands clasped behind his back. "But I want, ah, to know my function in this mission. Why am I along, Mr. Pineda?"

"I just told you. Just listen. Say as little as possible, and if you feel impelled to speak, remember that you are to make no commitment whatever for N'Louisiana."

Foch-Giraud stopped pacing. He stood at the foot of Pineda's bunk and looked into the diplomat's face. "Then why was I sent? I am to say nothing, to negotiate nothing? I could be at home, performing my military duties at the Presidential Palace!"

Leon sighed. A passing wave of nausea gripped him for a moment and he moaned, then answered Foch-Giraud. "Youngerman wants military allies for N'Alabama. You understand that of course, Brigadier."

The military man nodded.

"And you understand, Brigadier, that N'Loozy is not in the least prepared to become embroiled in Youngerman's idiotic war against N'Haiti? Do you understand that?"

Again the nod, slightly less forceful this time. "Then, sir, why send a military officer to the conference?"

"For appearance's sake, Brigadier." Leon's head had begun to ache. The discomfort started so subtly that he could not establish any moment when he had gone from the zone of non-pain into that of pain. He only knew, now, that his ears rang, his sinuses were trying to push his eyes from his head or as an alternate to burst through his temples, and his neck was growing sore.

"N'Alabama has been a valuable trading partner for us," he continued gamely. "And the President and the secretary both feel—I think they are right—that we don't want to offend N'Ala."

He sighed and turned on one side. The pain in his head abated slightly but that in his stomach grew worse. He could feel himself grow pale.

"Are you all right, Mr. Pineda?" Foch-Giraud said. "Shall I summon aid?"

Leon waved away the suggestion. He drew a deep breath and resumed speaking. "The trouble is, we don't want to offend N'Ghana, either. They are even more important to us. Minerals and products N'Loozy lacks. Important markets for our own production. Interworld Babbage alone—ahh—," he moaned, fell back against his pillow, panting.

Foch-Giraud had begun his pacing again. "Why don't we just proclaim our neutrality for the duration of the war, then?"

"No, no," Leon grunted. "Historical accident, Old Earth geography, foolish history, young man. Old Louisiana was once part of a bloc of earth states. Ah, why don't they teach you children anything in school?

"Old Earth traditions, color blocs, colony planets grown from ethnic stock. N'Lithuania, N'Latvia, N'Singapore, N'Equador. Foolishness. Carry all the hatreds and prejudices of Old Earth to the new worlds, leave the old planet to the Pan Semites.

"N'Loozy is one of very few worlds with varied ethnic strains. Do you realize, Brigadier, that ambassadors from the old white-bloc planets insist on dealing only with white-stock N'Loozians? And black-bloc ambassadors, with black-stock?

"Asians, others, don't care. We're all odd and different from them, so it doesn't make any difference. But the people who see themselves mirrored in N'Loozians . . ."

He shook his head, then stopped when the pain leaped to new intensities. Leon moaned.

"I never—I—," Foch-Giraud stammered.

"No, you never would," Leon grumbled. "You should have seen the ceremony at which the N'Jajan ambassador presented his credentials to the President. The protocol people had fits arranging the choreography of that, to save face for the ambassador and keep him within the odd boundaries of his planet's code . . . and to get him through the ceremony still, and get his credentials officially presented.

"At one point–," he stopped and chuckled, stifled the laugh when his stomach knotted again, "–oh, oh, at one point the secretary suggested that the President use a white stand-in or even appear in makeup. He vetoed that himself for fear of insulting our black partners."

"Then one thing I don't understand, Mr. Pineda."

"Hmm?"

"Why are we going to N'Ghana? Why did we book passage with these, ah, New Australians for a stopover instead of a direct ship to N'Alabama?"

"Ah, Foch-Giraud, they didn't teach you anything. Don't call these sailors Australians, youngster. They aren't. New Australia and Yurakosi are completely different places. One white, you see, and one black.

"The Yurakosians are a proud people, and they have a culture and history that far antedates the arrival of white people in their Old Earth homeland. They regard the Australians, new or old, as latecomers and boors. Not to mention criminals.

"Yurakosi is their home."

"Then they're not like me?" said Foch-Giraud, holding a black hand before his face.

"Ah, they don't teach young people anything nowadays," groaned Leon, turning his face into the pillow on his bunk.

4. Disappearing to Other Parts

Jiritzu stood on the spar Miralaidj and he had been sharing, lifted one foot and locked his ankles around the spar. He tuned his radio and tight-beamed a quick call to Bidjiwara.

Then he threw his weight forward, falling toward the hull of *Djanggawul*, and toward the bulk of N'Jaja below. His ankle swung around the spar. Bidjiwara pushed herself upward from her handholds, flinging both arms straight ahead.

Their hands caught each other. Jiritzu swung on around the spar, Bidjiwara's mass adding to the momentum of their swing. When Jiritzu again stood upright he clutched tighter with his ankles, released one of Bidjiwara's hands—she was directly over his head now, feet uppermost—and grabbed the mast with his free hand.

Bidjiwara clutched his free hand even tighter, swung around their wrists as a fulcrum and landed on the spar. She threw her arms around Jiritzu's waist and hung on, giggling and gasping for breath. For a moment it crossed Jiritzu's mind that she had a childish romantic feeling for him, but of course she was of the Kunapi, Miralaidj and Jiritzu of the Aranda, and that was all that there could ever be of that.

They sat down on the spar again, Miralaidj, Bidjiwara and Jiritzu. They all had their radios on now, and they could hear the proceedings down in the passenger tank even though they couldn't see what was happening there.

Wuluwaid's voice they could hear, attending to the mechanics of the airlock and getting the meat inside; Captain Nurundere was of course present too. Everyone knew it would be old Wuluwaid's final sail—he had no intention of letting himself be treated like ballast, he was going to work every leg of the voyage. Captain Nurundere, of course, was duty-bound to welcome the meat aboard and see to their welfare.

Captain Nurundere and Wuluwaid had their radios on even though the atmosphere of the passenger tank would have carried their voices directly. Using their radios, they could be heard by the meat even before the passengers removed their helmets—and also, the two officers, Nurundere of the Kunapi and his half Wuluwaid of the Aranda, could be heard by all the crew of *Djanggawul*, a method of informing the crew of all that transpired.

The officers held their positions by merit and experience, but officering was merely a job for sailors, no different from the job of membrane rigger, mess chef, or any other. There are no differences of class among sky heroes, and officers hold no special comforts nor keep secrets from their fellows.

High on their spar, the blackness of space above and the radiance of N'Jaja below, Miralaidj and Bidjiwara and Jiritzu listened to the events in the passenger tank. They could hear the turnings, scraping, and clanking of the airlock door, the hiss of free air moving from the tank into the lock, then being replenished from the reserve supplies of the tank.

Heavy, metallic footsteps sounded as meat emerged from the airlock into the passenger tank, thick shoes rattling against hard flooring, sending echoes off the curved metal roof. The number of clanks was surprising—the N'Jajans and their allies were a larger party than Jiritzu had expected to transport. But for all that, things were satisfactory. The tank was large. More passengers meant more revenue for *Djanggawul* and ultimately more trade goods for Yurakosi.

When the last of the meat had come through the airlock and it had been resealed, Wuluwaid and two or three duty sailors moved to help the meat out of their helmets and suits. Jiritzu could hear them working at this task, made needful by the clumsiness of the meat's protective garb and by the problems the meat would have in seeing inside the tank, through the heavily shielded faceplates of their helmets.

The first of the meat had removed his helmet and exclaimed something as he caught sight of the sailor who had helped him to remove it. The meat's accent was thick and made understanding difficult, but his words were something to the effect of, "Bigaw! Han zoffa me, baw!"

Jiritzu wondered who had been helping the meat. Baiame? Kutjara? Young sailors, but strange that the meat would think either of them a child. Well, perhaps an N'Jajan custom.

Rasp! Thump! Other helmets came loose from their collars, more meat were helped from their clumsy protection. Captain Nurundere addressed himself ceremoniously to the leader of the party of passengers. His voice correct, his words those dictated by the serious custom of Yurakosian space sailors and their officers, Nurundere spoke.

"Welcome, honored passengers, to our ship *Djang-*

gawul. Place yourselves in the care of sky heroes. The Great Mother will guide and assist us in protecting you from demons."

There was the brushing sound of Captain Nurundere drawing from his waistband his captain's *rangga.* In his spirit Jiritzu could see Nurundere draw a *maraiin* in the air with his magic stick.

To Jiritzu's amazement he heard the voices of the strangers raised in laughter! Not that he himself believed seriously in the magic of the *rangga,* the sacredness of the *maraiin* patterns or the picture stories etched on sky heroes' *tjurunga.* Not to believe was one thing, but to insult the sacred traditions of one's hosts by laughter—that was scandal.

"You baws pretty funny!" a stranger's voice said. "Owzbow gettin an officer down hya swikn talk seerisly?" It was difficult to understand parts of his speech.

But *Djanggawul's* officers seemed to understand.

"I am Nurundere," spoken formally, "I am the captain of *Djanggawul,* your transporter and protector, sir."

"Ya?" the stranger's voice came. "Ya? Yibuncha nigras," he said, great astonishment in his speech. "Zevybody on thole damn ship nigras?"

There was a moment without speech, only the sounds of shuffling feet and persons continuing to remove spacesuits, then the stranger went on.

"Hey, you!"

Jiritzu could not see the meat's movements, but clearly he must have addressed himself to the captain's half, for the voice of Wuluwaid came through the sailors' radios. "I am the half of our captain," the old man said. "If I can assist our charges, they need but explain their requirements."

"Yeh, you ole baw," the stranger said. "You done look lacka nigra. Wuss gone on hee?"

"Nigra?" Wuluwaid said. "I don't understand."

There was the sound of more shuffling, some murmuring among the new passengers. Then their leader spoke once more.

"You mean to tell me—," his accent lapsed and resumed "—that this whole ship . . . that there black boy is really the *captain* of this ship?"

Wuluwaid made a sound in his throat as if disturbed deeply. "I regret that I am as grayed-out as you see me. My half Nurundere is more fortunate in his blackness."

"Ahdoe get it, ahdoe get it," the stranger's voice said. "But oreye, oreye."

Then there was confused speech, as several of the meat spoke at once, men and women tumbling over one another's words. There were chunks of sentences, words merely. "Na really nigras," one voice said, and another used the word Australia.

Captain Nurundere explained briefly but courteously to the passengers the background of the sky heroes, a bit about their world Yurakosi and their ancestors of Old Earth.

Very shortly sailors set about to withdraw from the tank. Wuluwaid made arrangements with the leaders of the meat, a man called Ham Tamdje, to provide a mess chef for the tank. This is a negotiable part of any journey—sky heroes prefer to leave the meat to their own devices as much as possible, but if they are willing to pay, and desire extra services, the services are provided.

Soon Captain Nurundere, old Wuluwaid, Baiame and Kutjara were settled in the airlock. The door from the passenger tank was sealed. Then, from his post high on the spar with Miralaidj and Bidjiwara, Jiritzu saw the airlock open to the deck of *Djanggawul*. The four sailors emerged in file. Captain Nurundere was first, his woolen cap pulled over his head, his face as he looked upward for a moment clearly showing its growing grayness beneath the broad captain's striping of his cap. Then came old Wuluwaid looking nearly white of skin, he was so grayed-out, and then the two young sailors Baiame and Kutjara.

They separated to their posts. Jiritzu heard radio communication links becoming activated, *Djanggawul* clearing with Port Upatoi control center. Every sailor on the ship must have had radio contact with the net at that point, for without any command being issued from the captain or any other officer, sky heroes swarmed up and down masts, scattered across the decks of *Djanggawul* checking lines and equipment, moving to duty stations preparatory to getting under way.

Miralaidj touched Jiritzu in parting, dropped hand-under-hand down the mast, little Bidjiwara following close behind. She threw one glance quickly back and Jiritzu could not restrain a smile before the two of them reached deck.

Then he flung himself off the spar, diving headfirst for the deck below. There is no regulation against this kind of diving, and of course it is quite safe in deep space. A bit riskier in port, to be sure, but Jiritzu was confident that he could gauge his acceleration and flip again above the deck, landing on flexed knees, rolling and springing erect again on the deck, breath coming fast in his close-air envelope, blood racing with the involuntary response of his body to the few seconds of free-fall.

This was the life of the star sailor, the crewman of the membrane ship! The ground squirmers who never leave their little mudballs, the sealed-ship spacemen who crew the heavy agonized-matter ships—what can any of them know of this moment?

Jiritzu ran to the dogging locks that held *Djanggawul* to the bulk of Port Upatoi, and with other Aranda and Kunapi sailors worked the heavy gears and seals open. The task completed, they scattered to voluntary stations as *Djanggawul* made ready to move.

For himself Jiritzu selected a handhold near the bow of the ship. It was slightly precarious, and here in port where they hung momentarily within the gravity fields of both the artificial moonlet and N'Jaja itself there was none of the assurance that a sailor would be carried along with his ship should his hand lose its purchase.

But no membrane sailor had ever been lost under such circumstances—they of Yurakosi do not rely upon mechanical devices or elaborate regulations to assure their safety. Every Aranda and Kunapi is thoroughly schooled in the ways of space, everyone is expected to keep his or her body in good condition, reflexes fast and mind alert, and to take responsibility for his own safety. Every sailor on *Djanggawul* knew that, from little Bidjiwara to old Wuluwaid, and each bore responsibility for himself.

At the stern of the craft the agonized-matter conversion was taking place. The converter at the tip of the rod of superdense matter chewed off a microscopically small bit of the stuff, passed it through the terrible process and gave off the brightly glowing cherry exhaust familiar to sky heroes.

Djanggawul began to move.

She pulled away from Port Upatoi. The gigantic disk of N'Jaja slid away. *Djanggawul* was still in orbit even though she had broken dock with the artificial satellite. Now she moved faster around the equator of the planet, pulling into higher orbit as she swung around the globe.

By the time she reached the center of nightside, cities gleaming below looking like stars across the night, *Djanggawul* was ready to swing away. She pointed her prow out of orbit, dropped her tail toward the center of the planet's mass, and with a final spurt of reddish glow the converter was switched off.

The ship was coasting now, N'Jaja's sun eclipsed by the bulk of the planet. Without need for any signal the membrane riggers began scrambling up the masts to unfurl *Djanggawul's* sails. By the time she had cleared N'Jaja's shadow, coasting silently on the momentum of her matter converter push, the sails would be spread and ready to catch the solar wind that would carry *Djanggawul* to her tacking point near Yirrkalla.

But even before Jiritzu began his work in the rigging he stood for a moment on a spar, one hand braced against the mast, gazing straight ahead of *Djanggawul* in the direction of Yirrkalla. The sight was one he had seen countless times in his life as a sky hero, but still it brought his blood rushing and made his heart pound with thrill.

The far stars and galaxies were spread before him: the seven stars that early sky heroes had seen as the beak, eye, fins, gill, and tail of the Baramundi fish; the swirls of glowing intergalactic dust whose colors had suggested the legendary Rainbow Serpent; the formations of the Greater and Lesser Wallaby. He stood for a moment with his radio switched off, a mere score centimeters of close-air separating him from infinite vacuum, the silence of the galaxies in his ears, their splendor dazzling his eyes.

And he wondered: What is it like to be an ordinary man?

Were one not born to sail the membrane ships, were the cells of one's skin not blessed with protective melanin that permits the people of Yurakosi to do without radiation shielding, what meaning would there be in life?

And in that distant time when he would be grayed-out—how could Jiritzu face life as a ground-squirmer, even on Yurakosi where sky heroes could retire with honor? He saw himself then, husband to Miralaidj, father of many sons and daughters who would sail membrane ships. Perhaps Bunbulama lived through her child. Wuluwaid would do the same after this voyage was complete.

But to be an ordinary human, to travel as meat on a membrane ship, knowing sky heroes, knowing of their lives but unable to share their experiences—what could that be like?

He looked back at the deck of *Djanggawul*, saw his fellow sailors working busily to rig sails for the solar wind. He switched on his radio, caught the flow and rhythm of work, joined in. The labor was strenuous and precise, a joy to perform. By the time it was finished the crew were ready to assemble on deck for the day's ration of reconstituted grog.

There is no day or night in deep space, so deck-lights and rigging-lights glow throughout a journey. To keep the ship working the crew are divided into watches, each watch with its own officers—and the captain, a member of no watch, responsible for the conduct of all.

Sky heroes are few and precious to humanity; their safety on voyages is placed above all else except that of the meat, for the tradition of Yurakosi holds that the host must extend himself to any degree to safeguard his guest, and passengers are guests aboard the membrane ships even though they pay for that privilege.

The annals of Yurakosi bear no greater shame than the story of Elyun El-Kumarbis, a Pan Semite of Old Earth who bought passage on the membrane ship *Makarata* sailing the great elliptical route from NGC 7002 to Al-ghoul Phi. A black man of Ghanaian descent, Elyun El-Kumarbis purchased sailor's garb and a close-air generator and donned them in a private room at Port Hussein.

When he boarded *Makarata* along with the other passengers, wearing a standard protective spacesuit, no one could tell that he was out of the ordinary. Inside the passenger tank of *Makarata*—the ship is still in service—Elyun El-Kumarbis found some inconspicuous corner, removed his spacesuit, mingled with a group of crewmen who had entered the tank on routine tasks, and exited back to the deck with them.

Elyun El-Kumarbis managed to stay on deck for nearly a quarter-hour before he collapsed from radiation. He was carried below deck and treated at once by the ship's medical officer, but he died within the hour. The captain and watch officer responsible for the incident were immediately ordered by vote of the crew to spend the rest of the voyage as meat. When they reached Yurakosi they were shuttled down to the surface and never again permitted to leave the planet, although both had many years of melanin still in their cells.

But Elyun El-Kumarbis, tradition tells, spent that last hour of his life raving of the beauty and the joy he had known. His last words were pleas that he be permitted on deck again, which was not done, or that he be buried in space, which request was granted.

5. At Elmina Castle

Port Takaradi loomed beyond the viewports of *Makarata* as the membrane ship swept with silent grace into orbit around New Ghana. The planet gleamed beneath the membrane ship's hull, green continents alternating with glittering oceans, the duotone varying only as the wispy bands of cloud systems and the all but insignificant polar caps of the planet drew a white covering over parts of the green and blue.

As *Makarata* was tethered to the orbiting station, Leon Pineda felt his traveler's malaise begin to evaporate. He knew that the effect was wholly mental. If anything, the great membrane ship's gait under sail was steadier than the constant swinging and shifting she underwent at tether. A native of the vacuum realm, the membrane ship danced and trembled in port like an unbroken stallion forced to accept the unwelcome restraint of a bridle and bit.

Makarata was like a beast alive, yearning for the feel of the starwinds in her sails, the friction of sparse-ranging hydrogen atoms bounding from her flanks as she drove the channels from blazing sun to sun.

Leon wanted nothing more than to slide through the hollow tether and feel the relatively stable solidity of Port Takaradi's decks—no, *floors!*—beneath his feet. That, and shortly thereafter the even more comforting sensation of standing on the ground of New Ghana, a solid planet's thousands of miles of soil and rock holding him up.

He made his way at the earliest possible moment to the tether-lock, ready to transfer to Port Takaradi with only his briefcase of working papers, leaving his other sparse traveling gear on board *Makarata* for the continuing journey to N'Alabama.

His stay on N'Ghana would be brief; *Makarata* would remain at Port Takaradi, loading, unloading passengers and freight while Leon and his military aide Planetary Guardsman Brigadier Foch-Giraud conferred with N'Ghanaian officials. Then they would shuttle back to the membrane ship and she would cast off tethers, unfurl sails, and make for N'Alabama.

Foch-Giraud, splendid as ever in scarlet tunic and gilded frogging, appeared at Leon's elbow. "Eager for *terra firma,* Mr. Pineda?" The officer chuckled in a friendly manner.

"Yes," Leon sighed. His anticipation had improved his feelings but his stomach and his head still knew that they were on the swaying, rocking membrane ship. "I'm surprised you know the phrase, Brigadier."

"Oh, yes," Foch-Giraud burbled. "As the space cadet said to the flight instructor after his first suborbital mission ended, 'The more firma, the less terror!' " The officer doubled over with gales of laughter, stopped when he received an icy stare from Pineda.

"Old military joke, sir. I'm sorry you didn't enjoy it."

"That's all right," Leon sighed, "I'm sure you're the wit of the Planetary Guards."

"I am rather in demand at the club, sir, as a matter of fact."

"Well, I can't condemn you for military humor, then, since you're a military man yourself. Perhaps it just doesn't strike civilians as funny, that's all."

They shuttled down and stopped at the N'Loozian embassy. Leon, feeling himself once again, briefed the ambassador on his mission to N'Alabama.

"Two questions, Mr. Pineda," the ambassador said when Leon had finished his explanation, "matters I don't quite understand. Perhaps you would illuminate me before we proceed to the castle. Not only the foreign minister but President Moshi-Nzima himself wants to meet with you and coordinate our policies."

"Go right ahead, Mr. LeMoyne. You'd better understand everything before we confront Jekki."

Foch-Giraud interjected a single word: "Jekki?"

"The President of New Ghana," the ambassador said. "Dr. J.E.K. Moshi-Nzima. Everyone calls him Jekki. But–," turning back to Pineda, "–why are you coming here to talk to N'Ghana if our government has sent you to confer with Youngerman on N'Alabama?

"And–," he turned momentarily toward Foch-Giraud, making a sort of half-bow as he did so, "–why in the world, if we're trying to make nice with N'Ala, are you taking a black officer as your military aide?"

Leon sighed as if tired of explaining the same facts over and over. Still, he was accustomed to it. And as long as he could feel good solid earth under his feet, he could put up with anything.

"Very well," he said. "First, Mr. LeMoyne, as you and I know so well although perhaps Brigadier Foch-Giraud imagines otherwise, diplomacy is a game of little other than double dealing. N'Louisiana plays the game as cleanly as she can–cleaner than most powers do—but it's a fact of life that you don't put all your cards on the table for every player to see.

"You tell some of the players some of the truth, some of them lies, some of them a mixture of the two, and some of them nothing at all.

"It happens that our government is on good terms with the N'Ghanaian regime, which is an important relationship for us to maintain because of the value of our trade with N'Ghana."

"For that much understanding, please give me credit, Mr. Pineda. I am the N'Loozian ambassador here, you know."

Leon coughed apologetically and looked at Foch-Giraud. The Brigadier was studying the decorations on his tunic in a floor-length mirror provided out of embassy funds. He was adjusting the golden thread-work of his fourragère.

Shaking his head, Leon turned back to LeMoyne. "Of course. The point, LeMoyne, is that we want N'Alabama to save face, and to do that we must say that we are supporting her. But we don't want N'Ghana to be taken in by the same show we put on for the benefit of N'Alabama. We are here—," he gestured toward the preening Foch-Giraud, "—to be certain that Jekki understands what's going on."

LeMoyne folded his hands contemplatively. "All right," he said, "but why a black? Isn't that going to be a slap at Youngerman? It's standing policy to send black ambassadors to black powers and whites to white. That's why de Pauger is our regular rep in Letohatchie and that's why I sit in Accra. My good fortune, of course, considering the climate here and that in Leto, but as a bi-ethnic society we use our options very carefully. Why Foch-Giraud?"

At the mention of his name the Brigadier turned and said "Eh?"

"Nothing, Brigadier, I was merely asking Mr. Pineda a few questions before we leave for Elmina Castle."

Foch-Giraud turned back to the mirror.

LeMoyne took Leon Pineda by the elbow and steered him through a carven doorway, into a smaller room. He closed the door behind them. "Why a black military aide?" he asked again quietly. "And why in particular this brainless peacock?"

Leon cleared his throat. "Ah, Brigadier Foch-Giraud is of excellent family background, you understand, LeMoyne? Politics is politics."

LeMoyne looked grim but said nothing. Pineda continued.

"He was hand-picked by the President himself and the secretary. I was not consulted. But the choice of a black is a calculated risk. The secretary hopes to get a message across to Youngerman and his friends, that automatic enmity is not the only possible response of hetero-ethnic encounters. We can't *say* this to N'Alabama, they'll be mortally offended. But if we can make a tacit statement . . ."

He gestured to suggest continuity of thought. Then said, "As for the selection of Foch-Giraud, why, aside from domestic reasons, he *is* a splendid specimen who will look impressive and say nothing. He may not be too bright, but he knows how to keep quiet, which is actually better, for this mission."

LeMoyne said, "An intriguing attempt. But do you think it will work? Do you think the N'Alabamians will buy?"

Pineda shrugged. "Who knows? Meanwhile, our job is to make old Jekki understand what we're attempting, so he can make properly angry noises when we give Youngerman our verbal support—but not go seizing N'Loozian property on New Ghana, or mess up the flow of trade between our planets!"

6. Last Night in Letohatchie

Well he didn't like the hot dust blowing, crusting and it made him have to blink a lot standing still a gentleman doesn't move under the circs but you can blink yes by the end of the whole thing it's like sleeping too long the dust tears get caked up and make a gritty crusty blob at the corner of your eye where the nictitating eyelid would push it clear if you were a frog (too late—you're not). He knew that afterward he would have a chance rub the two places one at a time it would hurt (pull scratch) but only for a moment and the dust-crumb would come out, get it between the last joint pad of thumb and forefinger of each hand it would roll into a nifty sphere so what?

Mean, what do you do with a perfect sphere (two in fact) three-four millimeters in diameter composition gritty dry outside (no sweat left) moist inside (tears yes) made out of 70% red cruddy N'Alabamian dust blown into your eye at parade by the hot wind 30% white man's tears (yeah) (saline content) listening to a would you be*lieve* it commencement address oh no!

How about that speech! Brilliant! Original! How about we gotta sacrifice to win brave surn manhood to protect pure white pussies from the nigras (ever see one who didn't slobber clutch after a white c*nt?) carry the war to the enemy put the nigra back in his place make N'Haiti pay for atrocities *and*

and

and grit in your eye. *Sheeh*!

So who ever said commencement was supposed to be fun anyhow tradition is what it is. & N'Alabama is strong for tradition good surn tradition all the way from O'Earthtime days before the furgem Jewrabs conquered the world when O'Alabama was an independent damn O'Earth *nation* bajeez with independent damn *al*lies: O'Miss O'Jaja O'Boerepublic the nigra knew his place *then* you bet basaintgeorge.

Well he stood there attention he was a good gyrene raring to get into space into war and fight the good fight for god and planet and little baby heads of shiny golden curls (that would grow up to be a *piece* you follow? a *piece*) who ever said he needed—whoever said anybody needed—a commencement speech to tell him to blast the damned uppities out of black space back to their stinking N'Haiti till the papadocs learned their place again . . .

. . . some bigbellied senator from furgem Talladega or someplace? Sheeh! What if it was the furgem governor himself what could he say about the war that everybody didn't know already anyhow? That we better win it or there'd be buck nigras walking free on N'Alabama's sacred soil and before you know it some cunning black nigra kid's playing pop-o with some innocent golden-haired little N'Alabama baby and you know what happens *then*! Minority groups at the polls! Two-party elections and furgem minority groups trading off damn *votes* for concessions the same thing that happened on O'Earth before the furgem Jewrabs pushed everybody else out and left the colony worlds to shift for themselves. Who needs speeches?

So after it became overwith he went with Gordon Lester Wallace III and Freddie. School out, all the eager boy graduates had their diplomas and a handshake from Senator Belly from Talladega (he knuckled his eyes between mitting them) and off to barracks for fresh undustied uniforms and awayaway it's over but he was gone already by then with Gordon Lester Wallace III and Freddie to Letohatchie for a time.

Down the red rut road to Letohatchie by whining two-wheel gyrocar and Gordon Lester Wallace III and Freddie said to him—How about it sarge?—and turned waiting for an answer.

He didn't.

Gordon Lester Wallace III and Freddie grunted and looked ahead no use bugging him that was obvious. What if he was just tired. Or grumpy. But if Gordon Lester Wallace III and Freddie had done something wrong that got him mad, ah, that was another matter and better let sleeping sleepers sleep. He knuckled his right eye it hurt (pull scratch, yes) and his left (yes) and rolled two gummy spheres three-four millimeters in diameter between the last joint pad of thumb and forefinger of each hand and threw them away dustodust they rolled whined down the red road.

7. Empty Places on Both Sides

Two standard days—merely a matter of watches in space—after *Djanggawul* left Port Upatoi the captain announced a ceremonial dinner in honor of the ship's passengers. The tank had been furnished, in accord with the passengers' wishes, in luxurious style. One of the three decks was devoted to dining salons, a bar, a lounge and an entertainment area.

A second was partitioned into private quarters for the N'Jajans and their guests. The third was set up as an artificial outdoor environment, with thick plant life and even a small constructed lake.

With Nurundere at their head, wearing ceremonial crimson plumes in keeping with the ancient Australian practice, a group of men and women from the crew trooped through the deck airlock and emerged into the passenger tank. Yurakosian chefs had taken over the passenger galley hours before the meal, preparing a lavish dinner of old-style dishes.

The long white-covered board was set with places for Aranda and Kunapi on one side, N'Jajan and other passengers on the other.

Captain Nurundere's seat was at the center of the long table, on a small dais; opposite him sat the senior member of the party of passengers, an N'Jajan ambassador called Ham Tamdje traveling to the big war conference on N'Ala.

Captain Nurundere rose to his feet at the beginning of the meal: a tall, imposing man, still with the mark of the sky hero on his face despite the loss of most of his melanin, his clothing a set of common sailor's garments with only the head-plumes of an ancient Aranda chieftain to mark his rank.

Opposite him stood the N'Jajan Ham Tamdje, a man with too much flesh on his face, pale skin marked with red veins in his cheeks and on his nose. He wore a suit of some local cloth from his home world, a sort of yellowish vanilla color, with a white shirt and a piece of colored cloth knotted around his neck.

The crew women in Nurundere's party were dressed as were the men, but those of the meat wore odd gowns that hung to the floor, most of them also coming only part-way over their bosoms; the effect was altogether as if their clothing was hung three or four handbreadths lower than intended, and threatened to fall to the deck at any moment.

Nurundere made the same welcoming speech Yurakosian captains had made on membrane ships for scores of years—the pleasure at carrying distinguished travelers, concern for the comfort and safety of guests, the sky heroes' sacred trust.

Ham Tamdje looked a little uncomfortable during the captain's remarks, then he made his reply: that the passengers appreciated the hospitality and the good food and booze and everybody sat down and the food actually came.

Jiritzu found himself seated opposite a woman who introduced herself as Missy Julietta Culpepper. She was an administrative assistant to the plenipotentiary from N'Tensi. She had wavy yellowish hair and a great deal of pale flesh that seemed to quiver any time she moved. She asked Jiritzu what it was like to be a membrane sailor.

"Work," he told her. "Sometimes it is lonely, sometimes companionable, and very beautiful when we are outside."

She wanted to know when she could go outside.

He explained that she could not—except in a spacesuit.

She said sky heroes were unfair to their passengers just because the sailors were black and the passengers white.

Jiritzu tried again to explain why passengers needed protective suits. He told her the story of Elyun El-Kumarbis.

She said, "But he was just a dirty nigra."

Jiritzu said, "It would happen to anyone who ventured outside without protection. Anyone except a pure-blooded descendant of the old Australian aborigines. Not even hybrids—there have been a few, there were some in the early days of the membrane ships, deliberate attempts to increase the number of sky heroes, but they did not have the protective melanin. "Only we may go."

"You're as bad as a Jewrab," Missy Culpepper said.

Jiritzu said, "As a what?"

"They were an Old Earth people. Full of uppity notions. Thought they were better than anyone else. And full of nosey do-good ideas about nigras bein' equal of whites. We learn all about Old Earth races in school on N'Tensi."

"What happened to the—Jewrabs?" Jiritzu asked.

"Oh, they got together and made that damn Pan Semitic Empire."

Jiritzu reacted with surprise. "Ah! Then Elyun El-Kumarbis was—"

Missy Julietta Culpepper said, "Yes. They took over Old Earth after everybody else left."

Still, Jiritzu did not understand Missy Culpepper's object. He kept at his meal, along with the others, the pride of Kunapi chefs. The passengers provided beverages, not reconstituted, but brought whole from their home worlds. Mostly whiskey.

The meal wore on. At the far end of the table some of the meat and some of the crew were leaving their seats, disappearing to other parts of the passenger tank.

Missy Culpepper said, "What I mean is, you Yurakosi people seem to think you're all so special because you can go around the way you do, and you won't let anybody else do it!"

"It is not our doing," Jiritzu said, "it is a quirk of nature. Wild fortune for us, a cruel joke on everyone else, but not our own doing."

Missy Culpepper turned to a man sitting beside her. "Tell this boy," she said, pointing at Jiritzu, "tell him what's going to happen if they won't give up their damn secret!"

The man drained a glass of whiskey and tapped himself on the shoulder. There was something hard and bulky under his jacket. His speech was slurred and hard to understand. He said, "Breakin' bread with nigras, Julietta. If Ham din tell us himself back in Upatoi I'da never thought we could do it. But Ham says—," he stopped and wiped his mouth with his sleeve, "—Ham says we could really do a job if we could have our own membrane ships.

"So we gotta find out how to sail 'em.

"Or else!" he said, and reached for a bottle to fill up his glass again.

Jiritzu said, "There is no secret!"

Missy Culpepper and the man beside her looked angry but did not say anything else aloud. Jiritzu wanted to talk with Captain Nurundere about what had been said; he considered radio but the crew had turned them off during the banquet: there was no need for them, and the noise would have been a distraction.

So he rose from his place and walked to Captain Nurundere's place, and put his hand on the captain's shoulder and said very quietly that he needed to talk with him. Such requests do not come often among sky heroes, and when they come they are treated seriously and quickly.

Captain Nurundere said a word to Ham Tamdje and rose, and he walked with Jiritzu a distance from the table and Jiritzu told him what the two passengers had said. While he spoke with the captain he scanned the table. There were many empty places on both sides. Nurundere said, "I suppose the meat have invited our brothers and sisters away to try to get our secret from them. Hah!"

He turned from Jiritzu and strode back to where Ham Tamdje still sat in his yellow-white suit. The captain spoke and although Jiritzu could not understand what he said, Ham Tamdje's face grew for a moment very pale, then an angry red as he replied to Nurundere.

The captain said something more to Ham Tamdje. The N'Jajan rose from his seat. Captain Nurundere took one step backward. From the seat beside Nurundere's, his half Wuluwaid arose.

Ham Tamdje reached inside his jacket and pulled

out his hand with a small, old-style explosive gun in it. He pointed it at Nurundere.

"All right," Ham Tamdje spluttered. "All right, if you damn nigras are gonna keep your damn secrets, some white men gonna show you your place!" He pointed the gun straight at Captain Nurundere.

It was a moment of shock. Jiritzu's mind very nearly refused to accept the reality of what he beheld. The meat were—were what? Were attempting to seize control of *Djanggawul*!

But why?

They were being transported to their objective. The sky heroes were, in a sense, nothing other than their hirelings anyway. What did the—mutineers? hijackers?—what did they want?

They wanted something that did not exist: the secret—the secret!—of survival in deep space without protective suits. Anyone could survive the vacuum, that was possible ever since the invention of the close-air generator, but the hard radiation would kill any human not of Yurakosian stock. There was no secret—it was a simple fact, a part of reality—yet these people were demanding that the secret be given to them, demanding at the point of a gun.

"Ya'll tell me rat now or you one dead nigra!" Ham Tamdje slurred at Nurundere. The captain began to explain still again that there was nothing to tell. He gestured to emphasize his point. Ham Tamdje raised his gun higher.

Across the gray face of Wuluwaid emotions flashed one after another. As Ham Tamdje squeezed his trigger old Wuluwaid launched himself at the N'Jajan, arms outstretched.

The weapon fired with a roar that echoed off the curving roof of the passenger tank. Old Wuluwaid crashed down on the white linen that covered the long table. In the moment when Wuluwaid had thrown himself at Ham Tamdje's gun, Jiritzu had flung himself after him.

Ham Tamdje stood, clearly shocked by the result of his own rash act. In an instant Jiritzu had seized his gun and wrenched it from Ham Tamdje's grasp, pointing it not at the passengers but at the floor to show that he had no intention of firing.

Captain Nurundere ignored both Ham Tamdje and Jiritzu. He bent over his half, Wuluwaid. He turned him over so that he lay face up on the table but it was clear that Wuluwaid was already near death. He had taken the heavy old-fashioned bullet in the middle of his chest. Blood was pouring from the wound and his face had faded from its customary gray to a deathly white.

Even in these few seconds his rasping breath ceased.

Up and down the length of the table something resembling a miniature war had broken out. The passengers had come to the banquet armed. The crew were without exception unarmed—membrane ships are craft of commerce not war, and Yurakosi had made neither pacts of alliance nor warfare in her history.

Very quickly the rattling shots ceased. Sky heroes lay dead on the deck of the passenger tank. Meat armed with old-style guns rounded up surviving sailors, Captain Nurundere included.

For an instant Jiritzu considered using Ham Tamdje's gun to continue the fight against the mutineers but did not, at last, fire a shot. He thought, perhaps, of the sacred concern of sky heroes for their charges, even under these extreme circumstances, but chiefly he saw no gain in firing a few shots against so many armed enemies.

Ham Tamdje stepped before Jiritzu, took back his gun and whipped it across Jiritzu's face. Ham Tamdje's expression was one of contempt.

"Nigra coward!" he snarled.

Should Jiritzu have shot Ham Tamdje, then, while still he had held the gun? To what end? To kill a passenger?

Ham Tamdje's own conduct might well have forfeited for him the right of hospitality. Jiritzu might have been held blameless. But it had seemed at that moment that the battle, such as it was, was over. To have killed the N'Jajan would have been merely gratuitous.

Within minutes now all of the captured sailors were forced into two cabins, men in one, women in another. Radios were taken from them, as were their close-air generators. The star sailors were told that armed guards would wait outside the door of the cabins in which they were penned. The door was slammed.

8. On the Ground

Jiritzu looked about the cabin to see who was with him—more than a dozen men including his half, Dua. Captain Nurundere and Wuluwaid were absent, as were many others. Wuluwaid, Jiritzu realized, could not be there—he was by now in the Dreamtime. Nurundere, when last he had been seen, was unharmed.

Jiritzu called out to the others, "Where is Nurundere? Does anyone know what happened to him?"

A Kunapi machinist, Watilun, said, "I saw him as we came in here, standing with the meat Ham Tamdje. He seemed unharmed."

Of the crewmen in the room Jiritzu determined that he was himself the most senior. Sky heroes are an egalitarian lot: they pay little heed to rank or position. Still, for the purpose of the moment someone was needed to lead, or at least to coordinate the efforts of all.

Jiritzu assigned two men as door-watch and called the rest to confer in a far corner of the cabin. Of them all, most were too shocked to contribute to the discussion, but Dua and the machinist Watilun put in their shares.

"We must think this through," Jiritzu began. "Can we assess the situation? Can we devise our response?"

He felt pompous and unnatural acting as leader, but the others took him seriously.

"We men seem uninjured, Jiritzu. There seem no wounded–those not killed outright are uninjured. Probably the same is true among the women. We are divided now into two groups, and Nurundere is held separately. Ham Tamdje must have wished to parley with him, that is why he is kept away from the rest of us."

Watilun looked at the others. "Some of us and some of the meat had left the dinner before the shooting began. They may still be fraternizing on the nature deck."

"Unless they were lured away," Dua added, "for some purpose."

Jiritzu said, "I think not. The meat were carrying weapons but I doubt that they planned that battle. Some of them seemed very surprised when the fight began."

Watilun said, "And there are still the duty-watch, on the outer hull."

"They must know that something is wrong," Dua said. "Even with our radios turned off, the sound of the shooting must have carried through the hull to the upper deck. They would have tried to make contact by radio and they would have had no reply, or spoken only to a passenger."

"That is all as it may be," Jiritzu said. "But what should we ourselves do now? We can wait for one of Ham Tamdje's people to come in and tell us what they want, or–"

"No!" interrupted Watilun.

And "No!" echoed Dua. "We must act!"

"Good," Jiritzu responded. "I agree. But *what*? What *can* we do?"

Dua looked at a loss, so Jiritzu turned to Watilun. "Have you worked inside the tank? Is there anything we can do to get out of here, either back into the big room or to the outer deck?"

Watilun rubbed his head with both his hands, concentrating. For the first time Jiritzu studied this Kunapi: strong features, bushy hair, skin still dark with unused melanin. He seemed a competent man and resourceful.

He said, "I have worked on the collapsed matter rod, tuning the positioning fields, tank and hull braces. I have worked on the converters."

"How do you get to the rod?"

He rubbed his chin. "Normally, from the deck to the converter at either end of the ship, then along the field braces. But there are service ports to give access also. Let me look over here."

He stood up and walked to a bulkhead near the corner of the cabin. He knelt and worked for a few moments on the base of the wall. A section of wall-base came away, and with it a panel of flooring. Beneath was a large rectangular plate, sealed heavily at the edges. There was brightly colored lettering on the face of the plate.

"Mother," Watilun spat. "Those meat took my close-air gen. I can't go down without it. For that matter I daren't open the seal at all—this cabin will go to vacuum if I do!" He sat back on his haunches and closed up the floor and wall sections he had removed.

"All right," Jiritzu said, "that won't work. What other ideas do we have?"

"We can try to overpower the meat when they open the door," Dua suggested.

"That's a desperation plan. We should be able to do

something on our own, without waiting for the meat to do something first."

A sailor nearby asked, "What if we just wait? What would happen then? What do they want?"

Jiritzu sighed, not at the question but at the irrational meat whose actions had provoked it. "These passengers refuse to accept the fact that they can never be sky heroes. They want the secret of withstanding radiation in space. I suppose as soon as Captain Nurundere tells them the secret they will free us and go on with the trip."

"But there is no secret to—" The sailor stopped himself.

Jiritzu nodded, his feeling one of bitterness tinctured with a wry humor.

In the silence that followed they could hear a stealthy sound from somewhere beneath their feet. Watilun ran to the bulkhead and again opened the section leading to the seal beneath the floor. There the face of little Bidjiwara looked up into the cabin, full of youth and excitement, missing any sign of fear.

Watilun and Dua pulled her into the cabin. Bidjiwara said, "One of the women knew how to get under the floor from our cabin. I came first as I am the smallest. The rest will follow when we send for them."

"That will do it!" Watilun exclaimed.

The others faced him, their questions needing no words.

"You go back," he said to Bidjiwara. "I think we may yet be saved, but we will all have to be in this cabin first."

"How can it be?" Jiritzu asked.

Watilun turned, very solemn of mien. "If we do not regain control of our ship what actually will happen?

How serious the result? What price is justified to save our ship?"

Jiritzu's brow wrinkled in thought. "I suspect that the N'Jajan Ham Tamdje is little short of mad. If he fully realizes that there is no secret, he and his fellows might do anything. They will be outraged. They'll be as if mad."

He took a few paces, staring at the floor, then returned. "If they refuse to accept the truth that we tell them—they'll be equally desperate. They'll try anything to learn what they think we're concealing from them. They must think that they can use membrane ships in their stupid war. I suppose they could, if they could man them, and they don't want to accept the fact that they simply cannot man our ships."

A crewman cried, "How can we stop them?"

Watilun said, "We can kill them." He looked around the cabin. No one spoke. "We can assemble in one place—here or in the cabin where the women are held. There are enough ordinary furnishings in these cabins—the meat didn't clear them when they shoved us in—I can easily rig a booby trap to open that floorplate when the door is opened.

"Once that happens—," he made a sweeping, downward gesture with both his hands, "—the air from the main passenger tank goes right out. The only safe place in the tank would be in a sealed cabin. And as far as we know, the only people in a sealed cabin are ourselves—and our women."

"What about Nurundere? And what about all of us who were off with passengers, who had left the banquet before Ham Tamdje showed his weapon?"

Bleakly, Watilun said, "They will be lost."

Bidjiwara was sent back to the other cabin, to summon the women.

Soon they arrived, moving softly between the floor-like deck plates and the bottom hull that surrounded the ship's axial rod.

They heard the plan.

Some favored proceeding, others preferred to wait and hope for a less lethal solution. The crew on watch, they hoped, would use radio and learn that something serious was wrong. They would seal the airlock to the tank and make for port.

During the argument the cabin door was flung open and the captain was shoved in. The meat didn't even look into the cabin and see that the population had doubled.

With the door slammed behind him, Nurundere advanced to the center of the cabin and seated himself. There was blood on his face. His clothing was torn.

He said, "They're mad. They refuse the truth!"

"What happened? What did they do to you?"

"I was questioned by Ham Tamdje and a few of his close associates. This doesn't mean anything." He wiped some of the blood from his face. "Just some scratches obtained in a scuffle. But they intend to take this ship to their port, back to N'Jaja, if we won't give them the secret of protection in deep space.

"They plan to take us hostage, murder us one by one, rape all the women to produce a race of tame hybrids if nothing else works, or force us to breed for them, get a race of slave star-sailors!"

He stopped, and there was only the sound of breathing in the cabin.

Then Jiritzu said, "Watilun has a plan." The captain asked what it was. Watilun told him.

Nurundere pondered a long time, unanswering. "I would prefer to avoid that," he said at last. "Killing passengers, even these, and losing sky heroes as well. If there is any other way, we should seek it."

"I agree," said Watilun, "but what other way is there?"

Nurundere faced Jiritzu. "Your thought?" he asked.

"Captain, they took your close-air and your radio?"

Nurundere nodded.

"Did they attempt to communicate with the deck?"

"Several times the deck tried to call us in the tank. Ham Tamdje ordered his people not to answer."

Dua said, "But what about our fellows who left the banquet? They would still have their radios and their close-air generators."

Jiritzu nodded. "They would! Then they would have heard the deck calls? And they would surely have heard the shooting! What are they doing now?"

For a reply the lights in the cabin flickered out.

"That must be it," Nurundere's voice came through the blackness in the cabin. "The deck must be acting to help us now. Watch officer should be, *mm*, Uraroju. Good, she'll do the right thing!"

From the tank beyond the cabin there came shouting and the sounds of running and tumbling. "Uraroju cut the power to the tank," someone said. "That means that the door-seals are open!"

There was a sound of movement toward the door, but Nurundere shouted, "Wait! Don't just push out there! We need a plan!"

There were ten confused replies at once.

Nurundere said, "Just to run out would be futile." As if to emphasize his words there came the sound of renewed shooting. "From the noise out there the meat must be disorganized," the captain said. "We should get out of this cabin as quietly as we can—in case they decide to slaughter their prisoners. We need to recover our close-air equipment, we have to find out where they've put the generators.

"But first, get away from this cabin. Spread out, make for the nature deck. We can count on Uraroju and the deck watch but meanwhile we have to avoid the meat and their guns."

They got through the doorway safely.

The meat who had acted as guards were gone. On the passenger deck the sailors could see almost nothing. The tank was completely sealed. Panels for space-viewing built into the curving roof over that deck had been covered over when the power was cut by the watch crew.

The passengers had not planned for total darkness and they were stumbling and crashing about, shouting. The Yurakosians had a great advantage now: equally blinded in the dark, yet they knew the arrangement of the tank, were completely at home aboard *Djanggawul* with its odd gravitic effects.

Jiritzu led Bidjiwara by the hand, she on her first voyage in space. They found their way from the cabin, moved across the deck. By the varying strength and pull of the dense rod that provided the ship's gravity, they could gauge their distance from the angle where the decks were joined.

With the passenger tank's power system turned off, the air they breathed was becoming stuffy. At once the plan of Uraroju became clear: if the meat failed to recognize the signs, they would fall unconscious along with their captives. But if they understood what was happening they could outfit themselves with close-air gens.

The crew on watch would come through the airlock. If they found the tank filled with unconscious bodies they could disarm the meat, confine them. All would recover. . . .

If the meat were using close-air, more blood would flow.

Jiritzu dropped to the deck, drew Bidjiwara down with him. Together they crept toward the airlock.

He detected a heavy chair, crept around it, moved across an open area with Bidjiwara's hand clutching his. He reached forward with his free hand and felt the edge of a heavy, hanging cloth. The gown of a woman passenger! He froze!

There was a startled gasp and the woman pulled away as if terrified.

Jiritzu held his breath as long as he could, then exhaled slowly and resumed creeping toward the airlock, Bidjiwara still with him.

After a few more meters his hand encountered a still leg covered with tight trousers. He pressed Bidjiwara flat to the deck, held her in place for a moment to communicate the need to remain still, then ran both his hands up the figure he had found. He moved slowly, silently, but almost at once realized three things: the person was dead, she was a woman, she was a sailor.

Explosive bullets had taken out her belly.

Jiritzu felt her hair: long braids. In the total blackness of the tank he ran fingertips over the *maraiin* on her cheeks. He did not know the meaning of her sacred patterns, but he recognized them nonetheless. This was the body of Miralaidj.

Half a sob escaped Jiritzu—he felt Bidjiwara grasp him in the dark. Miralaidj dead. Wuluwaid dead. Jiritzu had no thoughts of the Dreamtime. They were simply dead.

Miralaidj's Kunapi half Bidjiwara was now more than ever Jiritzu's charge. He could not stop to mourn, he could not wail a song of grief. He could only draw little Bidjiwara in a half-circle away from the body. Surely she must wonder what had happened, what Jiritzu had encountered, but he did not stop to tell her.

Now they were near the airlock. Now Jiritzu caressed the face of little Bidjiwara, hoping she would remain quiet until the coming struggle should end. Jiritzu's ears were beginning to ring, his breath to come short in his throat. Colors swirled in the darkness.

Surely this must be the approach of unconsciousness through deprivation of air. Surely all the meat, unused to conditions aboard membrane ships, were by now sprawled unconscious in the dark. Now Uraroju and the others from the deck watch must come through the airlock, moving quickly, to disarm and capture the mutineers before they died—yet also before they could recover.

The ringing grew louder in Jiritzu's ears, but before he lost awareness he heard the machinery of the airlock working, heard the first hiss of air from within it. In his spirit he could see the heavy lock opening. A sailor held a portable deck-light, and now Jiritzu could see, not merely in his spirit.

The light shone into the tank. Dead and unconscious bodies were scattered about, but before the airlock stood a single silhouette: gross, weaving, the edge of a sleeve of some nearly white cloth highlighted by the flare from the airlock. And in the hand emerging from that sleeve an old-style explosive gun.

One N'Jajan had divined the plan of Uraroju. One who had not been able to warn the others—or who had chosen, in his growing irrationality, to remain silent. One who had strapped to his leg a close-air generator and was ready to fire at the sky heroes coming through the airlock.

Jiritzu drew a deep breath of still-stuffy air, rose to his feet as the figure of Ham Tamdje of N'Jaja spun clumsily forward. Jiritzu flexed his knees, gauging the gravity at this point, and launched himself across the deck toward Ham Tamdje. No person other than a membrane sailor could have made that leap, but any experienced sky hero could have done so.

For a moment Jiritzu felt almost as if he were leaping from spar to deck in the free-fall of space. There was a blaze of light as Ham Tamdje fired his gun, a hot impact low on Jiritzu's leg, then the sailor crashed into Ham Tamdje's fat body and they tumbled to the deck. Now there was little struggle. Ham Tamdje was soft and unaccustomed to space, Jiritzu was hard and well at home. The wound in his leg would have mattered if he were standing, but as they rolled and struck each other, gouged and squeezed there on the deck of the passenger tank, it meant little.

Jiritzu struck the N'Jajan, the deaths of his fellows now coming to him, the death of Miralaidj before his eyes and his spirit. He could wail his song of grief now, could wail and scream at this fat, pale chunk of meat, could batter this flabby head against the deck of *Djanggawul's* passenger tank until the hands of sky heroes pulled him away from Ham Tamdje and the sailor could see the pulpy mass he had made of *Djanggawul's* senior passenger.

When the other meat were confined to their cabins the sailors in Uraroju's watch found the two in which the crew had been held. Their walls were marked with scores of scars where weapons had been fired—the meat had tried to massacre their captives when their situation became desperate. And now began the melancholy business of recovering the bodies of crewmen and women killed during the earlier battle, among them the bodies of Wuluwaid and of Miralaidj.

The sky heroes were buried in space.

They were far from the first membrane sailors to die in the deep void, far from the first whose bodies were committed to the stars, to drift forever while their souls returned to the Dreamtime.

The body of Ham Tamdje was set aside for delivery to his friends. Some ground-squirming N'Missan became head of the party of passengers, under cabin-arrest by Captain Nurundere.

And the sky heroes who survived began the great tack at Yirrkalla, near the three beacon suns, the most difficult and most critical portion of their voyage. Shorthanded, Nurundere called upon every available hand. Jiritzu's case was delayed to the end of the voyage; meanwhile he must do his share, wounded leg or no: he was one of the finest membrane-riggers in the fleet!

But afterwards. . . .

Jiritzu, Aranda, Yurakosian, had killed a passenger with his bare hands.

That Ham Tamdje was himself a murderer, armed, and ready to kill more sky heroes, was of no matter.

Surely there would be no criminal charge against Jiritzu, but equally surely he would never again sail as a sky hero.

The meat would be delivered in shame to their destination. They would be left at Port Corley circling New Alabama, left in disgrace, to be dealt with as their planet-squirming fellows might see fit.

And after *Djanggawul's* return to Yurakosi? Jiritzu would be put aground, would be sent into Port Bralku and from there shuttled to the surface of the planet to seek out poor Bunbulama and tell her that her man and her child were in the Dreamtime.

And then, his skin still rich with melanin, he would live as a ground-squirmer in a world of grayed-out elders and black-skinned children.

Or would he? More likely he would choose to climb the highest mast of *Djanggawul* and cast his close-air gen to the deck, and launch himself as far into the void as his muscles could send him.

In theory a very strong sailor could break free of ship's gravity and be lost in space. It has never been done. It would be a suicidal act.

But Jiritzu looks after his wounded leg. It is not a serious wound, and he keeps it well cleaned, and during every watch he exercises to keep his muscles strong. Before *Djanggawul* reaches Port Bralku the wound should be healed.

A ground-squirmer while still so young? The sky hero who killed a passenger, so marked for all his days? Jiritzu, whose beloved is in the Dreamtime?

Standing atop the highest spar of the tallest mast of *Djanggawul,* beneath his feet the starwind-bellied membrane sails, above his head only the blackness and million glittering suns and elsewhere in space the whispered, silent progress of other membrane ships—will Jiritzu climb down, return to port, ride the shuttleship, squirm forever on the ground?

A very strong sailor might break free of ship's gravity and drift forever in deep space. He could return to the Dreamtime.

9. Up Crikkingwood Stairs

Parked in a dirty alley in downtown Letohatchie (don't knock it if you've never tasted Letohatchie fried mudhen) and set a clever device on the gyrocar to set off an electric current and hold any burglar there till they got back Gordon Lester Wallace III and Freddie and he would find the bastard there maybe with a few hours of writhing first and see what they would see to do with him. Humane? Keep your nose clean and it won't get tweaked, that's what! Whose rights are you worried about, the victim or the thief, answer yes or no.

Gordon Lester Wallace III and Freddie wanted to go to a bar and no delay but lost out. Nope—he said—round the block once first.

Gordon Lester Wallace III and Freddie got very brave:—Why?—

Lucky-lucky, no blastback. He said—Look, tomorrow we're gone maybe, yeh? Got the nice boys their bars now who needs tough sarges any more, who? Use skullpower Gordon Lester Wallace III and Freddie—direct address no less! yes!—what will we get in the morning, tasty breakfast for jesusakamitey? Maybe!

—Orders!—A long speech that for him Gordon Lester Wallace III and Freddie felt surprised. Impressed, would you say? He said more!—No sentiment in you Gee Ell Wow Three & Freddie? Round the block once first last look at Letohatchie. Tomorrow who knows deep space off to N'Haiti or someplace else.—

Gordon Lester Wallace III and Freddie shall we say acquiesced.

Once around it.

Alquane was down (N'Alabama was Alquane VII dontchaknow) and the sky was a dark park for stark. No moon tonight not ever in fact except when . . . well, don't let it bug you. No moon tonight. Streets of Letohatchie no emptier than usual one fat man brushed by as Gordon Lester Wallace III and Freddie swung up cruddymuddy sidewalk *with* companion.

Fatman was short (5′2″? 2′5″? 52″? Short!), blondheaded long straggly strips of hair pasted down across his forehead a few tips jiggling delightfully before his *left* eye (not so gritty in the city) perspiration (must have been officer material, eeyems sweat) too on that noble brow helped. Fat fat he jiggled as he waddled as he walked but the sarge (not to mention GLWIII&F) didn't mind, watched his big behind, a find, they jostled for a moment feeling final fast last night in Letohatchie but only *once* around the block fatso goom-bye.

Wanna guided tour? Tag along. He knew Letohatchie inside in did he cadre get to know the towns that way. Here: corner bar (pinkred word startles: B A R) clashing red beersign pick your brand in dirty stapaglass window inside full of smoke, off duty renes sitting at fakewood tables glasses m bottle m soggy nappies all over. Other fakewoods, townies, grumpysullen pyech don't like each other comprehend?

Look: he knew this town. *Knew* it inside in, you know that now. Think he and Gilloowoo3 and Freddie went in there?

Pyech!

Next door Piggy Peggy's Pussy Parlor, big pink sign, local John Darn leaning against wooden doorway whistling sweet and low.

Pass it by sarge and companionship.

EATS next. He knew EATS from first day in Letohatchie. Bad EATS, door in back, oldest established stinking crap game in Letohatchie, run by oldest established ex-spacer in Leto, no crookeder than others, give a man a break he saw that bentfin boomer on his shirt, spacer gyrene trader all, oldest established looked out for deepmen, others beware.

He wore the fin forgot how many missions by now (sprickled skin said a lot a lot) Gordon Lester Wallace III and Freddie had been out too but last night in Leto, last night N'Alaside, who wants to squeeze it out boning for suckerbucks eh? Mean, what goodr bucks on a hotter in deep? *T*h*e*r*e a*r*e n*o w*h*o*r*e*s a*b*o*a*r*d N'A*l*a*b*a*m*a n*a*v*y.* Commercial ships were of course a whores of a different choler. (Same color, though.)

Nice little weapons shop, self-surf washery. Onononon.

—Where we going?—asked Gordon Lester Wallace III and Freddie.

— —

Gordon Lester Wallace III and Freddie didn't know what to do to say. Don't squeeze that was good policy he was a good man an all white guy but temprous so don't squeeze but what are you going to do stand there on cracked sidewalk (fix it postwarse of course) with your thumb zup waiting—Whatcha wanna do?—

He replied!:—Mmnnph.—

Gilloowoo3&F looked at him puzzled. He jerked a finger over one shoulder, moved his head—Mmnn. Articulation supreme.

Moved down sidewalk past ugly fronts GorLesWalTriF in tow, looking at ugly town, streetlights yellow-brown (fixem postwarse) some even worked, peep in windows: military supplies (one-fourthmaster was out of stock bentfin boomers two months, three? local merchant had aplenty, yes: old story, yes); Letohatchie Noozan Sundried selling plenty girlie piks, fukfuk boox, strip strips, You Too Can, noozes.

Noozes: WARGOZWELL ENEMYFALLZBACK BLACASUALTIZRIEZ PAPADOCS LOZING GLORI-WHITE SPACEFLEET NEET TREET.

Y Bi Noozes? Headlines allasame allagame allafine allatime. Win win win. So: Why no fixem sidewalk-cracks, streetlights, build some houses, kill some lowzes, and some schools? Afterwarz uvcorz.

Between Letohatchie Noozan Sundried m Leto Lower Mane St Comp Svcs Inc (kipunx, tab, 9th generation central processor you knit/Y'll U Ate Computing) he stopped *crkk*!

Turned quarter circle on crackedwalk pushed open a dirtywood door with a frosted dirtyglass panel set in its *upper* half turned knob pushed open door walked into hallway (what need to say it was *dingy*?) and started up crikkingwood stairs.

Gordon Lester Wallace III and Freddie followed.

—Going up?—Gordon Lester Wallace III and Freddie asked.

— — he replied.

Gordon Lester Wallace III and Freddie did not exactly qualify for MOS +*intellectual*+ where else to go, hey? Open a dingy door there are steps going uuuuup and he starts uuuuup crikking & Gleewo3+F asks—Going up?—

Pyech! Wrelse Gloowoo Threeneff slidewaze? Pyech!

Up he went crikking every steppina hotdim hall crik followed crik by crik Gordon crik Lester crik Wallace crik the crikcrikcrik and um, Freddie up to the first landing second floor (first floor, European style, O'Earthtime days) reached a landing & stopped.

GLW3&F2.

Nuthermuther dirtydoor loose dingy brass knob stapaglass pane in *top* half frostordirty anyway he couldn't see through (so what he knew) old overpainted mailflap slot set in wood a few inches (European style, O'Earthtime days would have said *centimeters*) below stapaglass he tapped it with starsprickled finger didn't linger door opened just a wee crack he saw a dingy brass chain smoke m people beyond no furners all good surners by their looks glasses m bottles 2 & music thumpathump bump it sounded highly encouraging *as*:

:eye in face opened wide peered through crack at him; eye *his* face peered back in slowly closed (other stayed open) shut didn't stay shut opened again (think a whink?); othereye inside shut-opened (sink a wink?) mustabin the code of the ills door shut a moment *clattk* must be chain coming off door opened again (link a wink?) big fella stepped back let *him* in Gordon Lester Wallace III and Freddie following close behind they made their way to a nempty fakewood table pulled up chairs saddown *and*:

:over came a waiter nice looking surn boy goodpure N'Alabamian stock short though (5′2″? 4′3″? 43″? Short!) pretty yellow hair plastered flat on his skull perspiration held a few straggling locks on his forehead a few tantalizing tips toppled tepidly toward his *left* eye and fat too a find a big behind don't mind.

Waiter looked at customers.—?—he said trippingly.

—Fine old Jack Daniel's charcoal filtered slow-mellowed golden sipping whiskey please with sufficient glasses m napkins you may leave the bottle thank you here—said *he* pointing at the fakewood table top with a finely manicured middle finger (the remainder making a fist).

The waiter said—!—and departed.

He took Gordon Lester Wallace's hands in his own two for a moment, looked into GLWIII&F's eyes, then around the room, found the band (they weren't playing merely staying for the moment): One hornist holding hollowed heculan headbone horn, guava marracist, rhythman with blackskin drumset taptatapa-ing quietly to himself.

Drinks came, sampled same, wartime shame *but* good booze good news. Trues?

Emcee stood up, *he* looked, Gloowoo3&F dida same. Emcee a fat pee, short too, big ass, big mass, yellow hair plastered where on his forehead, couple tips of couple strips hanging over his *left* eye, spotlight spanged on him dressed in plainbuttoned war surplus grays (no bentfin boomer of course) dark gray damp patches at armpits m crotch, perspiring in spangspot waving arms up and down pointed straight to sides fingers extended (don't cough he won't take off) couple times *till*:

:noise level dropped couple deci damn bels emcee worked his mouth couple times perspiration on his forehead glinted in the spangspot he said—and now ladies and gentlemen (no ladies visible present but who ever really *knows*, you know?) Ueer proud to present Miss Merriass Markham (one shrill whistle) to dance our National Anthem!—applause.

Gee Ell Woo Three and Fee lookin round, taken in that there nifty audience, all fine lookin N'Ala types, mostly Leto townies, lossa blond fella, eyes poppin at one odd trio (and in thatole bunch, that's saying a fair mought, donchagree?):

:Lillo man, gray thatch a batch, rummy tummy appearzing m atsizame table a tall skinny fella, longish-locked, hairbrushed back, deli damn cut boned Gee Ell Woo Three and Fee could almosta, not quite pre-bops but almosta, nearly could say, ahem, not to seem un*kind* yall mind, but considerable, arr, effeminate to the eye but that ain tall, recall:

:sittin twixtemz a—you'll never be*lieve* this—sittin twixtemz a, why it's in fuckin credible wearin some kinder fancy damn military lookin with braid m buttons m fleppy lepps m jingles m dingles m bagoozies here's newzies a big muthah co-co-co-coon! Lackta swoon!

One eyepop m *zop* lights stop m who can tell who's on top?

10. Our Own Little Mardi Grass

They dropped away from Port Corley in the shuttle, Leon clutching the railing around his couch for support, knowing that his face was ash-white and streaked with perspiration, his hands shaking and stomach heaving, the ringing in his ears and pressure of his sinuses overpowering.

It was a pleasure.

It was always a pleasure to get away from deep-space craft. This time he and his military aide had been hustled through their reception at the orbiting station and loaded directly onto the shuttlecraft that was taking them to the surface of the planet. For Pineda, the only pleasure that exceeded the relative solidity of the shuttlecraft was the anticipation of setting foot on the planet itself, even though it was going to be New Alabama.

He felt himself gradually relaxing, the knot in his intestines smoothing itself out, the pressure within his head gradually diminishing, his heaving breaths becoming steadier and more relaxed, a pleasant intake of nourishing air instead of the desperate gasps provoked by his body's irrational response to deep-space conditions.

He wiped his brow with a huge pocket kerchief, jammed it away again and turned to look at his aide. Guardsman Brigadier Foch-Giraud sat his own couch as if posing for an official portrait, his scarlet tunic gleaming and uncreased, the thread-of-gold fourragère, frogging and shoulder-boards impeccable, his trousers creased to perfection and boots shined to an incredible luster.

"You understand the situation below?" Pineda asked Foch-Giraud.

"Mr. Pineda, of course."

"Well, tread lightly on this world. There isn't another black man on the planet. They regard all blacks as brutes and fiends, their automatic enemies. You have to show them otherwise."

"I understand, Mr. Pineda."

Leon grunted. Perhaps so, perhaps Foch-Giraud would perform admirably. Still, he wished that he had been consulted both on the basic strategy he was called upon to implement, and on the selection of his military aide. He was far from certain that Foch-Giraud made a good object lesson for N'Ala.

The conversation lapsed—as it usually did with the Brigadier. Foch-Giraud, somehow, seldom seemed to have a great deal to say on any subject. A dialogue with him tended quickly to degenerate into labored speech on one side and dull inattention on the other.

It was a relief, when the shuttle skidded to rest on a long, red-dirt runway at the New Alabama Spacerine Fort Sealy Mae, to debark and look around for N'Loozy's ambassador to N'Alabama. Leon stood with Foch-Giraud at his side, drinking in the bright morning of Letohatchie township.

The sun of N'Alabama, Alquane, was a giant disk in the sky, intrinsically cooler and dimmer than

N'Loozy's or N'Ghana's primaries, it served its sole inhabited planet equally well as a result of N'Alabama's closer orbit. The result was a day-star that seemed to dominate the sky by its sheer size, but that provided no more overall light or heat than men were accustomed to wherever they chose worlds to populate.

The shuttle was tractored to an unloading area and Leon started down the ramp, Foch-Giraud at his elbow and half a stride behind. A small party of greeters stood nearby. One of them, a tall, slim woman of Pineda's age, detached herself and strode to the end of the ramp, clasped Leon's hand as his boots touched N'Alabamian soil.

"Pineda," the woman said, "right on schedule." Her eyes flickered from Leon's face to Foch-Giraud, then back. *Sotto voce* she added, "Is the secretary completely unhinged? Are you trying to get us all lynched by the damned loonies?"

"Everything for a purpose, Adrienne," Leon replied softly. Then, "Madame Ambassador, may I present my military aide Planetary Guardsman Brigadier Foch-Giraud. Brigadier, our ambassador to New Alabama, Madame Adrienne de Pauger."

They shook hands. Then with a loaded glance at Leon, the ambassador escorted them the few paces to the greeting party. She introduced Leon and Foch-Giraud to the N'Alabamian foreign secretary and to Milburn Mitchum, mayor of Letohatchie.

The N'Alabamians exchanged handclasps with Leon, looked at each other in puzzlement, waited while the foreign secretary and Adrienne de Pauger conducted a whispered exchange, then gingerly shook hands with Foch-Giraud.

They climbed into an oversized groundcar and the driver sped off down a red rut road that led from the spaceport and Fort Sealy Mae to the town of Letohatchie itself.

"Ah unnerstan we pulled you away fum your Mardi Grass celebration," the mayor of the town drawled, leaning half over his seat toward Leon.

"More urgent business, Mr. Mayor," Leon replied. "A small enough sacrifice."

"Wal, mebbe your ambassador'll show you around our town some. Miz Adrienne is the belle of the diplomatic corps hereabouts, you know. And we're mighty proud of our town, you know. Why, you might say we've got our own little Mardi Grass right here in Leto every night of the year."

Leon looked at Adrienne de Pauger, then replied to the mayor. "I'm sure that would be most delightful. But perhaps I will be tied up with preparations for the conference. Just an old stick in the embassy, I'm afraid."

"Ah, well it does start tomorrah. Well, you'll have a good time here, Mr. Pineda, we're mighty proud of our town."

"I'm certain your pride is fully justified."

They rolled past rows of scrub vegetation and flatland trees, the wheels of the car kicking up billowing clouds of red dust from the dirt road. The windows of the car were sealed to keep the grit out, but by the time they reached Letohatchie and the car pulled up at a ramshackle wooden building, Leon felt the perspiration on his brow turned to thin mud with the admixture of red dust. His eyes itched and his clothing was dirty. The others in the car seemed in little better shape except for Foch-Giraud, who climbed out, dusted himself briefly and seemed to resume the impeccable parade order he had displayed since their first meeting.

"Our embassy, Leon," Adrienne said. "You've never been here before?"

Leon shook his head. "I've seen worse, believe it or not."

The greeters made their farewells and the car pulled away, presumably heading back to await another shuttle from Port Corley. As the vehicle moved off Leon could read Mayor Mitchum's lips as he repeated his phrase about Letohatchie's own little Mardi Grass.

They went inside the building. Foch-Giraud was shown to his quarters, Leon accompanying Adrienne to a small office where they sat down and opened Leon's briefcase to spread working papers over a desk top.

"The conference convenes tomorrow," Adrienne remarked. "Do we need more time to prepare?"

Leon shook his head. "We're set. The President and the secretary have set policy, with which I fully agree. I hauled our military peacock through Accra and showed him to President Moshi-Nzima. We're well established there. Jekki will howl when we announce our support for Governor Youngerman, our embassy in Accra will have some paint splashed on it and the N'Ghanaians will issue a frostily proper expression of regret over the incident coupled with a sizzling condemnation of our tilt.

"But nothing will happen."

Adrienne nodded. "Well, if you have full confidence." She offered Leon a drink, he asked for tea and Adrienne ordered a pot. Then, "How are the things that matter going? How is Sophie? How is D'Arcy?"

Leon brightened and told Adrienne the news. "All unofficial of course. D'Arcy is keeping her secret."

Adrienne took Leon's hands in hers and squeezed them.

There was a pounding on the door. Adrienne opened it and Brigadier Foch-Giraud entered the room. "Don't wish to interrupt you," he said, "but have we plans for the evening? I really would like to see Letohatchie and the perpetual Mardi Grass the mayor spoke of."

Adrienne de Pauger sighed and said, "I'll arrange an escort for you, Brigadier. N'Alabama's most famous exotic dancer is performing in Letohatchie currently. You may enjoy her act."

* * *

Spangspot shot emcee disappears room is all dark a moment sound of rustling here m there surprising shrill giggle from one nearby table rustle too from center floor (emcee departing?) sudden drumroll from blackskin set (rhythman must really love his work *pang* and a *whang*!) fanfare on heculan head-bone horn and maracas rattle new spangspot *pows* on and somebody's init:

:Miss Merriass Markham a zoftic miss must be pure N'Ala blood but spangspot color is . . . ? . . . blue-green gruebleen gives her skin sheen (all glistered) unnatural coloration (bad taste that) standing at attention quivering salute.

What she wear? Tight brazeer on big big bosom, too tight, flesh welts above and below, must be shall we say, ah, uncomfortable for the poor leddy Miss Merriass Markham, cinched in back, bright bruegleen brazeer looks like rubber (?!) two highly attractive cutouts large pink (?) aureoles (howcinya *tell* in this light?) protuberant nips pazowie that must tingle it's too tite see the red (this lite?) line below nothing on her belly but a wee bit would you say protuberant (pregnant?) actually kind of voluptuous (think of that belly belly-to-belly with your belly—a navel orgasm?) and tights, shorts that is, same blue squeezing gluebreen rubberlooking oh! holdin that roundbottom Miss Merriass run your mind past that behind my! what a lotch of crotch mmmmm! *he* liked that thought *whooeeee*! Miss Markham he gave Gordon Lester Wallace III & Freddie a handsqueeze apeez watching Miss Merriass Markham stand all atremble with patriotic fervor as the three-man band struck up by damn, suh! *Digze* and in a couple beats Miss Markham *began*:

:quivering for *real* in time to that glorious tune her proud patriotic ass slamming slidewaze in tune to bump-bump-bump-bubu-bump-bump-bumbump feet planted proudly on that fine N'Alabamian wooden floors knees apart m bent her arms extended forward toward the audience and quivering quivering in time to the stirring strains of that glorious old tune soon she began to work her hips her hair (glorious golden waves sweeping over softwhite shoulders the kind of tyke a soul has to like her daddy must be proud to grab a handful of *that* stuff) swaying too in time and rock that pelvis hey (are we sufficiently discreet do you think?) all day.

He took a drink of golden smooth Jack Daniel's sipping whiskey bless the old land N'Alabama's soul must be in there somewhere the patriotic air slammed to a close with Miss Merriass Markham slamming a backbend (she was lithe) hands on floor behind her feet hot in the spangspot allover wet salty sweat the audience cheering to a man (no ladies *visible* in the audience but do you ever really *know*?) venting pure patriotic fervor m appreciation of artistry. Mmm?

He took a Gordon Lester Wallace III and Freddie

shoulder in each hand, shook companionship. —Here—he said to GLWIII&F—want know where I take you? Here for a last night in Leto.

Gordon Lester Wallace III and Freddie expressed appropriate impressedness. Now, wouldn't you?

Emcee was back on the floor now waving arms up and down fingers splayed his warsurp grays (plain buttons of course, and definitely no bentfin boomer) looking darkwetter where they'd looked darkwet before the spangspot had changed back no more bleegruen yellowbrown now on him (went nicely with his plastered blond hair one might suggest) grinning broadly his fat face but keeping his teeth clenched and making little folding-unfolding motions at the waist and neck (bowing? nodding?)—Thank you thank you ladies and gentlemen—he said (no ladies visible in audience but did you *know*?)—Miss Merriass Markham will be back momentarily I'm sure you want to see more of her much much more (snicker) and I'm sure she wants you to see more of her so in just one moment after everyone has had a chance to refresh himself for a moment—he stopped lights came back on in the room the emcee disappeared but:

:*he* remained at fakewood table with Jack Daniel's (reserve quality) and companionship.—That all?—asked Gordon Lester Wallace III and Freddie.—That all? Thought she was stripper. This our last night, maybe, on N'Ala, thought we'd get some satis damn faction not a tease.

—Wait—he said.—Looko there—pointing, table across floor had five men, three sitting, two standing, standing two looked alike, short, fatties, blond hair plastered over each *left* eye, two more *sitting* at table, one tall, palepalepale, feminishly looking, agitatedly moving jiggling up and down in fakewood seat, clutching at arm of companion *whō*:

:*he* looked again, touble-daking not for faking, coulda swore bah gore, mushy bin weirdo lights in here coz thato cato niz fancy what kind of luna damn tickle uni damn form coulda sworeez black, black, jussa bigra nigra as in Miss Merriass Markham zupposie haven-rack but:

:the third bird haveya heard medium size chubby man gray hair lay across table arms on table wearing nondescript business (looked like) suit not moving drink spilled across table washing face in booze (o dream, dream, to bathe in JD Sippin Grade) from nondescript medium sized chubby jacket backet covered nondescript nocolor business suit (looked) protruded what appeared toobie dagger handle he was (to coin a phrase) turned off.

Two fat shorties (short fatties) lifted nondescript medium sizer carted him from table disappeared into unknown preserves trailed by tall skinny ladylookin fella & splendo-uniformed can you, can you possibly, can you possibly be*lieve* a nigra both um bobbing agitatedly.

–So?–G etc. said.

–Tomorrow–he replied. –Ueebee gone, orders for . . . wanta guess, Gordon and so on? Try? Where? More training work? Not likely. Offplanet, hey, by by N'Bama hey. Where do you think?–

–?–

–Deepspace? Vacbattle papadocs ready to board? Killanigra once a day gyrene hasta earn his pay. Ready to invade N'Haiti?–

–Mmn.–

–Think the warle spread? N'Anguilla? N'Azteca? N'Tonga?–

—N'Haiti probably. Deepspace on a hotter don't think sarge?—

—Mmm. Drink y'booze. —He gestured again. The empty table where the three men had sat and two stood was empty not now.—!—

Bandback *brrrm, c'chkkkk,* sound of heculan headbone horn, lights down spangspot on emcee again waving arms as ever moving mouth—Thank you ladies (do you *know?*), gentlemen Miss Merriass Markham and assistant will now present a patriotic pageant in honor of N'Alabama her glorsy spacerines—sound of applause in room audible through thick smoke also sound in one corner—no no yes oh—(do you know for *sure?*) spangspot off emcee rustle movement in dark and a *pow:*

:light back on babypinkspot playing on golden curls Miss Merriass Markham strolling in center lowcut *low*cut frilly gown tightfitting cloth begins just above nipple showing pink circle protuberance through cloth every *pore* by bang tight waist and flaring skirt hooped out and ribbons frills to furgem *floor*—Sheet!—loud voice from dark room shuff mumbles Miss Merriass Markham only smiles in circle *as:*

:second spotlight pangs on edge of floor shows a nigra brute Gordon Lester Wallace III and Freddie and even he do double take—Ha?—but no, look, he's white only daubed, daubed, could they pay *you* to trick out as a coon buck? *You?* How much?

Sheeh, one never knows, does he?

Fake coon in a red red spotlight Miss Merriass Markham prances to and fro looking ever whichaway but not at him he inches up on her audience tense and silent inch there's some quiet tense music how can the headbone horner concentrate inch up on that symbol of pure surn lily lady parasol over shoulder gloves over elbows and the nigra:

:*pounces* from behind drags Miss Merriass Markham to him black black dirty she screams he bats parasol clatters Merriass Markham struggles nigra paws, claws *lookit* him drool smashes Miss Markham to the floor reaches, she screeches, nigra bends, rends, rips Miss Merriass's frilly gown *rip* down the back she rolls cloth falls away from big pink rubies round boobies nigra growls audience howls *and*:

:whimpering half-naked surn womanhood backs away from slobbing black animan backs he lunges an arm claws at hanging cloth at pure white womanhood's waist *r-i-i-p* nigra swings arm away in triumph pink and white shreds hanging from clawlike beasthand Miss Merriass Markham no longer fearing stands straight in spangspot eyes flashing bosom heaving as they say (mmm, hosom beaving) starkass naked pale white flesh pale in now-pale spangspot only spots of color her golden lox, dark eyes, red lips (open, panting, love those bodiorificesheymac?) and red nips and that curly triangle pub hair like night delight and what's that?

Curled around her jelly hip what's that black what's that? Round it goes around that sweet soft crotch that lovie V and up around her hip and back O Underline the Arse and back between and around and what? A handle it has she grasps and uncoils a whip (a bullwhip a buckwhip) and upraises't in the spangspot and lookit *lookit* that face that joy that maidenhood defended boyoboy o *lookit* that coon *now* willya see him cringe see him crawl

he *knows* his place

but she won't let him off that easy Miss Merriass swings that whip and *tchapp*! lookit that nigra roll hear him whine *phwapp*! O good O God O finefine-fine O go Miss Merriass and *crack*! O look o look his back the red the people lose their mind the cheers and screams and hips, hips working, losing minds, pelvis grinds tears, cheers the nigra falls, Miss Merriass Triumphant calls defiant independent slogan:

Never!

Lights out, rustling sighing moaning and house-lights uuuup roomful of men (well . . .) sitting drained, Miss Merriass and troupe not to be seen shortfatblond emcee in centeroom waving arms up and down blinking mouth working no sound at first (but who cares? a great audience, not a dry crotch in the house!)—Thank you thank you Miss Merriass Markham thanks you please note ladies (hmm) and gentlemen that the nigra was accredited member Actor's Professional Guild qualified simulator available weddings, confirmations, funerals, this is, after all, a respectable establishment drink up ladies (?) m gentlemen thank you.—

Well the Jack Daniel's sippin was about done by now so he poured a few drops for Gordon Lester Wallace III and Freddie and finished up the rest himself and smacked his hand down hard on the table some money in it bills and coins made a good solid sound on the fakewood and stood up, up too Gordon Lester Wallace III and Freddie, followed him to the door past the (one might so dignify him) *maître d'hôtel* a short man with the cutest blond strings crossing his pate plastered with perspiration (or sweat as they say) on his forehead and a couple strands dank dangling before his *left* eye and—Thank you sir O thank you—as they passed through the dirty door with the stapaglass panel (the extra O thank you for a sweet tweak in a sensitive spot) and onto the landing.

—Base now,—he said.

—Yes,—said Gordon Lester Wallace III and Freddie.

They scapp-scappered down dingy stairs out dingy door at bottom retraced steps past quick glimpse at Leto Comp Svcs peered into Noozan Sundried (last edns now on sale N'ALA TRIUMPH BLACKS FALLING BACK RUMOR N'DESERET TO ENTER WAR TREASON TRIAL IN TRUSSVILLE passemby), military supplies (needny bentfin boomers?), Piggy Peggy's (eyecorner glimpse of John Darn entering establishment), and EATS and B A R.

Gyrenes back to two-wheel gyrocar and !whatchaknow! clever electronic device done *caught* somebody (short man and fat with platnum locks) see'm *writhe* willya?

GLWIII&F watch as he keys off clever device, writher falls, he chexm—No fun this bucketkicker—he gets in gyro, G+ in back seat, 'noff we go on the red rut road and to (but of course!) beddie.

Darkness in barracks, he listens:

—Deepspace, do you think?—

—N'Cathay?—

—N'Yu-Atlanchi bet.—

—Invade, invade N'Haiti show furgem papadocs.—

—Think we'll ever get back on O'Earth?—

Sniggers. From sarge's private (well) cubicle:—Orders tomorrow. Now quiet!—

Rustles and sighs.

11. From the Bizonton Pylon

The climb from the Rue Margarite to the hoverail depot was long and difficult, and for the thousandth time Christophe Belledor mourned the long discontinued vertiflot service. Discontinued, perhaps, is not the correct word. When there was not the money or manpower to perform routine maintenance, the vertiflot became increasingly erratic in its performance, carrying passengers between the street and the hoverail platform less and less reliably, until it had finally been abandoned as too dangerous to continue.

Already, many N'Haitians, Christophe among them, had had narrow escapes from too-rapid descents or from ascents that had suddenly reversed their direction. A few unlucky Bizontoniers had tried the device once too often, and had not escaped its failure.

Ah, well, such was the war effort. Someday things would be better, the vertiflot would be repaired and restored to service, and patient, hardworking citizens would be rewarded.

Christophe stopped halfway up the pylon to catch his breath. He was no longer the young man he once had been. As well, as well. All citizens could contribute, each in his own way. Too old to serve in the starfleet, still Christophe could fill his desk at the Ministry, freeing a younger man to fight for N'Haiti. And he could bear arms at the regular drills of the Planetary Guard, ready to defend his world against invasion if it ever came. But for now . . .

Christophe shuffled forward, climbing the steps of slowly crumbling concrete, philosophically observing the tired citizens about him, their shabby clothing patched and threadbare. Ah, another sacrifice for the great effort. When N'Haiti is free to turn her energies to peace once more, things will be better. There will be new clothing, dwellings will be repaired and new ones will be built, and the vertiflot service will function once again throughout the commuter network of the Compagnie Nationale des Chemins de Fer d'N'Haiti.

But today, ah, Christophe Belledor reached the platform at last, made his way to the rear of the crowd waiting at the edge of the flatbed for the hoverail to take them to N'Porprince. Christophe recognized several of his fellow commuters but did not try to strike up conversations. Soon, if there had been no breakdown, perhaps at Bahon or St. Marc, the train would arrive. Then there would be a rush to get aboard, for trains did not run as frequently as once they had and those who missed one sometimes could not wait for another, and had to walk to work.

When the hoverail finally arrived Christophe was fortunate—he managed to crowd into the front car and stood wedged between a fat man he had seen many times but never spoken to, and the attractive daughter of his neighbor Leclerc, Yvette. She smiled at him as the sway of the car moving from the Bizonton pylon forced their bodies together for a moment. Christophe felt flustered, tried to look away and pretend he had not noticed the young girl or her reaction to their accidental contact, then grinned in embarrassment as she giggled at him.

After the hoverail had halted in N'Porprince and the crowd of workers had forced their way off, he relived the brief and wordless exchange as he walked through the stuffy passageways connecting the central hoverail pylon with the Ministry. He stopped at the stall of Maurice in the lobby of the Ministry, looked at the morning's *Haitian* and almost purchased a copy. First, though, he counted the few plastic sous in his trousers pocket and decided that someone in the office would have a copy.

He took his hand back from his pocket, walked past the wooden stall with a shamefaced, "Bonjour, M. Maurice."

M. Maurice's reply was a snarl which Christophe did not quite manage to avoid hearing as he started up the stairs. Eh, even the Ministry of Military Manpower Procurement could not obtain repairs for its vertiflot in wartime. The scurrying about that had taken place, the shouted commands and helpless shrugs that had been exchanged when word arrived that none other than the Premier was planning a visit to the Ministry, and would have to climb wooden stairs to reach the office of the Minister!

The Premier had reacted surprisingly. No vertiflot, he exclaimed, well, in wartime we must all sacrifice. And, taking the trembling arm of the Minister he had walked up flights of stairs to confer. Word had spread and with it relief—the Premier had not complained of the broken vertiflot. The Minister's neck was saved. Department heads were spared expected tongue-lashings. Employees breathed easier throughout the

Ministry. Such was war, and such was the operation of the Government.

But this day was another day, and with it there came another problem. As Christophe contemplated the staff study he was to complete editing for the Deputy Minister he clucked in his mouth and shook his head with worry. The pleasant thought of Yvette was eradicated by the stern problems of manpower procurement and the folly of the Deputy Minister's plan.

With the study, the promising career of Marius Goncourt would come to a sudden end as the Minister came to realize fully the nature of M. Goncourt's proposal, and with M. Goncourt would fall his staff, including—most emphatically including—Christophe Belledor.

Winded and perspiring, Christophe reached the landing of his department. He leaned against the doorjamb for a moment and wiped his forehead with a tattered pocket kerchief, then entered the large room. Most of the others had arrived ahead of him. Madame Bonsard, the secretary and receptionist, greeted him with an unpleasant smile and, "Bonjour, M. Belledor. Madame Belledor, she failed to waken you this morning?"

Christophe tried to smile as he walked past the desk of Madame Bonsard, but did not speak to her. He glanced at the clock as he passed beneath it. Eh, 0700 hours already, he was late once again. He turned to speak: "The hoverail, Madame Bonsard, there is nothing that one can do, you know. Perhaps you will not . . ." He caused his voice to trail off in quiet hope, but already he could see that Madame Bonsard was marking the hour of his arrival on the weekly personnel report.

"Wartime, M. Belledor," she said. "We must all do our bit, eh? Surely you would not wish me to falsify an official report of the Ministry."

Christophe shook his head and made his way to his desk. This day, he could tell already, would not be a good one. Another lateness ticked on his card, and the way it felt, eh, this day would be a hot one. But chiefly, there was the study of the Deputy Minister to be grappled with. Christophe fumbled in his pocket, drew out a group of keys, sorted them until he found the one he wanted and bent to unlock the drawers of his wooden desk.

Again he paused to wipe perspiration. Ah, when the war was over there would again be air conditioning in the offices of the Ministry. Such a pleasure it would be then, to arrive at work on a steaming day and perform his duties in the cool air of the machines now standing idle for lack of service and parts, and for lack of power to make them function even if service and parts were available. On such a day, to go home cool and refreshed to Marie-Auedda, on a hoverail not so crowded as they now were, and down a vertiflot. Well, one must wait for peace.

He reached into a locked drawer, removed a brown pasteboard folder and placed it on his desk. From the next desk a voice asked, "Is that the famous report of M. Goncourt, Christophe?"

"The very one," he replied. "When M. the Minister sees this, we are all finished. Deputy Minister Goncourt, Belledor the staff assistant, Madame Bonsard, all of us. You also, Phillipe." Christophe nodded sadly.

"Come now," Phillipe teased. "It is not all that bad. How can it be, Christophe?"

M. Belledor sat for a moment, his eyes fixed on the cover of the report. Then he turned his chair to face

Phillipe. He leaned forward. "You do not take me seriously," he said, "but I will tell you what M. Goncourt is proposing. Then you will not think so lightly of it."

Phillipe looked with mock alarm. "Christophe, is the report of the Deputy Minister not marked with a security level? How can you discuss it then?"

"I am sure that you are a spy, Phillipe. Everything you know goes directly to N'Montgomery, of course." He snorted. "You have the same clearance as I or you would not be in your position one hour! Now, do you wish to know what the Deputy Minister has in mind?"—he tapped the folder with the fingertips of one hand—"or do you not?"

The other nodded. "Yes, yes, tell me what he proposes," he said, a supercilious look crossing his face.

Christophe paused. Then, "You know, Phillipe, the manpower demands of the war and the general effect it is having on our economy. We must support not one but three national efforts at once. To fight the enemy we must man our ships with spacemen of every sort—officers, gunners, maintenance crews, boarding brigades, communications men, medical, supply clerks, cooks, everything!"

"Yes, yes," said Phillipe. "We all know that. So what?"

Christophe continued, undisturbed. "To support that direct effort of war requires a whole economy. Spaceship yards to repair battle and supply ships damaged by the enemy and to perform normal maintenance, as well as to build new warcraft to carry the battle to the *blancs* of N'Alabama.

"Weapons manufactories. Ammunition plants. Training and supply bases for our forces. Medical facilities for wounded. Transportation and supply systems. A constant stream of replacements and support. Do you know, Phillipe, there are between six and seven N'Haitians in and out of the planet's military force to support each space soldier actually in combat?"

Phillipe showed impatience. He grunted a bored yes.

"Well then," Christophe went on, "that is still not all. For beneath our military effort and all that goes to support it, N'Haiti must still maintain its own basic economy. We sacrifice such luxuries as the vertiflot and the comfort of cool air in the Ministry, but essential functions must be maintained or there will be no economy to support the economy that supports the military!" He placed his hands conclusively on his knees and leaned back, looking triumphantly at the younger man.

"Eh," shrugged Phillipe, "I still say, so what? You only mouth the commonplace. Everyone knows this. Is this the sensitive report of the Deputy Minister? It is the weekly project of the sixth-year school child. Christophe, you disappoint me. Deputy Minister Goncourt disappoints me."

"No, no," interrupted M. Belledor, "you are always so impatient, Phillipe! Now wait. M. Goncourt sets forth the obvious in his report, true enough, but it is necessary as background for the Minister. M. Antoine-Simone is not too clever, do you think?"

Phillipe conceded.

Christophe went on: "N'Haiti must support three complete economies then. M. Goncourt designates these the pure military, the military support, and the civil support economies. Each requires finance, planning, control. Each requires its share of our planet's resources. Most of all, each requires the efforts of the people. A farmer on La Gonave–"

"What has the moon to do with it?" Phillipe interrupted.

Christophe brought his fist into the palm of his hand angrily. "All of N'Haiti has to do with it! Do not interrupt! A man who is farming on La Gonave is not working in the factories of Miragoane! A munitions worker in Miragoane is not serving on board the *Toussaint l'Ouverture!* A marine aboard the *Dessalines* is not tending crops on La Gonave!" Panting, M. Belledor slumped back in his swivel chair.

Solemnly his companion said, "The profundity of M. Goncourt does not fail to astound me. Christophe, we are indeed fortunate to be in the department of the Deputy Minister." He leaned forward and slapped Christophe on the shoulder, roaring with laughter. The office turned and stared. Madame Bonsard clucked disapprovingly and jotted a note.

Christophe fumed angrily. Finally he spoke. "Phillipe, you, an employee of the Ministry above all citizens, should have an understanding of the biggest problem of the war. We lack manpower to support three demands at once. The fleet of Grand Admiral Gouede Mazacca suffers terrible losses. So do the cursed *blancs*, but you know the *blancs*, Phillipe, they breed like beasts.

"Gouede Mazacca demands new troops, La Ferriere does not delay to provide them. The pool is dry, Minister Antoine-Simone is called upon. Ah, well, all the strong men of the planet are at work in the war economy. Out they go, off to Grand Admiral Gouede Mazacca on the *Jean Christophe*, off to fight the *blancs*, off to become casualties. But the military support economy cannot be neglected, eh? Ships, weapons, power plants, ammunition—they must continue to flow! So: where do the workers come from? From the civil economy!

"Have you seen the reports of Governor Faustin, Phillipe?" Christophe went on without waiting for an answer: "He is running the great agricultural stations of La Gonave with old men, women, school children. No wonder food is short. Without a strong civil economy, the war supplies will not long flow. Then . . ." Christophe shrugged.

Phillipe said, "And Deputy Minister Goncourt has a solution?"

Christophe picked up the pasteboard-covered report. "He thinks he has. I think he is perhaps mad."

Obviously interested at last, Phillipe said, "And his plan?"

Christophe leaned back once more, luxuriating in his advantage over the younger man. "You take me seriously at last, eh? Well then, answer me some questions and then I will answer yours."

Phillipe leaned forward. Christophe said, "Do you know who is Dangbe? Ayida-Oueda? Have you heard of Papa Legba, of Ayizan, Tokpodu, Zo, Heviyoso, Kpo, Agone, Gbo?"

Phillipe sat mystified, silent.

"None of them?" Christophe asked. "Not one?" The other shook his head. "Have you never visited the Gran Houmfort Nationale, Phillipe?"

Again, a shake of the head. "Christophe, I do not know what you are speaking about. Those names. But I have visited the Gran Houmfort from time to time. It is the great museum of N'Haiti. What is the relation of all this to the war?"

"Phillipe, Phillipe, ahh." Christophe paused for dramatic effect; a plain man, still he did not mind the moment of suspense, the attention of an audience of even one person.

"Surely, the Gran Houmfort is a museum. Obviously you have not visited the wing devoted to O'Haitian culture. You have never heard of the great *vodus* of O'Haiti, of O'Earth. You have never heard of Gbo, great *vodu* of war, of Heviyoso, *vodu* of storm, of Legba, *vodu* of fertility. And you have never heard of Dangbe, *vodu* lord, king of all.

"Phillipe, you do not know that in O'Haiti the *houmfort* was the shrine of the *vodus*. You never heard of the rites of *vodu*, the sacrifice of the black rooster, the ouanga bag, the danse calinda, the zombie?"

The younger man broke in. "This is madness, Christophe! Does Goncourt think to provide Gouede Mazacca's fleet with crews of *zombies*? He is insane! It is all insane!"

Christophe sat quietly. He waited for the excitement to pass from the other. At last Phillipe sat quietly, also. "Tell me it is not so, Christophe. The Deputy Minister cannot be so mad. He does not seriously propose this insane magic."

Christophe tapped the pasteboard on his desk slowly. "Yes," he said at last. "Deputy Minister Goncourt believes that he can make the ancient legends real. Not by magic. He calls upon no *vodu* spirits. He works with the Department of Medical Science. He proposes to use resuscitated space casualties from both our own fleet and the enemy's to fill our needs.

"He claims he can do this by implanting a small sea creature found on an undisclosed planet at the base of the cortex of the casualty. And, Phillipe . . ." He gazed directly into the eyes of the other man. ". . .

Phillipe, he has initiated a pilot study of this madness. The parasitic creatures are already being harvested."

Christophe leaned back once again. After a few moments, Phillipe turned away, to his own work. Christophe opened the pasteboard folder on his desk, drew a blue pencil from the top drawer, and began marking punctuation and spelling changes for Madame Bonsard, who would mech-write the final version of M. Goncourt's report to Minister Antoine-Simone. Christophe sighed as he wrote, and his mind wandered to the earlier encounter he had had with Yvette Leclerc.

12. The Bright Sea of N'Yu-Atlanchi

Ch'en-Tch'aa-Zch'uwn writhes slowly, drifting supine in the shallow saline fluid that covers and penetrates all of N'Yu-Atlanchi. Her extended limbs, little more than vestigial after forgotten generations of weightlessness, retain still sufficient muscularity to guide Ch'en-Tch'aa-Zch'uwn from eddy to eddy as the heat-currents and multilunar tides of N'Yu-Atlanchi carry to her endlessly varied sensations. At times, she turns soft, cartilaginous hands, like rudders, directing herself, choosing to be carried by this stream or that, occasionally meeting a current sideways-on, rolling, the alternation of refracted sky and shallow sea-bottom creating a whirling spiral of visual sensation upon which she meditates long after its cessation.

Ch'en-Tch'aa-Zch'uwn is small for a S'tscha. Her large, flat eyes have seen the chief moon of N'Yu-Atlanchi die three times, the lesser moons no fewer than twice nor more than four score times. Like all S'tscha, she emerged from the womb of the All-Mother a living speck, little more than a blastula devoid of limb, the many nerve endings which now permeate her epidermis then fewer in number and more sparse in distribution.

She does not know how long she spent in the sea-filled, glowing crystalline caverns and grottoes of N'Yu-Atlanchi. She does not know of the seemingly inexhaustible parthenogenetic fertility of the All-Mother. It is possible to question the very designations: N'Yu-Atlanchi, S'tscha, Ch'en-Tch'aa-Zch'uwn, but if only for convenience, they may be used.

She does not know of the crippled high-speed traveler of metal that bore her distant, giant, human ancestors to N'Yu-Atlanchi.

Certainly Ch'en-Tch'aa-Zch'uwn does not think of herself as human. It is debatable whether she thinks of herself at all, or whether she thinks at all.

She senses.

Touch, odor, flavor, these are no longer differentiated. The skin of Ch'en-Tch'aa-Zch'uwn is populated with nerve endings. She feels through her skin, feels the warmth of NGC 7007 the sun of N'Yu-Atlanchi, feels the comforting buoyancy and saline intimacy of the nutrient waters upon and to an extent within her body at every point. It is, in a sense, very like sexual intercourse, but endless, except as her life will some day end, and without beginning, except as sensation began for Ch'en-Tch'aa-Zch'uwn at the instant that she quickened, a fatherless zygote, within the womb of the All-Mother in the buried, drowned centermost grotto of N'Yu-Atlanchi.

Her role is confused. Ch'en-Tch'aa-Zch'uwn is female, at least in the sense, and to the extent, that the offspring of the parthenogenetic All-Mother inherit all their chromosomes from that undeniably female parent. Is this three-centimeter-long child of the All-Mother then a living yoni, somehow inverted, presenting all of the moist, sensitive membrane of its calling passages to the total caress of the universally-penetrating sea? Or is she a living lingam, male though female, enveloped in the perfectly and wholly receptive brine? Her role is confused.

On the chief satellite of N'Yu-Atlanchi, often visible to Ch'en-Tch'aa-Zch'uwn, a minuscule blemish marks the soil of one small area that would assay an iron content slightly on the high side of normal, were there an assayer present, which there is not. One of the lesser moons of N'Yu-Atlanchi sustains upon its otherwise barren face a machine that is broken and does not function. The machine has been there as long as the iron has been on the greater moon of N'Yu-Atlanchi, but as the lesser moon is without atmosphere the machine has neither rusted, nor corroded, nor been torn by the green fingers of patiently indomitable vegetation, nor been pulverized by rain, nor crushed beneath snow, nor squeezed by ice.

It will not last forever. It is battered daily by photons from NGC 7007 the sun of N'Yu-Atlanchi. Radiation from more distant luminaries pushes it down into the unyielding rock of the lesser satellite of N'Yu-Atlanchi.

It is, really, a race, were a sufficiently patient observer present to appreciate the competition.

Consider: radiation batters relentlessly at the functionless machine, the relic. Will it pulverize the metal, powder the glass, crush the crystal, demolish the circuits, cause implosion, dismemberment of molecules, disorganization of atoms? Or will the lesser moon of N'Yu-Atlanchi interrupt the slow, relentless process; will the airless satellite draw close to its primary, closer and yet more close until it disintegrates, hurling its dead burden into the sea of N'Yu-Atlanchi, or, perhaps, into independent orbit?

More competitors in the race. Will meteoroid arrive, make smithereens of the machine before nature removes it from independent being? Will new intelligence arrive, driven by agonized matter, to retrieve the prize? Will NGC 7007 spoil the sport by flaring all to a crisp?

It is a perilous race, but Ch'en-Tch'aa-Zch'uwn does not think about that. It is debatable that she thinks at all. She senses.

Touch, odor, flavor, these senses are now one. She has no distinguishable nose. Long ago her ancestors discarded nostrils, lungs; their bodies learned to terminate ontogeny at that point which features gill slits. Long ago, this was even before the All-Mother came to her fruitful rest in the centermost grotto. Given enough time these too were abandoned. The omnipresent sea of saline warmth could provide oxygen as well as protein. Some distant ancestor of Ch'en-Tch'aa-Zch'uwn had learned to draw total sustenance directly from the enveloping wet.

With that went the mouth also.

Only remained the eyes of the S'tscha, the large, flat eyes placed proportionately far apart on what was once, ancestrally, a face, eyes that, too, were slowly becoming undifferentiated from the surrounding tissue, their photosensitivity becoming distributed, rods and cones appearing now here and there among the crowding nerve endings that made up the skin of each S'tscha, and ears, the sensitivity remaining still to an extent in vaguely distinguishable spots to either side of the head, but this function, too, becoming spread, increasingly with each generation, across the surface of the skin of the S'tscha.

Thus the All-Mother, refining her product, or, perhaps, the opposite of refining.

Ch'en-Tch'aa-Zch'uwn drifts slowly beneath NGC 7007, sensing visually upward. The star visible above her is green, blazing strongly through a sky of yellow. This Ch'en-Tch'aa-Zch'uwn has seen many times. There are clouds, yes; the rich sea of N'Yu-Atlanchi is not exempt from the law. Water, bathed in strong sunlight, shall vaporize and ascend sunward. This is the law. Humbly the waters of N'Yu-Atlanchi obey.

They vaporize, they rise, they recondense, accumulate into clouds. Clouds are not everyday occurrences on N'Yu-Atlanchi, but Ch'en-Tch'aa-Zch'uwn has seen them many times. She has seen the major satellite die thrice. She has seen, heard, felt/tasted/smelled rain. That is even more unusual on N'Yu-Atlanchi. It is not wholly unknown.

The rain on N'Yu-Atlanchi is fresh. The salts, the proteins, the free amino acids that characterize the sea of N'Yu-Atlanchi do not vaporize with the water; the clouds are pure, the rain is clear. To any S'tscha, rain is life's major peril. Cold it is, vapid, without the warm salinity to which the S'tschai are accustomed from the moment of quickening, without the nourishing impurities which are for the S'tscha life.

Once has Ch'en-Tch'aa-Zch'uwn known rain thusly. Drifting, caught in the lifelong surrender of her kind to her kindly environ, caught this day beneath a concatenation of clouds, the glare of NGC 7007 obscured, the warming rays interrupted, refracted, diffused, lost, suddenly cold despite the kindly warmth about her, Ch'en-Tch'aa-Zch'uwn knew something that might have been fear had her nervous system, surely thoroughly developed but so narrowly experienced, held any encoding identifiable as that emotion, or any other than a mindless content.

Then the drops had begun to fall. The water close above the eyes of the S'tscha was altered, their visual function revised from that of a faithfully planar semi-reflector through which the S'tscha viewed equably the calm sky and luminary of her accustomed day. Now the surface flickered, pulsed, broke into innumerable constantly shifting forms.

Concavities appeared, spread, overlapped, flattened; drops of rain created sudden moments of impact; the sound of individual strikings of raindrops as they violated the plane of juncture between sea and atmosphere impinged upon Ch'en-Tch'aa-Zch'uwn her ears, discrete explosions yielding to a patter, then a roar as the number of drops per surface unit per time unit grew from the discernible to the indeterminable.

Ch'en-Tch'aa-Zch'uwn her eyes lost their appearance of calm contemplation of the sky as their view was shattered and confused by the close-falling drops. She felt cold, the withdrawal of nurturing comfort at one with the new absence of nourishment in the sea water about her; in a state conceivably identifiable as desperation the S'tscha flailed the vestigial centimeter-long limbs left her by distant inheritance.

Unthinkingly flitting through the unfamiliarly cold and characterless fluid she spun one hundred eighty degrees about her unrecognized longitudinal axis, her sight whirling away from the darkened and broken sea surface, distant images spinning too rapidly for identification past her widened flat eyes, her attention arrested at last by the refractile crystalline seabed she now faced.

Light from NGC 7007 the sun of N'Yu-Atlanchi, green, returned sky color from the dome of N'Yu-Atlanchi, yellow, cloud tone, gray, menacing, sea coloration, aquamarine tint, rich, brilliant, darkened now by cloud and rain, reflected still and refracted also from the multiple surfaces of partially transparent crystal. Ch'en-Tch'aa-Zch'uwn, accustomed to the sight of light dancing from the crystals of the sea bottom, now, despite the vastly increased multiplicity of apparent sources caused by the increased diffraction of the rain-broken sea surface, grew more calm amidst the shifting shafts and glares of turquoise, aquamarine, blue, blue-green, yellow, gray; the movements of the limbs of the S'tscha desisted from their frantic quality, subsided to the calm, stabilizing sway more usually their characteristic motion.

Still, Ch'en-Tch'aa-Zch'uwn was imperiled by the growing concentration of chill and flavorless water produced by the continuing downpour of rain. That she thought is a dubious proposition at best; she was only vaguely self-aware, hardly distinguishing her body from her surroundings, her identity from her environment, her sensations from their sources.

That she determined, as the end product of logical process, to flee the menacing new element that altered her bath, that already was dimming her senses and sapping her vitality, is unlikely. Yet, flight was her course. Fluttering her weak and frigid legs to propel herself forward through the hostile environment, turning the tips of her forelimbs, once ancestrally hands, now soft, paddlelike, unmarred by differentiated digits, holding her gaze on the multiplanar refractive sea bottom she moved, seeking a break in the crystalline surface that would yield escape from the rainwater, entry to a lower grotto of the honeycomb crystal that formed the multiple shells and shorings of N'Yu-Atlanchi, that held the warmer, familiar, comforting fluid of Ch'en-Tch'aa-Zch'uwn her accustomed medium.

This way and that swam the S'tscha Ch'en-Tch'aa-Zch'uwn, the roar of falling rain assaulting her ears with its menacing fullness, the cold and deprivation of its waters stiffening the weak musculature of her limbs, slowly inhibiting the function of her countless nerve endings as it replaced the usual warm fluid interpenetrating epidermal tissue, numbing sensors, shorting out neural synapses as messages to the proportionately large central nerve cluster of Ch'en-Tch'aa-Zch'uwn grew fewer and fewer.

Ahead at last the S'tscha detected the small nonrefractive patch, the dull absence of reverberating crystal light that must indicate an opening through the sea bottom. Energies flagging, senses growing dim, she struggled forward, drew near, drew at last over the small opening. She turned the paddlelike flexible spatulates that tipped her forelimbs to brake her thin forward momentum, hovered momentarily over the small opening, roughly circular, in the crystal floor of the sea.

Beneath she could see more dimly, her eyes adjusted to the light of the uppermost surface of the planet, relatively brilliant as compared to the secondary grotto despite the dimming influence of cloud and falling drops. Hesitating only briefly as if to grasp needed resolution, she reached downward with forelimbs, down toward the sea-bottom opening, reaching as if to embrace the very fluid core of the sphere, then drew back, upward, simultaneously scissoring her legs, pushing against the coldly invading water as against a brace or truss, forcing her body into a position perpendicular to the concave surface of the planet, her head downward, and moving, now, with strokes of her forelimbs pulling downward, of her legs, pushing, moving down from the new cold world of grayness, of hostile unnourishing fresh water, downward toward the relative darkness, the warm and nourishing salinity of the inner grottoes, like a breach delivery reversed, the neonate longing to return to the protective interior darkness, to become unborn, a fetus, clutching itself, globular, inward turned, safe, unaware, untouched, unknowing, unquickened.

She did not lose consciousness. It is debatable that she was conscious at all. She sensed and reacted. As Ch'en-Tch'aa-Zch'uwn plunged through the bung in the outermost crystalline crust of N'Yu-Atlanchi in flight from the pursuing chill and deprivation of the fresh water her senses were dimming; as she penetrated to deeper levels the warmth and nourishing ingredients of N'Yu-Atlanchi its sea replaced the rainwater, pressing against the S'tscha, shallowly interpenetrating her tissues, restoring, repairing, comforting; the child of the All-Mother grew calm, her sensors returned to full receptivity and acuteness, her musculature to its usual vigor and strength.

Here in the uppermost refractive grotto of the world, soothed by warming moisture, Ch'en-Tch'aa-Zch'uwn floated, passive, the final kinetic residue of her escape converted now to a gentle horizontal rotation that yielded a slow twirling movement to her body, the images of crystal above and crystal below alternating with broad corridors, sea-filled, crystal-floored and crystal-roofed, wall-less, infinitely lengthy, stretching in all directions. From the sky descended daylight, filtered first by rare N'Yu-Atlanchian rain clouds, further tinted and diffused by seawater, then broken, scattered, thrown in violently varying directions by the uppermost crystal layer of the planet, beneath which floated the S'tscha, turning slowly, escaping from the rain.

Through other orifices in the crystal other S'tschai had escaped downward. Those caught by the rare downfall far from bung-holes, those whose reflexive responses to menace had failed them, they now were already returning their chemistry, in dissolution, to the waters, whence it would nourish other children of the All-Mother. Conceivably, borne by the vagaries of currents, blocked or guided as chance might have by the topology of the Ptolemaicly layered globe, some salt, some acid, some slowly decomposing organic molecule might reach the deeply buried All-Mother herself, might become absorbed into her fecund protoplasm, might, in course, be born again, a S'tscha renewed, resurrected, reincarnated, immortal.

And the S'tschai of the uppermost grotto, those uncounted neo-aquatics accustomed to the glittering lights of sky-refracted crystalline glare above, faceted radiant below, and new S'tschai arriving, nearing the end of their long, leisurely-paced migration upward from the grotto of the All-Mother, reaching this last warm ice-cave, short so little of that dumb and uncomprehending flat-visioned sight of the day-star and the night-stars, the major moon and the lesser moons, the home and the graves of unknown collaterals, and the quick refugees Ch'en-Tch'aa-Zch'uwn she and her fellows, these shared this liquid shell.

Recollection stirred. The grotto, recognized by Ch'en-Tch'aa-Zch'uwn, she had been here before, an unknown time ago, but long enough for her to see the greater moon die thrice. That had been as she neared the surface of N'Yu-Atlanchi, had neared the end of her own journey to the top of the sea, of the world.

Drifting, sensing, slowly revolving, the lights above and below endlessly alternating before her large eyes, Ch'en-Tch'aa-Zch'uwn is the unappreciating beneficiary of random occurrence. Floating, her gaze distracted by crystalline flashes, she encounters a small floating creature: longer than it is wide, vaguely cylindrical, quadrapoidal, soft, carrying a head at one end, flat-eyed, almost earless, densely nerved, floating, enblissed, unaware, it is a S'tscha.

The two observe each other. Ch'en-Tch'aa-Zch'uwn wavers gently her limbs, propels herself unurgently and without positive intent toward her sister. Likewise the other, easing through seawater, propelled by cartilaginous spatulates, flows vaguely forward. The two approach each other, align themselves to reversed congruence, drift slowly each toward the other, sense softly epidermal contact, the cylindrical torsos clinging each to the other with a pressure inconceivably slight, the legs of each pressing, gently twining about the forelimbs of the other, first maintaining the positions of the two, then, as body contact becomes increasingly firm, as forelimbs hold to legs, the faces are lowered, unaccustomedly, slowly working themselves into the semblance of a reciprocal embrace, holding closer each S'tscha to the other.

Slowly there follows a mitosislike process; the neural cells of each S'tscha divide, polarize, but, meiotically, producing no diploid chromosomes, spreading themselves, developing spiremes, threads piercing cell walls, crossing, sharing, passing coded memories each to the other, two S'tschai share experiences. Clutched in neural union, bathed in nutrient moisture, twin sister S'tschai renew identical heredity, add now identical lives.

To her sister gives Ch'en-Tch'aa-Zch'uwn her pilgrimage from All-Mother to the sky, her sensations of day-star, night-stars, moons, her quiet days and nights, the coming of clouds, of rain, its results visual, aural, tactile/aromatic/sapid, her return through the bunghole, her recovery.

To Ch'en-Tch'aa-Zch'uwn her sister gives her own life, similar, yet adding a sight uncomprehended: a figure vaguely, vaguely S'tschaoid, resting upright, the ends of its legs planted seemingly on the upper side of the uppermost crusting of N'Yu-Atlanchi, seemingly made neither of such stuff as are S'tschai nor of crystals nor of liquid, perhaps of the stuff of the satellites of N'Yu-Atlanchi, distorted by the sea, twirling, casting about a thing strange, large, flat, of close-placed lines, into the sea, then retrieving it, again, again, now plucking at it, removing, placing in a protuberance upon its trunk, casting again the thing of close-placed lines, then moving off, not swimming as swim S'tschai but upright, balancing somehow on its legs, and beyond the senses of the child of the All-Mother, the sister of Ch'en-Tch'aa-Zch'uwn.

The spiremes retract, the cell walls are restored, the neural union of the S'tschai ends; forelimbs unbend, legs untwine, slowly the two drift side by side until a stray movement of water pulls one away, they sense each the other still, drift, make small random movements of the limbs, become separated by greater and greater distances, are lost to each the other.

Ch'en-Tch'aa-Zch'uwn drifts supine beneath the uppermost crystalline crust of N'Yu-Atlanchi, her eyes absorbing sensory data, new memory now stored in her neural center but not analyzed. She neither wonders nor fears nor is pleased. She senses.

She does not seek a bung-hole above or below her but in time she arrives beneath one. Dimly through rich seawater she sees lights above: night-stars and moons. Vaguely she arches her form closer to the perpendicular, strokes languidly upward, levels again and drifts.

In time rises NGC 7007 the sun of N'Yu-Atlanchi,

brightening the sky, reflecting and refracting off sea and crystal. In time, floating supine, Ch'en-Tch'aa-Zch'uwn senses almost with startlement the strike all about her of the thing of lines, feels herself drawn, lifted, carried for a moment beyond the waters of N'Yu-Atlanchi. She is flooded for a moment by new and unprecedented data, as if being removed totally from her world. Her senses flash confused messages to her neural center. She hears sounds she has never before heard, sees visions unknown and ununderstood, feels/smells/tastes as never before she has.

All briefly.

She is plunged, uncomprehending, into yet another environment: close, warm, salt-moist, yes, but dark, totally for the first time in the life of Ch'en-Tch'aa-Zch'uwn dark, and yet with a tang of a new ingredient, a new sensation, and the feeling of other S'tschai about, more S'tschai than she has ever before encountered, but all quiet, and Ch'en-Tch'aa-Zch'uwn her own senses become less acute, less vivid, and she becomes less aware and she ceases to sense and to react.

13. Aboard the Starship *Theodore Bilbo*

'Namorning, Alquane up, gyrenes up, N'Alabama redin-white "colors" up the ole pole, sarge up, shine up, fix up, dress up, twenty-thirty push-up, goodnup, oak-hay, time to break the (reasonably) fast. Gyrenes line up, shape up, count off, march off, couterments off, bow down, chow down:

:grits, lard, corn bread, dawntime lightning (a mere drap), little little talk—passamuffins—mm—jug—mm—mm. Cadre here only, hung a many a man over this dawn this mawn and a bleary eye here or there, one enda bencha rutha seems distracted would you say, or ab-etc., thinking mayhap of a Miss MM or maybe futha nutha bench some gyrene shifting his sore ass thinks of Piggy's. Maybe?

Well get it down sarge, get it down, make a plite little belch and grab another something to swag or swig, it's the whole batch down the hatch act and a sniggery smirk at thought of old John Darn last at Piggy's well sloppies is better as none at all old John, none at all, but then why when better stuff is at hand (if you catch).

Follow up that delightful culination with a quick (but nonoptional) visit to the old chapel for a dose of

God's own. Shall we be epigrammatic and say Mass after Mess? No, we shall not.

Nonetheless Alquane that lucky old sun pushing his rays through stained glass winders depicting heart-rending scenes in the Shrine of St. Lurleen McQueen illumine soul-thrilling ranks of congregators in pew, pew, pew as chaplain heaves into view tew, mounts his pulpit (whatever turns you up) with visible risibles, gazes across gray-clad all spat and polished rows, officers' section shall sit upon thy rite ham, enceeyos upon thy laff and klenz the ole soul.

Sermon today, same subject as usual. Good to know God is on our side. Thanks, Pap old chap, crikies, think of going to war with Him in the ranks of *them*. How many divisions does He have, buy the weigh? Sing a few good old hymns (officers melody, eeyems harmony) like "The Old Ragged Crust" or "I'm Dreaming of a White Kiss, Miss." Dear chaplain does a couple of costume changes to melloharp and drums, comes out for his big finale in golden robes and pistol belt to introduce—Singing and Dancing His Way into Your Hearts—the ajjerant bird.

Bird stanz up to deliver orders of the day. Ptowie! Thus—This old fort this campa spacers gotcher marching orders here, See-O says to thank the cadre for a splennid job-well-dun, finest bunch of gyrene shavetails ever seed, pride utha fleed, mission over, staff reduced, here you go boys yule delighted to get back into the mysterious interstellar void and slap some punks for the glory of the N'Alabamian Weigh-a-life.—

—Waddeezay, wa-wa-wa?—axes crabby old esseffsee (reserve warrant O 'nee doesn't let anybody forget same you can bet) setting aside our sarge.

Our sarge snarls—Deep, man, we-all gonna gettanutha hotpot on the old bentfin boomer.—

—Oh,—exudes crabby. Not to go uncomprehended he repeats—oh.—

—Y'all find your list of duty stations posted on the company (just as one might anticipate, hath one but possession of the correct background) bulletin board right after Divine Observances,—sez the bird.

—Dis,—beloved chaplain commands unto his flock—missed!—

Cleansed of soul, lightened of heart, filled in the head with thoughts of God and Planet, our old sarge he looks at him's orders on the bulletin (right!) board after kirkey, seize a long row of names, ranks, serial twiddles, along upside of each bespeach a ship of the Crimsy Wabe, new duty stations for most of cadre, ship names m sine meants for each gyrene O m NCO lissed, restum must be stain on as cadre, 'll maintain post facilities pending renoola OCS program.

Our old sarge he looks, maybe not quite with twenny-twennies (no sprig chicken he no more but he keeps in good shape rest assured) but he gets buy with spectacles at leased. There's old friend Gordon Lester Wallace III gonna be a gunnery sarge upboard the old *James O. Eastland.* Our sarge once served upboard the *Jimmie-O.* He muses of nice times there. Yas. Goody, Gordie. Fun for fine. Other cadre buddies here and there doing this and that now and then. Freddie now, he's to be seen on the list nowhere, must be stain on as permy party. Owell, he'll blast no blacks that way, but it's a soft berth.

Sarge himself? Where's he to go? He won't be on the *Jimmie-O.* No. Sarge looks on list, fines him's name at last. Zippidie-doo-dah, sarge, you gonna be a weapons squad leader upboard the starship *Theodore Bilbo.*

[Aside: howcome smenny N'Ala ships barin' O'Missa names? Ponder that.]

Welletsee, welletsee, who is gonna be in that squad? And who is gonna be the platoon sarge? Squad leader worth his stripes, he *cares.*

Our old sarge he heads for the *TeeBee* stoppin by cadre barracks only long enough to pack a couple parsimonious suitcases [suitcases? well, call em duffles ef you like to] for space duty, grab a military gyrocar, fling him's *Bilbo* bags in, scuddle uccer tarmac to the *TeeBee,* cline upboard m finiz berth. Spacerine hammock's none 2 comphy, one must admit, but like rubbery jello, it'll do.

Sarge stoze gear, check sin, finezeez first man in from his section and dis*TeeBee*z to wait for others. He paces tarmac, gazes back m up at the *Theodore Bilbo* she's a fine figure of a ship. Tall, rounded shaft glisters in Alquane's pretty morning rays. Up at the top an instrument ring girds fuselage and atop that the conical command module replete with tippy-top cat's-iris command viewing station. Master ruby laser station there too, firing stream of hot singeing light to bathe foe when *TeeBee*'s aroused.

Crew quarters in the shaft, gun modules in the skin, and down at ground level mounted to the base of the shaft two giant globular fuel modules glistering m gleaming in the warming rays of happy old Alquane light, their contents of supercold liquified compmatter bubbling over surplus through safely valves, it hisses and steams in the Alquane warmth looking like clusters and curlicues of angel's hair around the globular modules and the base of the old *Theodore B.*

Finally sarge's squad trickle in. Nice boys, nice all, from fine ole pureblooded surn fammies O yes. Sweet blond hand laserman from Echola, articifer's mate from Eutaw, couple pincer-axmen from Coxheath m Salitpa, glow-mortarman from Gasque. anna sissant sarge outen Suggsville Center. A good crew all. That's important.

Our old sarge, he checked round summat, found altogether a fine bunch in that platoon of his except maybe one or two. Didn't like a zaprifle squad sarge alongside nohow. Fella name of Raff Slocomb. Knew him from cadre. Basserd wunt drink around, wunt whore around, *mean* SOB if you follow. Gotta watch for Slocomb.

Not too sure of the platoon leader too. Bad situ that, a good leader, he got confidence in the next layer too. An the next leader (platoon sarge was an ok, thank you) bein a shavetail just outen OCS. One of our boys no less sarge ponders (very thinky today wouldn't you say?), and he didn't like to toe too much for me. Mmm. Now he's platoon shavetail. Shavetail Snarp. Oak hay, will get on somehow.

Our sarge he lines up his men m inspexem good. Then alla board upside the starship *Theodore Bilbo*. Everybody checked in, gear stowed, strapped down, ready for deepspace.

Supercold, superdense fuel flows from those big hairy balls of the starship *Theodore Bilbo* into painboxes. Molecules are energized, atoms are squeezed, electrons are sheared from their primaries, crammed m jammed m slammed, whammed m bammed, shaped, scraped, raped, nuclei ripped apart, smashed into one another, forces whirling and driving madly, something becoming something else, something less, part of that something becoming nothing, energy produced, screams out propulsion tubes crying to the echoing deaf cosmos for relief, release, dying in an attenuating blaze of hyperenergized exhaust, thrusting the *Bilbo* away from N'Alabama into the dark vacuum that surrounds Alquane, thrusting, heaving, hurling her upwards.

Theodore Bilbo heads outward, outward, driven alone the planetary plane away from Alquane, shuddering, screaming as she goes.

This is propulsion by agonized matter.

On O'Earth furgem Jewrabs rule the world. Descendants of the citizens of that long-ago Federated Republic of Israel and Jordan ["Dinner in the diner, nothing could be finer, than to have your lox m eggs in Palestine," er, it was a big tourist attraction, that] that grew into a Pan-Semitic Empire, that Neo-Shem that spread and conquered and took. Growing population, *lebensraum* the Jewrabs echoed some forgotten hack politico of earlier times.

Great powers to stop 'em? Who?

The former United States of, uhh, where was that? Well, anyway, they quarreled too much with the old CCCP. Almost blue us *all* up. Happily the old Third Force powers woolen stand 4 that, disbanded them mothers back into independent units. Nation of Iowa, say, inn't rilly 2 scarifying. Nor, oh, Mountain Badakhshan Autonomous Oblast.

Czecho you can bet slovakia sure breathed easier. Also Iceland. Who's afraid of the big bad Georgians (Murrican *or* Sophie's wet)? Bunchezza farmers both.

Rest easy for a while. Neoclassical Cathay no problem; Innier too busy feeding starving millions for far'n ventures; Japan's new motto "Make money not enemies." Alla little guys rested easy for a while. Then the furgem Jewrabs took over. O'Earth, ta-ta.

Nameanwhile, howzabout colony worlds? Agonized matter goes fast.

No, you don't dig, man. Like, *fast*.

Like, think of what fast means to you. Now pretend that means *slow*. *NOW* what's fast mean? Oak hay? Now, *that's* slow. *Now* what's fast? You still there? Still following? Oak hay, now you have some idea of what's agonized matter driven spaceships fast.

So: colony worlds. Nation can't feed its people, can't pave its streets, can't school its kids, can't medicate its sickies, can't solve its problems . . . can always do the prestige things. Once upon a time, could have a jet airline. Once upon a time could have nukie-bombs. Now: everybody who's anybody, he got agonized matter driven spaceships. He got ships, what's he got next? Right! He got worlds.

So we got: N'Afghanistan, N'Albania, N'Andorra, N'Argentina, N'Australia, N'Austria, N'Belgium, N'Bhutan, N'Bolivia, N'Brazil, N'Bulgaria, N'Burma . . . yuwanna be bored, read an atlas. Also, we got N'Alabama, N'Alaska, N'Arizona, N'Arkansas and 49 more.

Also we got worlds colonized by religious nuts, diet faddists, hobbyists, political fanatics, sado-masochists, alcoholics, lotus eaters and a few hundred other kinds of loonies. *Also* we had a few worlds colonized by homosexuals of both types, but they didn't breed true in captivity and they died out.

Also we got colony worlds carrying on the electromagnanimous traditions of their ancestors including their loyalties and their hatreds.

And when the furgem Jewrabs finally take over poor O'Earth en its tirely, them colony worlds is left on their own. *With* agonized matter driven fast spaceships. So N'Alabama hates N'Haiti?

Our old sarge is on his way to war raght now!

14. Into the Exoneurobiology Section

" 'M. Goncourt, we cannot obtain the technical and fiscal support required to effectuate specified mission parameters!' *Merde*!" shouted Goncourt, pounding his fist on the grimy wooden desk top. "Nobody can get the support he needs, Trudeau! You know it and I know it. We're functioning in a bureaucracy and the trick is to do your job without the official backing you need. *I* give you my support and I'm your chief. I don't want to hear that officialese double-talk. Let's save that for Antoine-Simone and the rest of the clods upstairs. Let's speak plainly to each other."

Trudeau winced at Goncourt's outburst.

Goncourt said, "Well?"

Trudeau said, "I'm sorry, sir. I read and write so many tech reports that I'm afraid I'm beginning to talk like one. I take it you want this straight."

Goncourt grunted an affirmative. "I want a straight report on your specimen, and it had better be good. Manpower is breathing down Antoine-Simone's neck, and he has to produce on this boondoggle or he's in bad, bad trouble, eh? That means *we* had better produce or we're *all* going to find out what the far side of La Gonave looks like."

Trudeau gestured with his brown hands to express

his thoughts. "The specimen seems to be functioning properly. The control organism has been implanted in a fully thawed composite cadaver. Healing is taking place at an encouraging rate. I think I can get a response to aural stimuli now."

Goncourt rose from behind his desk, took his subordinate by the arm and propelled him through the doorway of the office. "Good! Let us see what wonder you have wrought, Trudeau. We may yet come out on top of this thing."

The two officials passed Goncourt's secretary, marched down drab corridors past frosted-glass lab windows and around corners. They paused before a door marked Exoneurobiology. Trudeau reached over and opened the door and they entered.

"Before viewing the specimen, M. Goncourt, I suggest that we view a film of the surgical procedures already followed." Trudeau rolled a screen down one wall, flicked a switch and the screen began to flicker. On it appeared an operating theater and surgical team. A rolling pallet was brought into the room, a sheet-covered form lifted from it onto an operating table. Throughout the scene the viewing room remained silent. When the sheet was drawn back a cadaver was revealed. The left arm and shoulder and half of the chest were missing, a jagged outline indicating the place where the body had been ripped apart.

Now the camera cut to the doorway of the room, showing another cart. As it was wheeled into position the scene cut back to the overhead view. The body already on the table now showed a clean edge in place of the former rags of flesh marking the extent of its wounds. "This is later, of course," Trudeau said. "The procedure takes several hours at present. That is one of the drawbacks that we hope to overcome with mass techniques."

Goncourt reached into a pocket in his sagging jacket, drew out a small pipe and charged it. "I want to see this fully," he said. Trudeau struck a match for him. Through blue-gray clouds the image continued to change.

"The second cadaver has been prepared as you see," said Trudeau. "The skin is contoured to match the extent of the first cadaver, with sufficient overlap to promote rapid growth. Internal organs are undivided—each is taken fully from one subject or the other." On the screen the two partial cadavers had been fitted together like parts of a jigsaw puzzle. Surgeons were adjusting bones, stitching nerve and muscle connections, attaching blood vessels like plumbers matching water supplies. The camera cut, cut, indicating repeated time lapses.

Finally the obvious chief surgeon waved two assistants to the task of suturing the skin of the massive pseudo-incision. After a few more minutes the screen became blank and Trudeau flicked on the room lights.

"Very well," Goncourt said, "a clever piece of surgery, a logical extension, however, of standard techniques."

"But the difference," Trudeau exclaimed, "the difference is that we are not merely moving a particular organ from a donor to a patient. We are actually combining parts of two nonviable cadavers to produce a complete individual."

"And he will live? He will function? Will this new patchwork man you have created be able to perform military duties? This is not an academic research grant, you know. We are supposed to contribute to the manpower problem, to the war effort."

Trudeau stood and looked Goncourt in the face. Goncourt's eyes were fixed on the bowl of his small pipe, which had gone out and which he was trying to puff back into life.

Trudeau said, "In the case of space casualties, this surgery is insufficient. When they are wounded in battle, when they are mortally wounded, the wall of the ship and the protection of their spacesuits both violated, the sudden vacuum and absolute cold produces a double effect."

Trudeau looked again at Goncourt. He had got his pipe going again, was looking into his subordinate's face with apparent rapt attention. Trudeau went on:

"The sudden physiological effects are terrific. At zero-pressure the lungs are instantly exhausted. Vomiting and evacuation occur. The bladder empties. There is danger of damage to the eyes, ear drums, blood vessels, all pressure-sensitive organs.

"But simultaneously the body is plunged toward absolute zero. In vacuum there is of course no conduction cooling, but radiant dissipation occurs at a fantastic rate. Even before pressure damage occurs, the body is quick-frozen. That is how we can obtain cadavers in such good condition."

Trudeau stopped speaking as Goncourt waved him to silence.

Goncourt said, "All very well, but what of the central nervous system? Can the revived cadaver function?"

"Not independently. The shock of death does something to the individual—we do not fully understand it, although we have tried attaching graphic readout devices to various CNS points in subjects and obtained astonishing results. They are apparently conscious of sensory input and probably capable of essentially normal mentation, but no voluntary functions take place.

"For this reason we have experimented with the creatures from NGC 7007. They seem to have evolved extremely complex and sensitive nervous systems, widely distributed generalized sensors, and yet to be without will or resistance. Also, they are small enough to be implanted at the base of the brain. They acclimate quickly, attaching filaments into the spinal column and brain. The bloodstream provides nourishment.

"Because these organisms are constructed as they are, they can be used as master controls for the subjects. By implanting one in a subject's skull, we can revive him and use him as a quasi-automaton for military or industrial duty."

"A quasi-automaton," Goncourt repeated. "Or a zombie." Goncourt sucked futilely at his pipe, knocked out its dead ashes and returned it to his pocket. He rose from his chair, said, "Very well, now let us see this laboratory wonder of yours."

In the next room the patchwork man lay on a hospital bed, breathing slowly. Clad only in pajama pants, the body showed its livid scar from neck to sternum, turning a neat ninety degrees to disappear behind the rib-cage. The flesh of the attached arm and shoulder was a different shade of brown from that of the rest of the body. From the temple of the still man an electrode fed a thin wire leading to a communication interface. A small computer, fed through the interface, controlled a graphic display screen, its surface a neutral green-gray across which moved sluggish waves of varying density.

At the sound of the footsteps of the two men the figure lying on the bed opened its eyes. The display screen flickered. On it appeared the forms of Goncourt and Trudeau. They were approaching the viewpoint from across a rolled-down bedsheet. Goncourt stopped, placed his arm in front of Trudeau to stop him. In the screen the figures seemed to advance an additional fraction of a step. The image fragmented, shuddered back into form to show them standing as they were.

"You see," Trudeau said.

From an audio device Trudeau's voice distortedly repeated, "You see . . ."

Trudeau stopped speaking. The device paused, then repeated a higher-pitched, "You see." Higher, "You see." Higher, "You see, you see–" Trudeau took quick steps, switched off the audio output.

"You see," he said again, "whatever the subject views or hears, we can read back out through the devices. We have a feedback problem with the audio, although there is no problem if we move the speaker to another room.

"At any rate," he continued, "sensory functioning is just the half of our achievement. Watch this."

He stood close by the hospital bed. "Raise your hand," he commanded the figure on the bed. It raised a hand. "Sit up!" The thing on the bed slid its legs over the edge of the mattress, pushed its torso upright with unmatched hands, waited.

"Stand," Trudeau said. The thing pushed itself off the bed, stood swaying beside it. On the graphic screen Goncourt could see himself, Trudeau, the room shifting back and forth as the dead-alive eyes moved.

"Enough," said Goncourt.

"Down," Trudeau commanded. Clumsily, the thing folded itself back onto the bed, guided by Trudeau's hands. When it was again supine the screen showed the ceiling of the room momentarily, then went back to gray-green as the eyelids slid shut.

Walking back to his own office, Goncourt said to Trudeau, "Very impressive. I'll have to strip someone else to do it, but I will get you some people and some money."

"Thank you," Trudeau said. "I'm sure this thing will work, sir."

"I'm sure it will," Goncourt replied. Completing the trip to his office alone, Goncourt again drew the pipe from his pocket.

15. Into the Great Hall

Flip calendar pages.

Things happen.

Gordon Lester Wallace III (a sarge himself, you know) scuffs red dust dirt dragging drearily drawn-faced outen the order office. –Okay, buddy,–he says to topper, –see you later.–

Gordie-boy m iz pal Adam A. Aiken amble crossen reddish dusty sward of Fort Sealy Mae, Letohatchie Township, Independent Planet of N'Alabama, Eugene Youngerman, Governor, ambling aimlessly around toward the NCO Club, kickin pebbles, spittin casionally and hummin under their respective breaths the Fort Sealy Mae strictly unofficial alma mater.

Adam, he sed–Gord, wappenta *Jimmie O?* Wuntcha poseta join the star fleet, go knock hell outen them nigra pigs on N'Haiti?–

Gord, he sed–Wuhmm,–or approximately that, pickin up the taciturn speech habits of a certain friend of his who shall remain nameless (seen as how he's been that to this point).

Gord, hez not sech a bad gyrene you know, ef you like gyrenes, ef you don't then close your eyes for a while and mebbe hill go away. With Adam A. Aiken. Least ways, Gordie been pickin up some of the speech patterns of his buddy that other guy and he don't say so much at first but Adam he persists—Well, Gordie, well? Off you go, now you're back, wappen? Big space battle? Ja kill any nigras? Ja getta see N'Haiti? Ja getta fuck any nigra broads?—

Gord, hez got that other guy's tendencies now but he don *persist*.—Wuhmm,—that was a good answer but now Gord, he gives in, that's iz weakness, he gives in and he sez—Yeh, we went up, yeh the *Jimmie O*, and the rest, we seen some nigra ships, we seen some and we zapped some. They zapped us. Wir back.—

Pretty good, Gordon Lester Wallace III. Not as good as that other fellow would do, but good.

Gord stops walkin and looks at the dirt (some grass too, some grass, not enough to keep a mowing crew busy much of the year but you know how manpower is on a gyrene post, all those guys around to keep busy and not much to do so maybe the topper senzem out to mow the dirt—you get on a dirt-mowing detail you think it's senseless never mind, just mow and keep your mouth quiet about it).

Gord don't say no more right now.

Adam A. Aiken he sez—We make out *bad*, Gord?—

Gord he don't answer but take a look in his face now, look in his eyes they don't look so great.

Now Adam he presses, very very deftly.—Hah?—he sez.

Gord, he sez—It was pretty bad, Adam, I think we lost. Least, we broke off and come home. M now Ole Gene he called in all the friendly planets for that palaver over to Leto. You pull that guard detail too?—

Adam sez yez.

They sprawl up the steps of the NCO Club and smarmily float inside the screen doors, find a table and set down. —Flipia 4 a Stonewall—sez Adam. Out of his grays comes a fine anglo-saxon-blooded hand holding a fifty-boll piece. He flips it in the air, it lands on the table top with a depressing clunk m spins a couple times there, flops over with a boll a cotton m a supered numeral 50 up.

Gordy triziz luck, gets a smiling portrait of some olden time fart lookin up and goes to buy two foamies.

Good many foamies later, Gord m Adam they float smarmily back out through the doors of the NCO Club. One um belches m neither's sure which it was.

Two good purebred surn N'Alabamian spacerine corps nonconditioned officers stumble m clutch at one another back to barracks and into sacks.

Whichever one belched before, t'other one does now so they even. That's good, nobody ahead nobody behind.

Lights off, eyes closed, snores m wheezes m N'Alabama whirls about that old axis.

Clock hands spin.

Alquane zaps brightness through screened stapaglass windows Gordon needs no wakener bettern Alquane. He gets everybody up & eaten their breakfast & back to barracks & spat & polished & into pressed new grays & outside & assembled & lined up & counted off & dressed right & marched around & interposition & reported in.

Captain Cal Koberly commanding, everybody onto the bus & they head down the red rut road, gyros twirlin, into Leto.

Letohatchie Town Hall, meeting place of the interplanetary conference. Wow! Neo-neoclassic architecture, gabled & porticoed, columned & terraced & stepped, & in front a (would you believe this, it's a test) Confederated Worm-morayeel, some old bearded jackass ridin an old hoarse carrying an old flag into some old battle on some old planet who knows where or what for?

N'Alabama spacerines line up making an honor guard, double ranks facing one another (sheee-*eeet* lookit that ugly bassur across from Gord!) all in fine old traditional grays with glistry brass buttons & a crowd of rednecked townies (see that fat old fellow follow a filly fondly facing for a feelup) held back by town *po*-leese.

Town *po*-leese, madgin that! White crash helmets m glistry green one-way eyemurrs, chin straps so you can't swipe that old pretty helmet from that old, that pretty *po*-leese boy. Sideburns m black leather jackets with studs spellin out patriotic mottoes (Rise Agin! No mongrelization! ((That'n barely fits.)) Never! Lawnorder! . . . and other patriotic slogans) silver studs for troopers brass for sarges gold for brass.

Tite pants, real real tite & big shiny boots, flying gloves & billy clubs & cans of insect repellent (or *some*thing). Why, those boys can't even move without creaking.

Well cops to keep the redneck townies (in their civvies & a large but expectable proportion of plainbutton warsurp grays) offen the gyrenes and the gyrenes to keep whoever in hell offen the backs of the official plenipotentiary ambassadorial representatives of the *friendly* planets.

First delegation rolls up in a siren-howlin jeescout gyrocar, red lights flashin, two-way radio cracklin & that jeescout slews round in the red dirt tween the Worm-morayeel & the Town Hall & the ambassador de-mounts. Hez tall & pale wearn white flannel civvies & a broad-brim planter's hat & he waves t'the gyrenes & the town cops & the redneck townies & he starts up the steps follerd by couple flunkies dressed alike unto him & carryin a briefcase & some other stuff & scurryin about in his dust & up the steps they start 2.

Halfway up Town Hall doors open & out comes Mayor Milburn Mitchum & a couple *his* flunkies looking summat flustered & Mayor he dances delightingly down the steps & seizes thambassador by the hand & turnin around he links up his arms like he prolly saw someone do it oncet in some ole newsclip & heen thambassador clompin up the ole steps & in the doors & outen sight jes quick enough as the ole jeescout soops off through red dirt dust (don't they never think of them poor honor guards standing there stranglin?) along comes another siren-blastin light-blinkin howler-hootin hooter-howlin jeescout with another ambassador & a couple more flunkies & it just keeps *up* like that, poor honor guards, poor town cops, seemin to be like all *morning* till everybody's there in the Leto Town Hall there near unto the Confederated Worm-morayeel (unless you deciden you wunt *bleeve* that, it's your option, buddy) & then something else happens.

Firstall, Gord & t'other honor guards, they haven seed no sine nor co-sine of their *own* pure surn N'Alabamian planetary delegation septin for ole Mayor Milburn Mitchum m shee-*eet* who pays any tention to *him* anyhow. Muss be they own delegation may been snuck in the back door r summin. Whose there, secastate, secawar, secacom, who knows mayen the Governor hisself (not so as to mention mayn't been some old senator from Talladega or someplace).

Let ole Gord wonder about that, you, now, you just relax & follow along, okay?

Come on!

Last official plenipotentiary ambassadorial representative delegation piles outen dust-churnin jee-scout gyrocar (see that arready, right?) & marches up steps of Town Hall ambassador arm-narm with Mayor Milburn Mitchum & into the Town Hall & the twin ranks of gray-uniformed shiny-brassed spacerine honor guards starten to peel off from the farthest end two steps forward right angle turn & marchen to the old Letohatchie Town Hall themselves marchin now in a double line splittin at the base of the Confederated Worm-morayeel (maybe it's just a big outdoor garbage bin ef you'd ruther bleeve that) & up the old Town Hall steps to the double doors & some civvy suburbs flunky opennin the doors form & they marchen right into the Hall & into the Great Hall meetin chamber & range theirselfs around the room (as rehearsed—you weren't thar) and standin at pray rest as honor guards (not to mention skeweritty) durin the meeting itself.

Which is very handy for Gordon Lester Wallace III ef he cares to hear what happens at the meeting, which who knows whether he does or not, hes just a spacerine sarge doin his duty as he seen it, right? But maybe hez interested anyhow.

There's a speaker's table in the front & there's a man setting in't & a couple flunkies around him & facing the speaker's table's a bunch of leetle tables & chairs & things like that & every one's got somebody settin in't & they're all buzzin & burbling around & everybody looken pretty grim spitin' a casional laugh hearn there & each leetle table gotten a pitcher ont fulla *some*thing & some glasses & there being a big one on the speaker's table & a glass for the fella settin there & some for *his* flunkies & the poor spacerine honor guards standing around the room, *they* dryeran all *hell* & nobody gives them no drinks but then who's this meeting 4, the meeters or the greeters?

Fat florid-faced fella at the main place he standen up now & he leanin ford close to a amplifier microphone inconspicuous stuck in fronna his place & he sez firstoff—Ahem!—

Or summin like that. Not really *Ahem*, no, but more of a throat-clear m call torder he'da done better rappen a gavel only nobody brought one (a head will roll for that as if an excuse were needed) so he says instead, approximately at least,—Ahem!—

Everybody looken up, & he sayin—Arr, weccum to N'Alabama & weccum t'Leto, a ben Eugene Youngerman, Governor this planet, & am dlited twelcome you.—

Polite hums and humphs.

—A hopen yall ben enjoin the hospitality, traditional surn hospitality, of N'Alabama m this lovely town of Letohatchie, hopen yall found our commodations satisfactory, little presents to your liking, bedmates cozy & friendly and alla that.—

Polite humphs and hums.

—Now we got serious business to transact. You all know the glorious past history of our peoples, fine surn traditions & practices of the past. No need to remind you of fine glorious past of our ancestors on O'Earth before the furgem Jewrab takeover.—

(No need but he reminded them for a longish while. Well.)

—What we asked everybody here to talk about is this little problem we got with, uh, them black bassurds, uh, N'Haiti. Now any fool knows a white man can lick a nigra in a fair fight, of course, it's natural. Innate superiority. We all learn that from first grade onward. Even O'Earth sociologists knew that. Pahneers like Audey Shooey, Henny Gart, Jawny Kimball, they knew that the human race was the highest creation of nature and that the pure-bred white man was the highest form of humanity.

—Now we got this little problem going with N'Haiti, & I can well imagine how some of you—Ole Guv Youngerman, he looken around to see who's pain attention & who's more interested in studyin his fingernails—how some of you—Ole Guv resumes—matt wonder how come we can't smash them nigra brutes with proven superiority of our kind.—

He stops for a smallish swig (depending on your measuring cup of course) of that nice fluid from the jug, looks around, ambassador from N'Missa seems to be asleep, ambassador from N'Transvaal plane some kind of under-the-table hands-game with the ambassador from N'Maddoxia, ambassador from N'Eensmyth maybe pain attention or maybe just staring abstructionously ahead. Ole Guv, he shaken a mane of white hair (worth many a vote, that, long hair bein okay if it's white one might guess) an resumes (or might we say reresumes):

—Way, lookitit like so: now no one would argue that a man in't superior to a varmint, whetherts a snarlin mean cuayo-peen biggerna plow-horse or a teeny varse. But a cuayo-peen, he gettin a man outen the open, he'll rip him up but good with his tushes & his spines. Or a varse, you get some varse in*side* you, you might be a goner too. That don't make no cuayo-peen nor no varse the equal of a man, but an inferior order a creation can be given special parz to overcome a superior order a creation.

—Now these nigras, you know no nigra never made nothing worthwhile in all of history, not on O'Earth, no, old Jawny proved that sentries ago, nor noplace else neither. Just nature's mistake, tryin out ideas, how to make something superior to the beasts of the field, old nature messed up once with the black man then got it right on the second try.

—But nigras, they got a natural instinct to kill & destroy, and I'll be perfectly frank with yall,—Ole Guv, he looken almost fit to cry now—we taken a thorough *whompin* in this war, and unless yall willing to see a sovereign planet of your own flesh and blood, a world of pureblooded surn white manhood, taken a whipping from a bunch of flat-nosed woolly-haired black nigra *savages* . . .—

Ole Guv, he flailin his hands now but he still in control & he pauses dramatically to let that last word sink in,— . . . yall *have* to give us some help. Now that's all there is to it.—

That's no shit, that's his bit, he done spoke and down he sit.

Well how long you wanter hang around some dumb-ass diplomatic conference listening to speeches? You can guess what happenin after that. Alla them ole ambassadors, they expressin sympathy for the sacred blood cause of the independent planet of N'Alabama, maken speeches all day long about solidarity and Them Nigras Cain't Be Permitted to Get Away with It.

But the ambassador from N'Missa, he say (summat sheepishlike)—Yall know we with you one hunnerd percent, Gene, but we get most of our heavy machine tools from N'Ghana. *They* stain outen this war, *we* stain outen it & we get along fine, but if *we* gettin inter it, then *they* gettin inter it, *you* no better off as before and *we* in bad trouble.—He go on like that for quite a while, but you gettin the message by now no doubt.

Ambassador from N'Transvaal, he rise in place, teetern a bit (that jug in front on his table been pretty down by now) and he say summin like this:—You cause is one of destiny, Governor Youngerman, and the white surn-blooded people of your planet have the unquestioning and unlimited support of the white boer-blooded people of N'Transvaal. As you know we haven a little problem of our own in gettin on with N'Kaffirstan. Now nothin we can't handle ourselves, understand. Ole Chaka CVII he a markable smart man for a nigra & we get along all right. And you know ole N'Kaffirstan, they happen to have the biggest & fastest space fleet in the entire N'Afrikaans sector.

—But I'll tell you the honest truth, Governor Youngerman, wud really rather not tread on ole Chaka's sensitive toes. Besides, now, we haven full faith and confidence in the ability of N'Alabama, proud, free m white as she is, to hole her banner unstained & her purity unmixed.

—A thank you.—And he sitten down and everybody kind of looken at him and applaud a teeny bit, and then looken at Ole Gene Youngerman and blushen a teeny bit and then the room getten to be pretty quiet once again.

Ole Gene, he don't give up but all he gets from anybody is expressions of solidarity (how much JD sippin quality will *that* buy you?) & maybe a half-headed pledge of some financial credits, which are nice but that's not what Gene was really tryen 4.

Well they marchen back out past the Confederated Worm-morayeel (or garbage bin, whichever you prefer to believe . . . if you don't like either, how about a bicycle rack?) & gettin back into their jeescout gyrocars & Gord-3 & the rest of the gray-uniformed brass-buttoned spat & polished up honor guards, including their commander Captain Cal Koberly (soon to be lieutenant) and GLW's pal Adam Aiken, they marchen back to Fort Sealy Mae bus & out to the fort & take the night off boys.

Gordon Lester Wallace III m Adam A. Aiken stain grays, they two bentfin boomers burnished, Gord haven a new hotpot on his boomer courtesy *James O. Eastland's* recent (albeit unhappy) encounter with nigra space fleet; they climb into Gord's gyro & head down that beloved ole red rut road to Leto, past familiar places, seen familiar faces, parken in the street where the elite meet t'eat (or EAT, that's near the B A R the longer-recollected set will recall). Gord puts a chumly arm around A. A. Aiken's gray-covered shoulders m takes him up that certain staircase & they get t'the dirtyfrosted doorway Gord winks conspiratorily at Adam & goes:

:*a-rap-a-tap-tap, a-rap-a-tap-tap, tap-tatty-rap-rap, rappy-tappy-tap*:

:or something like that. Anyway, it don't really matter none because nothing happens. He repeats the tarradiddle-de-de survural thymes, summat as he recalls his "erstwhile guru" (heh!) and friend, our ole sarge, having done, but is it a false recollection? Is it some smuggled half-boll dreadful Gord read behind the barn manly years ago rising t'cloud his mind with memories of unoccurred experiences? Leave us not spectorate on that subject too much.

Adam doubting, Gordon Lester he attempts to laugh it all off, maken a fist and on the wooden frame of the door pounden:

:*ker-whumph*:

(twicet)

:m footsteps inside, door opening a crack (chained)

m thoo the crack peeren out a face, not holy unfamiliar, fat, cornsilky colored hair pasted flat to forehead wid perspiration, huffin in his plainbutton warsurp sweatstained grays,—What can I do to be of service to you two obviously fine gentle, uh,—his eye flickers down Gord, across at shuhite, up Adam A., lites on A's face, smiles, cuts horizonally to Gordon's mug, m he completes syncopated word—men?—

Gord speaking:—Wanna show my buddy here your fine floor show, haven't seen Miss Merriass Markham in a long while, off in space fighten nigras, now I'm back . . .—Gord does rattle.

Blond feller:—I'm really sorry, sir, I don't know you and this is a private club.—

Gord:—Whadaya, etc.—

BF: (in essence)—Amscray before I call the uzzfay, oysbay!—

Adam A. Aiken: (not in these words)—Let's blow, Gord.—

Gord gives assent grumpily & down the creakies they creak.

Adam:—Howzabout a visita Piggy Peggy's Pussy Parlor, GL?—

So they do, picking respective ways through crapped-up broken sidewalk & crossen rotten busted streets beneath busted streetlights (Letohatchie has *not* been bombed). Outsiden the good ole 4P Gord sees that same ole Letohatchie town John Darn plain with his can of insect repellent (or whatever), leaning as usual against a (n even nonfunctional) lamppost.

Inside, G&A are greeted by Piggy herself in finest old tradition of surn hospitality.

—Mighty busy night, boys, alla these visiting firemen in town for the big meet over ta Town Hall,—Peggy sayen, fixin her little-girl blonde curls (they been slippin all around her face as she talks, noddin her head continually)—but we aim to please. What's your pleasure, boys or girls, S or M, plain or fancy, twosomes or whosomes, now or later, lesser or greater, front or back, top or bottom, bed or board, anal oral or genital, scental gentle mental or dental, thin or fat, this or that, etc.—

(Peggy, she always tries to provide her customers with what they want, that's her formula for a successful retail enterprise.)

Gord, aside to Ad—Leave this to me, Ad.—To Piggy Peggy:—Just a dark room, PP, a soft floor, shut our eyes, open the door & a pleasant surprise.—

Gord & Adam shortly lyen side-by-side, stark naked & all up for excitement (assisting one another in the preparations). Lights low, door opens slow, in comes someone maken a show.

She's a biggish lady, you bet; Gordon Lester's eyes at the moment are somewhat shut but he hears appreciative noises from Adam; Adam he says—Willya lookit that, Gordon.—But Gordon bein capable of delayen gratification he squeezesis eyes shut m says—I wanna feel it first.—

Gordon waits in his homemade darkwomb & in a minute he feels someone very surprising doing something very surprising someplace very surprising. He sayen something very original like (these are not his precise words)—What the fucken shitmother's going *on* here?—

From Adam Aiken an unexpected bit of inarticulation.

Gordon opens his eyes and speaks with shock:—Miss Markham!—

All hell breaks loose in which Gordon Lester Wallace III, Miss Merriass Markham, Adam A. Aiken, and one or more surprising objects are variously tangled & tied, conjected complected & connected, interspersed interjected & interspected, banged balled blowed & throwed, socked cocked & knocked, rolled cold & holed, dabbed grabbed & jabbed, permutated germutated & spermutated, dipped tipped cripped & whipped.

But no details. If you think this is a story off over which to get your rocks you're mistook.

Anyway, in the morning Gordon puts in for space duty again.

16. To the Nation We Know

Marius Goncourt personally verified the completeness of each conference kit shortly before the arrival of the first invited participant. Each had the usual lined pad and short pencil, the conference folder, the report of the preliminary task force on the experimental manpower resuscitation project, the meeting agenda and the departmental chit good for one free meal at the Ministry executive cafeteria. Seating was carefully arranged, nameplates present at each place, refreshments at hand.

After checking arrangements Marius waited in the hallway for the early participants. The first to arrive was Mme. Laveau. Goncourt greeted her, then asked a question: "Your superiors at Propaganda are willing to see this through? No last moment hesitation?"

Madame nodded.

Goncourt continued: "As long as it's just talk, they like to sound creative, aggressive, open to new ideas, radical thinking, but when it comes down to committing to action, you know how they are. Suddenly they go with the tried and true."

"Bureaucrats," Mme. Laveau said.

Goncourt nodded.

"Then what are we?" Madame asked.

Goncourt grinned ruefully, took her arm to guide her into the conference room. "Of course, of course," he said. "But N'Haiti is starting to fall apart. If some plan doesn't get us past this manpower crisis the *blancs* will be in N'Porprince within eighteen months!"

"What makes you think they are any better off than we?"

"Perhaps they aren't," he agreed. "But then, shall we fight the N'Alabamians until both planets collapse from sheer exhaustion? Be assured, Mme. Laveau, I lose no sleep worrying over the fate of the poor enemy, but I also take no comfort from envisioning N'Porprince and N'Montgomery equally in ruins, both planets decimated, both worlds in chaos, unable to raise and distribute food even, for inability to put workers where they are needed.

"A modern planetary society is a complex and delicate structure. You cannot just remove a few pieces and say, 'Well, most of it is still there, it should keep running nearly as well as it has.' That won't work. Take away too many of the skilled people who make the economy, the government, the law continue to function, and the whole thing won't just slow down a little or go a little out of kilter.

"We're pressing our luck now, both we and the *blancs*—they *are* human beings, you know. We have to get this thing cleaned up and return our attention to developing our planet and its trade and cultural relationships with others, or we're going to find ourselves back in some kind of hunting and gathering society. Well, maybe not quite that bad but . . ." he permitted his voice to trail off.

"I know all that, Marius," Mme. Laveau said. "Whose side do you think I'm on? It's just that resuscitation is such a radical solution, it's hard for people to accept. And our plan for selling it is even more radical. But . . . as you say, we are approaching a state of affairs where only a radical solution can save us. I think it can work, I have the backing of my Ministry, and if we can get through this committee, we're in business."

"The man who invented committees," Goncourt said, "should have been contraceived."

As he spoke the remaining participants in the meeting arrived: Goncourt's own deputy for Exoneurobiology, Trudeau; representing Grand Admiral Gouede Mazacca, Captain J.-P. Girard; from the office of Governor Faustin of La Gonave, Deputy Governor Laurence.

At last, Jean-Jacques Adolphe Antoine-Simone, Minister of Military Manpower Procurement. Short, balding, round-faced, huffing as he strode to the front of the room self-importantly.

All rose. M. the Minister gestured them to be seated once again. He spoke:

"Madame, gentlemen—you are all aware of the problem. Captain Girard can tell us how badly the space fleet of N'Haiti is in need of additional men. Space warfare produces casualties in alarming numbers. For obvious reasons we cannot rob the munitions industries of workers to meet the military needs, so farmers are drawn away. Now M. Laurence can tell us that La Gonave is stripped to the bone. Agriculture on N'Haiti itself is equally as bad off.

"M. Goncourt tells me that Doctor Trudeau and his people in exoneurobiology have devised a method of reviving space casualties and returning them to duty. Now I am only a simple man, a simple servant of the government and the people of N'Haiti, but even I can see that such a program, if it is successful, will still have very serious overtones in the area of, ah, let us say public relations. So I have asked M. Goncourt to work with the Ministry of Propaganda to prepare a strategy for gaining public acceptance of this use of, ah, let us say reanimated corpses. Goncourt?" He waved a hand at his deputy and seated himself.

Marius said only, "Madame Laveau has represented Propaganda in this project. I will let her present our plan."

The five men followed with their eyes as Mme. Laveau walked to the front of the room. She looked about, smiled slightly as her eyes locked with those of Goncourt. Then she began to speak, at first hesitantly, then less so as she worked into her presentation.

"We have all seen the remarkable work of M. Trudeau and his staff. Although his first subjects were only crudely animated, later experimental resuscitees have proved capable of performing routine military and industrial duties under supervision of normal persons. A certain percentage of space casualties, we have found, can be returned to useful assignments by the application of Mr. Trudeau's implantation procedure. A far larger number can be reclaimed by the application of salvage techniques.

"Our surgeons have long held that there is no reason for an otherwise healthy person to expire when the implantation of an artificial organ or the transplantation of a natural one to replace a single nonfunctional organ could return him to health. We have now applied this principle more radically. Providing only that the size and general tissue structure matches, and with the application of antirejection techniques, we can take extremities, trunk, head, internal organs, from any number of casualties, recombine them, implant one of the NGC 7007 organisms—and have an effective soldier or worker. These resuscitated individuals—," she stopped as Laurence interrupted her sentence with a single word:

"Zombies!"

"Yes," Madame Laveau resumed. "Zombies. Sooner or later everyone associated with this project comes to that. Zombies. And that is our problem in public relations. Will N'Haitians accept this seeming return to O'Earthian primitivism? My Ministry has studied this question, and we have reached conclusions in three areas, leading to a proposed course of action.

"First, we must consider the reaction of our own general citizenry. The war is less than overwhelmingly popular as it is, and a major program which was rejected by the public would place the government in an untenable position.

"Second, the reaction of the workers and military personnel who will be in regular contact with the resuscitees. Because the subjects seem to manifest no will or personalities of their own, we have concluded that it would be best to isolate them into units of their own—field crews, industrial work gangs, even complete spaceship crews, with normal humans only as supervisors. The latter will of course have to be selected for special psychological makeups facilitating this type of assignment.

"Third, the effect on the enemy. This is probably the most difficult aspect of the problem to consider, and yet potentially the most significant. If the enemy regards this program as evidence of desperation on our part, it will only encourage his war effort. But we believe that if we approach the resuscitation program from the right direction we can actually convert it into an effective psychological warfare weapon."

Madame paused. From his chair Minister Antoine-Simone, squirming with eagerness, called out, "Zombies, yes! Tell them the plan!"

Mme. Laveau gestured placatingly. "Very well," she said. "Yes, after long consideration we believe that this aspect of the procedure should be neither denied outright nor downplayed, but should be the main focus of our entire publicity campaign regarding resuscitees. We propose the full-scale revival of the O'Earth traditions of *vodu*, with public ceremonies emphasized, to gain support for the program as an authentic Haitian tactic. Further, we proposed to broadcast information on the resuscitations—omitting, of course, clinical data of potential value to the enemy. We contend that this will make the spaceships manned by resuscitee crews, which will carry special markings to make them visible to the enemy, objects of such terror that there will be a significant advantage to our forces."

M. Antoine-Simone said, "You think there will be full acceptance of this, Madame? Intellectuals, philosophers, the religious minority . . . they will all go along with this?"

"Perhaps not without difficulty, but all can be convinced. The intellectuals are aware that our war with N'Alabama is of the enemy's making, not of ours, that we are at war for our survival. They and the philosophers support the war—except for the total pacifists, who are opposed to it anyway—so their attitude toward the resuscitation program does not matter. We plan to emphasize the cultural and nationalistic aspects of *vodu*, the ties to O'Haiti. This should gain us their support as well.

"As for the religious, the problem may be more severe, but we must again emphasize the cultural ties to our O'Earth heritage. We may have to permit a few trappings of other mythologies to be grafted onto our *vodu* rites, but my Ministry's researchers assure me that in the historic practice of *vodu* there was a cross-mythologic flow anyway. The old *vodu* cult was based on a pantheon of nature gods originally found in a country called Senegal on O'Earth.

"*Blanc* slavers raided Senegal and its surrounding states to capture workers, and transported them to the nation we know as O'Haiti, our ancestral home. The slaves wished to retain their religion but to fool their masters they adopted some of the forms of the slavers' religion, and grafted them onto their own rites. So you see–," she paused and looked about the room like a lecturer making a point in an undergraduate class, "–*vodu* was a mix from the start, and we can use the same tactic as the O'Haitians to make *vodu* live again, serve again as the tool and focus of our national struggle against the descendants of the Christian slavers."

17. With the Mourning Tide

Nurundere, captain, ordered his lighter to be hauled from the storage deck of *Djanggawul* and fitted for use of Jiritzu. Sky heroes bent their efforts, sweat glistening on black skin, dirt of labor staining white duck trousers and gripping-soled shoes.

Much thought was given to their work and the reasons for it although little was said of the matter. The people of Yurakosi were not given greatly to speech: a taciturnity, self-containment was part of the heritage of their race, from the days of their desert isolation in the heartland of Australia, O'Earth.

The brilliant light of the multiple star Yirrkalla wheeled overhead; *Djanggawul* had completed her great tack and pointed her figureheaded prow toward home, toward Yurakosi, bearing the melancholy tale of her voyage to N'Jaja and N'Ala, and the death of a passenger, Ham Tamdje of N'Jaja, at the hands of the sky hero Jiritzu.

Djanggawul bore yet the scars of the attempt by surner meat to seize control of the membrane ship and force from her crew the secret of their ability to live unsuited in space. At N'Ala she had shuttled the surviving surners to the orbiting Port Corley, along with the bodies of those killed in the mutiny.

And now, passing the great tack at Yirrkalla, *Djanggawul* heeled beneath the titanic solar wind that would fill all sails that bellied out from the rows of masts on her three flat decks. With each moment the ship gained momentum. Under the careful piloting of her first officer Uraroju she would sail to Yurakosi on this momentum and on the force of the interstellar winds she encountered on her great arcing course. There would be no need to start her auxiliary engines, to annihilate any of the precious rod of collapsed matter that hung, suspended through the long axis of *Djanggawul,* where it provided the artificial gravity for the ship.

Sky heroes swarmed the storage deck of the ship, readying Nurundere's lighter for Jiritzu. They fitted the tiny ship with food concentrate, tested her recyclers, tried her hinged mast-fittings and clamped the masts to the hull of the lighter in anticipation of her catapulting from the deck of *Djanggawul.*

When the lighter was fully prepared, the sky hero Baiame went to *Djanggawul's* bridge to inform Nurundere and Uraroju. Others in the work party hauled the lighter from its place in the storage deck, refixed the now vacant moorings that had held the lighter, and worked the tiny ship through a great cargo hatch onto the main deck of *Djanggawul.*

High above the deck Jiritzu stood balanced lightly on a spar near the top of a mainmast. He was dressed like any sky hero of the crew of *Djanggawul,* in white trousers and canvas shoes, black knitted cap and turtleneck sweater; the costume declared by Yurakosian tradition to have been the costume of the sky heroes' ancestors on O'Earth.

A tiny radio had been supplied from ship's stores and strapped to his thigh was a close-air generator.

The oxygen-rich mixture that it slowly emitted clung to Jiritzu, providing him with the air he needed for breath, insulating him from the extreme temperatures of space, providing an invisible pressure suit that protected him from the vacuum all around.

He watched the cargo hatch roll slowly back onto the deck beneath him, the one of *Djanggawul's* three identical outer decks most easily accessible from the lighter's storage place, and watched his fellow sky heroes haul the lighter onto the deck. He kept his radio turned off, and by tacit agreement no man or woman of *Djanggawul's* crew, not even Jiritzu's Kunapi half Dua, approached the mast he had climbed or made any sign of knowing his presence.

Nurundere himself strode from the bridge of his ship to inspect the lighter now standing emptily on the deck. Jiritzu could tell him easily, not merely by his distinctive cap of white with its wide black band, but by his pale skin, the protective pigmentation of the Yurakosian almost totally faded now, whited out by the passing years and long exposure to the radiation of the naked stars.

Soon Nurundere would have to return to Yurakosi, give himself over to the life of a ground squirmer, crawl with the small children and the old men and women of Yurakosi, the only inhabitants of the planet whose able sons and daughters were desperately needed to sail the membrane ships between the stars.

Not so Jiritzu.

He closed his eyes tightly, turned his face from the deck below him to the blackness above, reopened his eyes.

Above him gleamed the constellation Yirrkalla, beneath which *Djanggawul* had made her great tack. The colored stars formed the facial features of the

Rainbow Serpent: the pale, yellow-green eyes, the angry white nostrils, the blood-red venomous fangs. And beyond Yirrkalla, fading, fading across the immensity of the heavens, the body of the Rainbow Serpent himself, writhing and curving across the void that separated galaxies.

A drop of sweat fell from Jiritzu's forehead, rolled to the edge of one eye where it stung like a tiny insect, then rolled on, enlarged by a tear.

He looked downward, saw that the work on the deck was completed, the lighter ready for his use. With heavy heart he lowered himself slowly to the deck of *Djanggawul,* avoiding the acrobatic tumbles that had been his great joy since his earliest days on the membrane ships.

He walked slowly across the deck of the great ship, halted before the captain's lighter. A party of sky heroes had assembled at the lighter. Jiritzu examined their faces, found in them a mixture of sadness at the loss of a friend and fellow, resignation at what they knew would follow.

Nurundere was there, himself. The captain of *Djanggawul* opened his arms, facing directly toward Jiritzu. He moved his lips in speech but Jiritzu left his personal radio turned off. The meaning of Nurundere was clear without words.

Jiritzu came to his captain. They embraced. Jiritzu felt the strong arms of the older man clasp about his shoulders. Then he was released, stepped back.

Beside Nurundere stood Uraroju, first officer of *Djanggawul.* Some junior officer, then, had been left upon the bridge. Uraroju was a younger person than Nurundere, her protective pigmentation still strong, barely beginning to white out; she would have many years before her as a sky hero, would surely become captain of *Djanggawul* with Nurundere's retirement to Yurakosi.

They embraced, Jiritzu for a moment closing his eyes, permitting himself to pretend that Uraroju was his own mother, that he was visiting his old people in their town of Kaitjouga on Yurakosi. The warmth of Uraroju, the feel of her womanhood, comforted Jiritzu. Then they released each other, and he turned to other men and women he would never again see, men and women who must return to Yurakosi with the tale of the tragic things that had transpired between Port Upatoi and Yirrkalla on the outward leg of their sail, and with the tale of the end of Jiritzu.

Watilun he embraced, Watilun the machinist and hero of the battle against the mutineers.

Baiame he embraced, a common sailor, Jiritzu's messmate.

Kutjara he embraced, Kutjara with whom he had often swarmed the lines of *Djanggawul*.

Only Dua, Kunapi half to Jiritzu of the Aranda, spoke in their parting embrace. Radios mute, Dua spoke in the moments when his close-air envelope and that of Jiritzu were merged, when common speech could be carried without electronic aid.

"Bidjiwara is not here," Dua said. None but Jiritzu could hear this. "The loss of her Aranda half Miralaidj is too great for little Bidjiwara to bear. The loss of yourself, Jiritzu, is too great for Bidjiwara. She remains below, weeping alone.

"I too have wept for you, my Aranda half, but I could not remain below. I could not forego our parting time."

He kissed Jiritzu on the cheek, his lips brushing the *maraiin*, the swirling scarifications born by all Kunapi and Aranda, whose meaning he, Dua alone of all Jiritzu's shipmates, understood.

Jiritzu clasped both Dua's hands in his own, saying nothing. Then he turned away and went to inspect the lighter given him by Nurundere. He found all in order, climbed upon the deck of the tiny membrane craft, signaled to the sky heroes on *Djanggawul's* deck.

Watilun himself operated the catapult.

Jiritzu found himself cast from *Djanggawul,* forward and upward from her deck, the distance between the great membrane ship and tiny lighter growing with each moment. He sighed only once, then turned to the task of sailing his new ship.

Beneath Jiritzu and the lighter, *Djanggawul* dwindled, her great membrane sails bellied out with starwinds, her golden skin reflecting the multicolored lights of the Yirrkalla constellation.

And above Jiritzu, Yirrkalla itself, the serpent face, leering and glowing its brightness.

He erected the masts of the lighter, fixed their bases on the three equilaterally-mounted decks of the lighter, climbed each mast in turn, rotating gimballed spars into position and locking them perpendicular to the masts. The sails, the fine almost monomolecular membranes that would catch the starwinds and carry the lighter onward, he left furled for the time being.

From the top of a mast he pushed himself gently, parallel with the deck of the lighter. He floated gently to the deck, landing with bent knees to absorb the light impact of his lean frame on the lighter's deck.

He opened the hatch and crawled into the cramped interior of the lighter to check the instruments and supplies he knew were there—the compact rations, the lighter's multiradiational telescope that he would bring with him to the deck and mount for use, the lighter's miniature guidance computer.

Instead, before even flicking on the cabin light, he saw two brief reflections of the colored illumination of Yirrkalla—what he knew must be two eyes.

He flicked on his radio and demanded to know the identity of the stowaway.

"Don't be angry, Jiritzu," her voice quivered, "I had to come along."

"Bidjiwara!" he cried.

She launched herself across the cabin, crossing it in an easy, gliding trajectory. She caught his hand in her two, brought it to her face, pressed his palm to the *maraiin*, the graceful scarifications on her cheek.

"Don't be angry with me," she repeated.

He felt himself slump to the deck of the cabin, sitting with his back to the bulkhead, the hatchway leading to the outer deck overhead, light pouring in. He shook himself, turned to look into the face of Bidjiwara, young Bidjiwara, she who was barely entering womanhood, whose voyage on *Djanggawul* was her first as a sky hero, her first off-planet, her first away from Yurakosi.

"Angry?" Jiritzu repeated stupidly. "Angry? No, Bidjiwara, my—my dear Bidjiwara." He brought his face close to hers, felt as she cupped his cheeks in the palms of her hands.

He shook his head. "I couldn't be angry with you. But do you understand? Do you know where this little ship is bound?"

Suddenly he pulled away from her grasp, sprang back to the deck of the lighter, sighted back in the direction of *Djanggawul*. Could he see her as a distant speck? Was that the great membrane ship—or a faint, remote star?

His radio was still on. He stood on the lighter's deck, shouted after *Djanggawul* and her crew. "Dua! Nurundere! Uraroju!"

There was no answer, only a faint, random crackling in his skull, the signals of cosmic radio emanations broadcast by colliding clouds of interstellar gas.

He dropped back through the hatch, into the cabin of the lighter.

He reached for Bidjiwara, took her extended hand, drew her with him back onto the deck of the lighter.

"You know why I am here," he said, half in question, half assertion.

She nodded, spoke softly a word in confirmation.

Still, he said "I will die. I am here to die."

She made no answer, stood with her face to his sweater, her hands resting lightly against his shoulders. He looked down at her, saw how thin her body was, the contours of womanhood but barely emergent from the skinny, sticklike figure of the boisterous child his dead Miralaidj had loved as a little sister.

Jiritzu felt tears in his eyes.

"I could not go back to Yurakosi," he said. "I am a young man, my skin still fine and black, protecting me from the poison of the stars. I could not become a squirmer, alone in a world of children and ancients.

"I would have thrown myself with all my strength from the top of *Djanggawul's* highest mast. I would have escaped the ship, fallen forever through space like the corpse of El-Kumarbis.

"Nurundere said no." Jiritzu stopped, looked down at Bidjiwara, at her glossy, midnight hair spilling from beneath her knitted cap, her black, rounded forehead. For a moment he bent and pressed his cheek against the top of her head, then raised his eyes again to the Rainbow Serpent and spoke.

"Nurundere gave me his own ship, his captain's lighter. 'Take the lighter, Jiritzu,' he said. 'I can unload at Port Bralku with the others, by shuttle. I need no glorious captain's barge. Sail on forever,' Nurundere said, 'a better fate than the one awaiting me.'

"You understand, Bidjiwara? I mean to sail the Rainbow Serpent, the tide that flows between the galaxies. I will sail as long as the rations aboard last. I will die on this little ship, my soul will return to the Dreamtime, my body will continue onward, borne by the Rainbow Serpent.

"I will never become a ground crawler. I will never return to Yurakosi. No world will know my tread—ever."

Bidjiwara turned her face, raising her eyes from Jiritzu's ribbed sweater to look directly into his own eyes.

"Very well, Jiritzu. I will sail the Rainbow Serpent with you. Where else was there for me to go?"

Jiritzu laughed bitterly. "You are a child. You should have remained aboard *Djanggawul*. You had many years before you as a sky hero. Look at your skin," he said, raising her hand to hold it before them both. No power lights were burning on the little ship, but the colors of Yirrkalla glowed white, green-yellow, blood red.

"Black, Bidjiwara, black with the precious shield that only our people claim."

"And your own?" she responded.

"My own pigment—yes, I too would have had many more years to play at sky hero. But I killed Ham Tamdje. I broke the sacred trust. I could sail the great membrane ships no longer."

He dropped her hand and walked a few paces away. He stood, his back half turned to her, and his words were carried to her by the tiny radios they both bore with them.

"And Miralaidj," he almost whispered, "Miralaidj—in the Dreamtime. And her father Wuluwaid in the Dreamtime. No."

He turned and looked upward through naked spars to the glowing stars of Yirrkalla and the Rainbow Serpent. "We should set to work rigging sails," he said.

"I *will* stay with you then," she said, "you will not send me away, send me back."

"Dua knew you were hidden?"

She nodded, yes.

"My closest friend, my half, Kunapi to my Aranda. Dua told me a lie."

"I begged him, Jiritzu."

For a moment he almost glared at her, anger filling his face. "Why do you wish to die?"

She shook her head. "I wish to be with you."

"You will die with me."

"I will return to the Dreamtime with you."

"You believe the old stories."

She shrugged. "We should set to work rigging sails." And scurried away, flung open lockers, drew out furled sheets of nearly monomolecular membrane, scampered up a mast and began fixing the sail to spars.

Jiritzu stood on the deck, watching. Then he crossed to another of the lighter's three equilateral decks and followed the example of Bidjiwara.

He worked until he had completed the rigging of the masts of the deck, then crossed again, to the third of the lighter's decks, opened a locker, drew membrane and clambered to the top of a mast. There he clung, knees gripping the vertical shaft, arms flung over the topmost spar, rigging the sail.

He completed the work, looked across to the farthermost mast, near the stern of the lighter. The Rainbow Serpent drew a gleaming polychromatic backdrop. The mast was silhouetted against the Serpent, and standing on the highest spar, one hand outstretched clinging to the mast, the other arm and leg extended parallel to the spar, was Bidjiwara.

Her envelope of close air shimmered with refraction of the colors of Yirrkalla. Jiritzu clung to the rigging where he had worked, struck still and silent by the beauty of the child. He wondered why she did not see him, then gradually realized, aided by the misty sidereal light of the region, that she stood with her back to him, her face raised to the great tide that flowed between the galaxies, her mind wholly unconcerned with her surroundings and unaware of his presence.

Jiritzu lowered himself silently through the spars and rigging of the lighter, through a hatchway and into the tiny cabin. There he prepared a light meal and set it aside, lay down to rest and waited for the return of Bidjiwara.

18. Aboard the Starship *Jimmie-O*

An NCO's bunk in a N'Ala starship is bigger than a breadbox, smaller than a phone booth (laid on end), shaped a little bit like a condom for a giant about seventy feet tall with a teeny-weeny baby bonnet attached to the open (or "nonbusiness") end. You slide into it (if you're an NCO aboard a N'Ala starship) as if your feet were the head of said seventy-foot-tall giant's dork and your head its base; then you put on your teeny-weeny baby bonnet.

This is all worked out because gravity is a variable rather than a constant in a starship. No matter how you mounted that bunk, sometimes it would hang you like a hammock, sometimes like a salami in a kosher delicatessen back on O'Earth. (You'd be surprised how many of those there are in these days of the furgem Jewrab hegemony, Yitzak ben El-Makesh, prexy.) Sometimes "up" is relative to the head of the starship, sometimes to its tail, sometimes to its longitudinal axis and sometimes to its skin.

Sometimes it's in free-fall. Those bunks work regardless.

Gordon Lester Wallace kept his three V's and toprocker when he gave up shore duty and went back on board the *James O. Eastland* with the spacerine detachment, but he lost his position—no squad leaders were needed and he wound up assistant squad leader in Lt. Jimmie Rainie's platoon, working for Sarge Bo Fallon. It wasn't a bad squad or a bad platoon, and what the hell, gyrene casualties do tend to get a bit heavy so there was a good chance that there'd be an opening for an experienced squad leader one of these days.

Mean, not that Gloowoo *wanted* to see Bo dead. Hale, a leetle wound would do it, providing it wasn't *too* leetle. Bo out of action for a while, Gord would be squad leader again, then when Bo came back from sick bay *he'd* be out of work! That was the way to do it.

There hung Gord sumpin up in the sack (bonnet tied neatly neathiz chin) merrily dreaming away of some nifty N'Alabama baby (Miss Merriass Markham perhaps or then again perhaps not) not too many hours outen Fort Sealy Mae Spaceport, chowed down, settled round, gear stowed, weapons checked out, checked in with CO, leader Bo, ship's records, chaplain, quartermaster, company clerk & a necessary minimal few others, happily snoring up a storm much to annoyance of a few early risers (?) when an eyeball-smiting beam filled the gyrene embunkment where he was embunked and poor old Gord he flinched away, eyelids squeezing together trine to make that light stop only it wouldn't and then a let's call it sound started & worked its way up into his ears from a point so low he more felt it in his teeth (danged back molars needed some dental attention but the N'Ala spacerines were a mought short of dental talent these days) vibrating his whole danged skull & working its way up into his crany danged um and shaken the whole thing until he felt almost as if the whole banging noise was pouring *out* of his ears instead of in and he shook his head nearly like a dragonfly flicking sideways through some summery sunlit air and even in that tied-on teeny-weeny baby bonnet he somehow managed to whomp hisself upside the haid on some kinder stanchion or beam anna *wham* he donged hisself unpleasantly, clicked his teeth, flung defiantly wide those previously tight-clenched eyelids staring into the damned ultra-blue reveille light and mumbled unintelligibly something to the effect that tough is tough but you'd think they'd find some gentler way of waking the spacerine detachment aboard the goddam *James O. Eastland* when it was time for chow in the goddam standard ship's time morning.

After chow they had a shape-up in the troop-marshaling area and the detachment commander, Colonel-General "Pissfire" Pallbox, addressed the men.

—Umen—Colonel-General "Pissfire" Pallbox (his real first name was not spoken allowed in the N'Alabama spacerines, you can bet your *ss)—Umen—(being somewhat repetitious)—are the finest fighting force in the N'Alabama spacerines.—

Up went bajeesus & saintgeorge a loud cheer.

—M the N'Alabama spacerines bein the finest fightin force in the en dammit tire planetary military establish fuckin ment. —He spit on the deck. Some swabby wone like that!

(Prolonged & stormy applause.)

—M the N'Alabama planetary military establish fuckin ment—his voice rising—being the finest fightin force among the pure surn white planets under God & His Son Jesus George Christ!—

—Yay!—everybody said to that, loud & with enthusiasm.

—M the pure surn white planets—ole Pissfire hollern rantin now, snappin his official spacerine issue galluses m turnin from side to side—bein the toughest, meanest, wild-spit-in-the-eye-&-kick-em-in-the-nuts bunch of ball-barren *men* in the entire furgem galaxy!—He jumped up & down with a red face & shoutin.

All the spacerines likewise.

Gord, he like to piss his pants when he heard that speech. That old Pissfire, now there was a leader bajeez, none of this weakwater and julep-sippin wheezes like you got from Milburn Mitchum or Eugene Youngerman or them other pansy-assed parlor ticians. Gord, he just stood there hoping to hear more.

Pissfire, he said—Now these here swabbies—and he paused for reaction, being a man who knew how to play to an audience, even of enlisted men—now these here swabbies, they got a certain technical competence, we gotta hand them that much.—he said, then paused again while a titter (pardon) swept the ranks.

—An ole Admiral Yancy Moorman, he tellin me this morning that these swabbies spotted some blips on their lookin glasses. Now some of them blips, we know what they are. I can tell you men now—he leanin forrard conspiracarily & emphasizin that word *now*—that we haven a general fleet mobilization & rendezvous today, m we been plannin, right, we been plannin what we all been trainin for m hopin for for all these years, we goin to land on goddam N'Haiti m teach the nigra papadocs oncet m frall they *place*!—

Spacerines cheerin an whoopin an huggin each the other (sometimes with a leetle more hug than you might think for spacerines, but what the hell, they wuz a long way from Leto) when they hear *that*, you can bet your sweet a*s. But then Colonel-General "Pissfire" Pallbox, he had summin else to add:

—But those *other* blips ole Yancy's boys seen—he let that *other* sink in a little bit—those *other* blips, they a bit farther off, m they straight on ahead, m unless ole Yance, he fooled mightily, he says he thinks they bein the N'Haitian damned space fleet! Now you men, you know what that means.—He stoppen & looken around once more.

—You know what that means! We can't go pissin away our military cream on their bap-a-lousy two-bit crummy planet m let their cruvvelin damned forces have a free pass at our sacred homes! Nossir! No cruvvelin black animan nigra goin lay one filthy paw on some innocent defenseless little golden curly-headed surn baby while Pissfire Pallbox draws breath. Are you with me?—

Oh, he played a audience well. They been howlin yet if he didn't raise his hand for quiet.

—Oak hay, men—Pissfire wrapped it up—we goin rendezvous as planned, but then we goin head straight at them cruvvelin black papadocs m smash the daylights out of that bunch of floating tin they call a space fleet. Before another sun sets—(he was talken meta damn phorically you realize of course, out there in the big glittery dark)—ole Goody *Maz*accy'll wish he been a waiter or summon else a nigra's fit to be, an not play-act at bein a admiral.—

He finished up his speech & walked off & the lesser brass took over & made speeches & then the damned company grade officers took over & *they* made speeches & finally the NCO's took charge & got everybody to fixing up their packs & spacesuits & practicing battle stations & calling out raider detachments & boarding parties & making sure they had their weapons at hand & ready to go & ammunition supplies okay & the chaplin went around & prayed over everybody &

gave em all a tweak below the belt & finally everybody had chow again & grabbed a little sack time cause you never know when you'll get a chance once a battle starts.

By late afternoon (according to standard ship time, you can never tell in space of course except on a civil liner where they keep dark & light hours but on a military ship it's light all the time & ready to go) Gord was "up" again, everybody was giving his lase-ax a final cleaning, everybody was talking in a kind of nervous undertone & Gord kind of quietly drifted off (one of the advantages of being a 3V & rocker without the responsibility of command) & headed for a window hoping to see the fleet rendezvous (he was still that much of a boy at heart & loved to watch spaceships land & take off & all that stuff) & kind of hoping that the swabbies would be trying out their holo projectors in preparation for fooling the poor stupid apes in the impending battle & at the same time wondering if he'd be fooled himself & not be able to tell the projos from the rest of the real fleet. Well, one thing for sure, if he saw another goddam *James O. Eastland,* agonized matter exhaust pouring out her asshole & red lase streaming out her slit & gun ports zapping & bapping, at least he'd know that *that* was a projo, that was for sure.

Found himself a nice window, part of a big old gun blister right there in *Jimmie O*'s flank. Gun crew'd been there & everything was all clean m polished nice. The emplacement was a big ole bapper, Gord figgered it for a sixty megapower go-go mounted right there to the deck & emplaced into the blister for better sighting & maneuverability, plugged in & charged up & ready to go when the whistle blow. Gun crew must all been in their bag-m-bonnets trynta grab a last nap m only one guard was left at the blister, nice chubby blond boy with a perspirey complexion & a tendency for his hair to get plastered onto his forehead name of Leander Laptip.

Gord he walked up m Leander said—See them points Gord?—m Gord nodded m grunted m Leander said—Ain't stars.—m Gord make a kind of grumphy noise m Leander said—They *ours* Gord!—

Gord he crawled into the blister with Spacerine Corporal Leander Laptip brushing maybe not nearer than necessary to get past and get a good look at those points and he said, full of patriotic fervor and enthusiasm—You right, Leander, they our fleet oak hay.—

Arms around each other and holding mutually onto that sixty megapower all shined up & ready for action go-go bapper for steadiness there in the stapaglassene blister & their heads close together four wondering eyes perceived the assembly (weren't they lucky to be on the right side of the *James O. Eastland*!) of the en just about tire N'Alabama military space defense force, swabbies & gyrenes alike.

How many ships? Gord, Leander they tried pointing out & keeping count, calling out names when they knew em m types when they didn't know names: sleek m speedy hit-m-runners darting ahead, destroyers, bigger, heavier armed but still light m maneuverable, tenders, communication ships, supply ships built like giant plasmetal balls:

:m sister ships of the *James O. Eastland*, giant elongated shafts bearing instrument rings m command modules at their heads, giant fuel balls at their bases: *Orval Faubus, Theodore H. Bilbo, Lester Maddox.* Gord picked out *Verwoerd.* Leander picked out *Goebbels.*

Forming up, forming up, commo beams crackling

almost audibly, data sensors humming, circuits m generators throbbing, troops preparing for the battle to come: *Long, Lee, Davis, Perez,* on they came. The pod-bearing *States Rights,* her bulging belly packed with daughter ships ready to spring into battle, gnats that would spread havoc among the enemy fleet. The space ram *Jackson,* N'Alabama's weapon of last resort, a space-flying shaft of almost solid plasmetal, crew quarters buried deep inside macrometers of padding m protection, if all else failed, lasing m zapping m bapping, *Jackson* could smash, headfirst, into any enemy ship, nothing in space could survive that impact m the *Jackson's* crew padded m strapped inside there would just wait for a retrieval team if they could make it outside themselves, m the flagship of the N'Alabama fleet, pride of a planet, painted pure glistry white with a giant portrait six decks high m a hundred meters long:

:*Lurleen McQueen,* flying out of N'Montgomery spaceport, proud m pure m altogether sure, bearing the finest of the finest, armed to the hilt, surrounded by a swarm of tenders almost audibly buzzing m bounding at her every move. Oh, that ship she was proud of her ass!

—What you think that ship cost, Gord?—asked Leander.

Gord looked, shrugged (rubbing up a little bit on Leander as he done so, but unavoidably let's be quick to note) m didn't say nothing.

—What you think this *fleet* cost?—asked Leander.

Gord took his free hand off the go-go bapper for a moment m rubbed his head, then he said—Dunno. Must be close on three thousand ships here, big ole battlebottoms down to those little pizmaiers zoopin around out there. Them damn parlor ticians planetside (he liked to pick up space talk when he got off the ground, being a boy at heart) surely know how to squeeze the ole taxes out of us, but they hardly do nothing with all the money but build ships, buy zappers m bappers, train soldiers m the like, for about as long as I can remember. Lemme see now . . . –he got deep in thought but didn't get through it cause the ship rocked:

:*kerwhup!*:

:alike to send him m Leander sprawling m struggling if they didn't have a good secure grip on the bapper m onto one the other. Then they heard a ship's siren sounding m in a minute ole Admiral Moorman's voice a-whipping through the ship's voice system:

:–Moorman here tention crew stations medially furgem papadocs clearly got some kind of longer range weapons as we calculated still beyond pickup gear but they gotta be northeast quadrant between thirty, thirty-four degrees, holos *on*, gunners ready m I turn command over to section CO's.–:

:m off he goes m there's bumping m bitching sounds m voices, noises, thumps m sommon sounding like a *urrkh!* m a familiar voice coming on:

:–Pallbox here listen all spacerines we gettin moren we an fuckin ticipated soonern we ex hubbadubba pected everybody to assembly areas goddam *now* by ee-vee-ay detachments we gonna augment firepower ex shittin ternally till the nigras get close m then we gonna go across m take the furgemothers assall!–

He shutten up, voice system crackled a couple-three times m shutten off, feet pounding, whistles sounding, people shouting, Leander he yell at Gordon–My crew coming now m you gotta go ole buddy.–he given G. Lester one sweet tonguing m away Gilwoo swooped coming round a corner passed Leander Laptip's gun squad pounding down the plasmetal corridor m Gordon Lester he making his way at top speed past his condombunk picken his pack m on his way fastern you can say Jackie Robinson m he going so furgem fast m he so sucken scared he don't know whether he mess his pants or just let a little nervous gas but he knows it smells bad in that sealed-suit but he's in place for a quick tense countoff.

Lt. Jimmie Rainie he's zoopin around in front checking who's there (everybody is) m all the squad leaders are dancing up & down making sure everybody's got his equipment, no use being present if you don't have your gear right, weapons ready, sealed-suit proper; everybody's okay though spacerine drill being what it is they've been through this beau coup times in barracks on drill field in the boondocks bivouacked away from camp and you can bet every time they ever hit black deep space.

:*kerwhup!*:

:that ship gives another shake, gyrenes jarred but everybody keeps his feet Lt. Rainie he hollers, his voice comes out crackly-plasmetally in everybody's headphones—You all oak hay? Stand fast men!—

They do.

Ship starts to buckle across her beam, ole *James O.* being in bad trouble, in perilous shape and those poor white boys they haven't even *seen* no black-as* papadoc ships yet but now everybody standing in unsteady slowly tilting ranks wobbling m wavering as gravity slips around up goes down m heavy-light swapping around m only grabboots holding those gyrenes steady to the deck but leaning m swaying m Gordon Lester Wallace the one two three he looks up m:

:*Great Balls of Fire!*:

:the core dinged ceiling/wall/hull utha ship's got a

rent in her up there thirty feet above his wondering head half a football diamond long m nearly as wide m on the other side of it up/down/out there [Gord he feel like he falling/flying/swooping out/up/down into that hole/flat black pool/sky/plane m he swooping in circles his head wobbling on his suddenly rubbery neck m his stomach sending up sour warnings of the taste of things to come meanwhile churning/burning inside m a humring in his ear(phone)s as Lt. Rainie's voice hollering (to be continued)]:

:gigant shapes huge glistry another *Jimmie O.* beside the *James O.* beside a ghosty wavery *Eastland* behind a bigabigabiga battlewagon oozy fat letters honor prow proclaiming *James O. Eastland* uptop a glowing gleaming phanty *J. O. Eastland* surrounded by a clustra *JamesJamesJames O.O.O. EastlandEastlandEastland* some solid some lucent m beyond Gord can see a *Bilbo*, another, another, waving, dancing, bapping m zapping away m *Longs* m *Lees* m *Faubuses* m *Maddoxes* m one *Lurleen*, two, three, wheel m:

:faway, faway, wayway past the holos visible at last the shiteaten N'Haitian nigra fleet:

ships m ships m ships
ships m ships m ships
ships m ships m ships
ships m ships m ships
firing, firing
swooping m dodging

rays, missiles, rams, coming from the nigras' ships, coming from the N'Ala ships,

noises in the headphones, sum um words, sum um not, loud m *Creesacappery* screaming m now a break, now a second unscreaming m now coming across the headphones Lt. Jimmie Rainie's (continued now!)

voice—You gyrenes, you surn men, nowsa time, on the hull, weapons up, now, now, up, lezgo!—in command still, Gord he's trained, he obeys, kicking his grab-boots, shloop! off the deck, up, outen that hole, ee-vee-ay time, out/up/down onto/into black deep/flat swoop/tumble m a quick spin, most a mini-orbit m clank! splank! onto the hull, onya belly, look up, through holos (*you men bin trained!*) m a one-man lase-ax ready to augment ship's firepower, looking up at nigra ships, *Creeso!* how many they must have holos too but even so how many they must have us five-to-four, four-to-three, three-to-two m now the two fleets they intermingling m:

:zapper m bapper fire crossing, singing m zinging, singeing m twingeing the ether itself, lightning streaks red, yellow, orange, glaring magenta, blood colors, flesh colors, missiles barreling by, striking *us*ships, *them*-ships, silent glary detonations, impact demolishments m:

:*kerwhup!*:

:the *Eastland* took another shot someplace Gord didn't see where only felt the whole sucken hull buck m thud beneath him m just as she settled down a might Gordon he readying his lase-ax once more there's the most incredible:

:B-L-O-O-M-I-N-G:

:as the *Lurleen McQueen* she musta taken a direct full-force blow right to the vitals m she goes *splowen* in all directions, plumes of fumes m chunks of guts m hull m hardware, guns m control gear, power plants m fuel supplies (that lady she had the biggest damn balls in the whole furgem fleet packed *full* of agonized matter!), sealed-suited spacerines blown out, twirling m snapping through blacuum some clearly dead, some not so, some clearly holed, some still looking sealed m now:

:sliding silently upside the *Eastland* Gord sees a shape, a hard-looken plasmetally thing, huge, biggern the *Eastland* even, close even to the blowed *Lurleen* m she's a clearly she's he knows he can identify her from Fort Sealy Mae dayroom ID posters she's a she's no doubt about it a gigantic damn nigra ship she's in fact that superwagon *Oh! Oh!* N'Ala spacerines call her, the *Annie Eyes*, the *Oginga Odinga* m on her hull Gord sees vast rectangular pullbacks inside battle-dressed armor-glinting starshine-lit black-suited black-skinned N'Haiti colleagues-in-arms Gord's co-pro's no mistakenem nigra spacerines m with a helmet-shaking common *roar*:

Lt. Jimmie Rainie's spacerine platoon kick off from the hull of the *Eastland*, grabboots shloop up off the hull, that blattering bunch of old Pissfire's finest, lase-axes light-lining m illuminated only by multi-originned starslight m the glints of their own lase-axes they see black-suited nigras leap fly/fall from that pullback opening in the *Oh! Oh!* sweeping up/down/out to meet them m with a crash the first two foes meet, lase-beams missed, chest-plates giving a radioed *clank*, pants m gasps of *Creeso* can you tell the sounds of killing of dying from those of coitus!

Now too late, forget that interlocked murdering pair, Gord too flying up/down a black-suited papadoc falling up to meet him, Gord sends a lase-beam, *sppssp!* across meters of blacuum, papadoc keeps coming but starts to fold, spindle, mutilate, Gord takes a good two-hander on his lase-ax, feels his own chest heaving, deep breaths demanded, adrenaline spurting through hot moist vascules, sweeps his weapon overhead in two hands, feels null-weight trained habits acting unconsciously, hips jerking into involuntary thrusts and a:

:*whap!*:

:Gord's lase-axhead comes down on the nigra's back armor with a pacifying thukky noise, armor m bone conducted right up Gord's arms to two much-gratified ears m Gord wrenchesiz l-a free m kicks papadoc's body spinning infinitely away m Gord looks around for new worlds to conquer m comes face to face with another nigra spacerine m:

:he brings an ax around m:

:he brings an ax around m:

:he opens his mouth in a silent shriek m:

:he opens his mouth in a silent shriek m:

:the ax, blooded m starlit, swings gracefully m:.

:the ax, blooded m starlit, swings gracefully m:

:smashing, m blood gushing, m a sound:

:smashing, m blood gushing, m a sound:

:a scream too loud too shrill m:

:a scream too loud too shrill m:

:red:

:red:

:black:

:black:

: :

: :

19. Aboard the Starship *Oginga Odinga*

: :
: :
:black:
:black:
:red:
:red:
:a scream too loud too shrill and:
:a scream too loud too shrill and:
:smashing, and blood gushing, and a sound:
:smashing, and blood gushing, and a sound:
:the ax, blooded and starlit, swings gracefully and:
:the ax, blooded and starlit, swings gracefully and:
:he opens his mouth in a silent shriek and:
:he opens his mouth in a silent shriek and:
:he brings an ax around and:
:he brings an ax around and:

The inside of his black space-armor stinking of terror and his own vomit, Christophe Belledor recovered from momentary unconsciousness. The body of the *blanc* marine had gone into a mad binary orbit with him, the two of them, the live and the dead, holding captive millions of tiny red glinting globules. More globules continued to pour from the ax-rent in the armor of the dead N'Alabamian.

Christophe kicked away the corpse, as he had been trained, using the equal-but-opposite force to drift back toward the main concentration of troops, his comrades and their foe, struggling and hovering between the *Oh! Oh!* and the *Eastland.* Corpses hung balanced in the small gravitational fields of the two great ships, or swung in long elliptical orbits away from the battle. Survivors on both sides dodged frenetically, alternately seeking to assure themselves that they were not about to be attacked and seeking enemies to attempt to beam down or ax.

Of the thousands of N'Haitians and N'Alabamians who had entered the battle, only the untouched and the dead remained—nonfatal wounds were all but unheard of in a vacuum-environment battle. Self-contained resealant systems in space-armor could handle the occasional micrometeoroid strike that might occur in hard vacuum, or might even close off a tiny puncture from a glancing beam or point, but any significant hole in space-armor produced quick death from decompression and fast freezing.

Christophe, circling in free fall, found himself again startled, face to face with another enemy marine. He valved slightly, thrusting toward the enemy. The enemy remained stationary, as if not knowing what to do. Christophe aimed his lase-ax, fired at the enemy's chest. He missed.

By now they were very close. The enemy raised his own lase-ax; as he did so Christophe saw the jagged shards at the beaming end, where some blow must have been blocked, saving the *blanc*'s life but also destroying his laser. Too close to beam again, Christophe raised his weapon to port, blocked the enemy's swing, attempted to come under it and jab to the pelvis but the N'Alabamian twisted and Christophe's blow landed harmlessly on the man's flank, sending a ringing vibration through his armor.

The *blanc* leaned sharply backward, spinning on his own axis, checked and started forward and down again, his ax a gleaming streak of white starshine as it sped murderously toward Christophe's helmet. Christophe tried to get his own lase-ax handle above his head to block the blow but he miscalculated and his mass slid "downward" leaving an open target.

The gray-dull chestplate of his opponent's armor splashed into sudden glory, glowing momentarily rust-red, then scarlet, yellow-orange, then back with equal speed through the spectrum. Even through his own insulated plasmetal suit Christophe felt the heat of the radiant energy. The enemy now floated away, performing a series of graceful back somersaults, lase-ax still strapped to one wrist, arms thrown backward and knees spread and buckling. With each revolution of the body Christophe could see the circular black opening where the laser had seared away the N'Alabamian's armor.

Too late to counter an attack upon himself—if one was coming—Christophe whirled to face the unquestionable source of the laser beam, but saw no possible origin of it.

He shrugged, checked his weapon, valved again toward the mass of space-armored figures that floated between the *Oh! Oh!* and the *Eastland*. For him the battle was over. For thousands of cubic kilometers around N'Haitian and N'Alabamian ships maneuvered and fired, rammed and dodged, disgorged miniature hornet-ships to harass the enemy and marines to board or to place skin-charges on enemy craft.

If this battle progressed like most, it would go on for hours, even for ship-standard days. Then each fleet would withdraw, the well ships guarding the withdrawal of the crippled, towing away what salvage they could scour from the wreckage of those ships, both their own and the opponents', that were too far gone even to stagger away under partial power and post-combat conditions.

One difference this time.

The *Oh! Oh!* was little damaged. *Eastland,* a hulk. Her command module had taken a partial ram. It lay crushed and opened against the instrument unit, itself hanging against the distant stars with one chord sheared completely away, the remaining ring lifeless, data-acquisition circuits silent, storage banks dead, processing modules hopelessly fused by fantastic overloads of random heat and power surges produced by monstrous laser rakes.

The long shaft was crumpled, drooping where some surface charge had blown in a jagged section, orbiting flotsam circling the equator of the ship. At the base of the hull one huge fuel tank was torn away, flung out of sight by the residual energy of whatever force had torn it from the shaft—an internal explosion, perhaps, set off by intense heat from a N'Haitian beam, or a ram where the globe was seamed to the cylindrical hull of the *Eastland.*

Dead. Perhaps salvageable. Whichever force was stronger in this sector, whichever fleet retained sufficient strength to board *Eastland* with a salvage crew, make fast for towing, protect their prize from the opposition until they had withdrawn out of range, would return to its home base with whatever weapons and equipment, engines and communications gear, intelligence data and flight-and-battle records she contained.

The hulk itself would be examined and evaluated. If reparable—she would spew her exhaust once more between the stars. As the *Eastland* if salvaged by N'Ala, as something else, *Duvalier* perhaps, or perhaps *Cleaver* or *Newton* or *Seale*, if by N'Haiti. And if *Eastland* should prove to be beyond repair, then still the plasmetal of her hull would be rendered and recast and emerge someday as something new, to lance down the stygian star-tracks and fight again for the eternal glory of N'Alabama. (Or N'Haiti, as the case might be.)

But one difference in this salvage operation.

Not merely the hulks of battered starships this time. Not merely the metals and esters and silicons. Not merely the fabricated goods. This time the men.

Between the star-glinting *Oginga Odinga* and the dead and crumpled *Eastland* the unit of Christophe Belledor was beginning once again to form. Christophe moved toward his place in ranks, noting the gaps in the disc-shaped free-fall formation. Far, far in the distance he could see other salvage-ready situations, illuminated ships nestled triumphantly near to dead hulks like triumphant beasts of prey near the dead bodies of their victims. Here Belledor could recognize the form of a N'Haitian victor, there a N'Alabamian. In the aftermath of interstellar battle a strange truce seemed to fall as the survivors, gratefully wonder-struck by the fact of their own survival, concentrated only on their own withdrawal and on the rape of their own victims. They did not choose to jeopardize their status as survivors with any foolish picking of fights with survivors of the other fleet. Belledor gazed into the distance: N'Haitian plundered

N'Alabamian; N'Alabamian plundered N'Haitian. One hulk swung about and for an instant, by some odd trick of optics, her name, marked in huge letters, caught a glint of light and became visible for the briefest instant: *Bilbo,* then was lost.

Inside Christophe Belledor's helmet the voice of his commander spoke, synchronized with the movement of the commander's arm. The instructions were clear. In company with his fellows, Christophe set to work gathering the shattered and frozen cadavers of the two space marine detachments. White and black, burned and axed, he collected them all. Those with only punctures in their armor to let in the drowning ocean of nothing, and those with organs roasted, and those with torn-away limbs and heads and chunks of torsoes.

What could be salvaged would be used or banked. The remainder, well, at least would not remain behind to leave a cluttered battlefield.

For a moment, Christophe entertained a stray wonderment: Now that the battle was ended, who had won? But then, the admirals and the captains, the generals and the intelligence staffs, were paid to determine such abstruse mysteries. He, Christophe, was paid to do as he was told, and to try to stay alive until such time as he could return to his comfortable desk, his comfortable wife, and his occasional pleasant encounters with the daughter of Leclerc. Meanwhile, Grand Admiral Gouede Mazacca probably knew who had won the battle.

20. Home from the Stars

'nifykin look outha portole sreely pretty, sreely pretty, lookna Port Upatoi swinging roun thole mudball, thole goodole place, it's maybe not the prettiest place na whole universe but nobody ever said it was, it was home though m that counted frole lot that swat Leander Laptip saw outha portole:

:N'Ala (as her sons wuz oft wont tcaller):

:N'Alabama (to be slightly more polite of expression):

:Democratic Autonomous United Planet of New Alabama (to be utterly quite ubsurbly formal):

:buthe thingz, here lay on his bunk a-lookin out the window, the portole, the plexipeep one of a good many that lined the length of the battlewagon battered m bruised m bumped m bunkered tho she be, *Leander Perez,* onetime pride of the fleet of N'Alabama, here lay Spacerine Cor dam Poral Leander Laptip.

What's with Leander?

Tbe assholelutely accurate about en the boy ent so spry just today, nfact hez pretty unhappy, despite pretty site of take a look therz old Port Corley a rollin m a bowlin around N'Ala from light sight t night site m night sight t light site m so bright m down on the ground summer banns are playing but:

:Leander Laptip slyininiz bunk looking out the (to be extraneously vernagulous)—window—nee sees a fungbodacious gorgeous old sun just hanging there going:

:hot:

:m going:

:bright:

:m Port Corley rollin m N'Alabama underneath spinnin m Leander looks down m he sees Leander m he's somewhatly de-one-might-say-at-least-slightly-pressed at what his singular functional remaining eye might espy. What he sees is:

:well what he is seen is:

:well this int pleasant just keep yo patched-m-buttoned *on*:

:mostly bandages frankly m a good many tubes m wires zoopin into m outa himself, which nobody much would like to see, maybe back on O'Earth the furgem Jewrabs got geriatric doodaddies like so but out ahere on the independent settled m spunk-assed new planets we hardly have anybody around long enough for that kind of tripe.

No'm.

N'Alabama Spacerine Cor fuckin Poral Leander Laptip from Eutaw Town hez a veteran gyrene now, hez bloodied his lance, done his dance, wet his pance m had his chance, hez gone to (meta-damn-phorically speaking) gone to France, found romance and earned iz grance cose hez been, to use the term of the day, holed.

Holed.

Not many casualties cummin from space wars. No'm, not so many.

Lotsa casualties *occur* but not many come home coz once you *holed* in a space battle, you harley ever recover, one *hole* in yarmer m you know what happens? What happens is:

:*zoop*:

:assaright, *zoop!*

Nifya wondering whassa *zoop!* here's the dope, here's the truth, here's the hope, hope of youth:

:*zoop!* that's your *air* blow nout, *pfff!* m what's left inside you vacuum suit, well to be excusably graphic about it, you vacuum suit so named for one reason lives down to its name for another, m there *you* somewhat suffering from oxygen starvation for a little while, yass, but true word, no turd, don't worry, only for a little while coz, lovey-dovey, you only gone suffer from oxygen starvation very briefly coz also you depressurizing *rapidly*.

Rapidly.

How rapidly? Well, this rapidly: *zoop!* Or *pfff!* All the same, all a shame, not a game.

Very, very few wounded. Dead a passel. Live, no hassel.

But every now m then some flukey lukey comin along, catching a matching, bash but no cash, after a crash, m here lays Corporal Leander Laptip coming home to Eutaw via Port Corley, let's give the little feller a great big hand.

He needs it, for sure.

Leander gets thattention of ship's doctors here aboard the good ole space battlewagon *Leander Perez*, something there about namesakes worth milkshakes, Leander *L* went to battle the furgem papadocs in the furgem battle of wevvafuckinell, who can tell, rode out there proud m tall a spacerine gunner on board *James O. Eastland* m back he came on board the *Ell Pee* ridin uneasy m unhappy not many others in the ship's sickbay.

But some.

Swarboy, swarboy Leander *L* lizaboard *Leander P* perspicaciously pondering what lizahead of him on little old N'Alabama land that he digs, when very shortly now he again sets his singular foot upon her red dust. He is depressed, distressed, and more than a mote impressed with the magnitude of the task that lies ahead of him.

Speaking of which still in orbit there what's still left m functioning of the good ship *Leander Perez* tether-docked to Port Corley wheels waltzingly out of the planetary shadow, the land terminator still downside N'Alabama's arcly horizon but up ahigh as *Leander P* she be, dawn crumples early and ole Alquane sunny ball smites Leander Laptip smack in his one functionary survivor m Leander blinks m turns away which . . .

. . . considering the assortment of rubber implements, plastic doodads, m metallic gimcracks various punched into, parted onto m screwed unto Leander's remaining anatomy is no mean feat nossir but he does it, he manages to swivel his remaining neck to get that one lubricated orb out of the path of the glare for fair.

Ponwhich it lights up as it lites down upon, surprise, what Leander instamoneously misgrabs as a looking damn glass but in one tick deduces no bajeesus m saint george it is not nossir neither no mirror mimage tall but a other person. Leander would sit up and gasp if he could but he does manage to explice something that sounds like this:

—whuuw—

:or thereabouts, which brings forth some kind of response, leastly a closed exposed eye goes flitterflatterflutter openshutopen m Leander finds himself lookin eye unto eye with a goddam pitiable mangled bangled dangled *mess* of a former person's remaining viability m Leander finks tombself:

—good krykie fime in shapes bad that poor fucker thissole boyd better cash it in m call it quits—

:but that other poor fucker laying there thinking prolly justabout the same thing, wouldntya think, about our poor laddy Leander m there's this kind of, not to be mystical about it or anything fruity like that but would you be willing to grant at least the metaphor if not the fact, *telepathy*.

And they both, after a momentary tension, the two poor bastards what's left of 'em giggle at each t'other.

Leander he looks m he quietly (coz that's the only way he can if at all) laughs.

And that other poor bastard lays there looking at Leander, each othem with one eye, lots of bandages, tubes, pipes, wires, gadgets, patches, stitches, whevva, they both of them, they just laugh a little.

And then they quiets.

And they gazes.

And they does, both um, a little bitta double take. M two eyes blink, one from each shelf where theyz laid m stayed, m they take again what we should call above all a triple take.

M laugh agin.

Coz hez a boy.

M shez a girl.

M that is funny coz they both pretty smarts m they knows about their parts and figure nohow arts gonna fix the mix for *these* hix.

Leander Perez erstwhile pride of the fleet (along with a couple others such as the big ole momma ship *Lurleen McQueen* as never made it back from thole battle at all) she go stain drydock as it were, norbit forry pairs even tho N'Alabamian battlewagons customarily rise and return to and from the surface of that there ole little planet such as at or near the ole dear never fear Fort Sealy Mae, but not now.

Leander Laptip finds what's left of himself transported to that ole orbiting loop, that interplanetary universal detachment, Port Corley, m in sick bay *there* while they tryne patch up what's left so he can return to a somewhat normal life back on the surface of the land that he loves a loyal son of N'Ala m since surviving wounded of space battles:

:here's Leander in sickbay aboard Port Corley being interviewed by some good old medic m the medic is takin a what they call medical history of Leander [only bout the seven zillionth one he's (get yo' gee hard baby) gin since heen listed in the N'Alabama spacerine corpse way back awhen] m the medics they already bin doon a good job on Leander, you kin believe that because *he* sez, first chancty gets twixt–evahad measles–m–evahad penny ciders, no nemmine thaparts gone now anyhow–Leander he sez:

:–Hey you old medic boy, whevva happena that lil ole gal was alayin in sick bay on bo *Leander Perez* wimme?–:

Ole boy medic he don't know, or he sez so, anyhow, Leander he feels pretty lonesome, pretty unhappy, but they work that boy over, gravity's light up here in Port Corley, sick bay here not very crowded, staff moderately adequate to supernumerarious, they fix him up with a bunch of physiotherapeutic procedures like warm baths, cool baths, dumbbells, exercisers, whatever they haven to hap around, m:

:one fine day (as such things are measured in space where stuff like that can be pretty much arbitrary if you want 'em to be) they take Leander down to the gymnasium m hitch him up onto some parallel bars, which is no easy proposition considering as there isn't a hell of a lot of him left to hitch onto those bars, bees got a whole arman hand and another chunk of one m parva torso so they get him hangin up there m:

:well, toobee doobee butterly frank it isn't that Leander's actually and immediately in acutely intolerable pain, again, he ain,

(they keep some fat ole molecules circulatin in his blood all the time, keeps that from happening)

but more, well, a sort of generalized malaise m discomfort, a sense that all ain't exactly right with him (which of course is quite the case) m he can't see too much of hisself even wiz one eye that he has left, but he's a game lil fella Leanders, so he letsem hitch him up there on the parallels m he starts what they call in medijarg, generalized preprosthetic musculaturial conditioning, or, as it's known familiarly to its friends:

☆ ***Toughening Up What's Left So We Can Hang On Hardware*** ☆

:m after a couple three eternities of unpleasantness Leander is hoisted back-down offen them parallels m dropped in a little gadget not a hole different from a shopping cart same as good wives use down in Echola, Gasque, Coxheath, Suggsville Center &cet knee gets a free trundle back to zward, which is a private room full of nutrogenic life support systems m all like that.

Leander comes out twice a day (so to say) for sessions the likes of that, minbee tween there ain't a hell of a lot frim to do, being incapable in his present condition to swim, play free-fall volleyball, whatever, but he does have his brain (or that major portion which do remain) soz to keep him occupied, satisfied, gratified m stratified the kindly crew, staff m therapists of the sick bay m medical rehabilitation station of Port Corley make available to Leander their own cultural materials.

Some of which he has a trifle of trouble with handling the physical aspects of, such as turning pages m pushing buttons but modern prosthetic technology works wonders, right?

Startin wif a threevee holo tape of N'Alabama's most famous and admired night club entertainer, eggs arctic danseuse, gooseloose, Miss Merriass Markham, dooner famous patriotic S&M act, live as seen in the finest establishments of Letohatchie m the likes:

:Miss Merriass wearn underneath her ole style surnbell friffles mere triffles, rubbery briefs featuring strategically placed cutouts here and there, m Miss Merriass first threatened wivva lil misceginaceous rape then whipping out her whip m given that yukkypukkysukky thing What Four.

Of alla this, nun is noo, nun is noo to Leander Laptip who bin raisen fine old N'Ala traditions, budda boy looks at it all with suitable admiration, aesthetic appreciation as it was, m one might even say, speculating as that's all one can do under the peculiar circumstances involved, as how Leander for sure would, soseta place this peckerously decorously, well:

:He'd get a rise out of Miss Merriass all right if he had any rise left to get out of her.

Oleander, he sighs over no rise, the reel ends anyhow m Leander turns his head wondering what he's goin to do next for diversion, it not being meal time right now.

He gets a fukbuk next: lossa nice pictures, no dialogue to distract the "reader" fromz vicarious fantasies, lozza nicetuff, ultra closeups, camera peeping right up there inside the vulva, implanted, vattery osperated, waiting for the arrival of Lord Glans, here he comes m there he goes m here he comes m there he goes m this transpires for a while, little cutaways nown then to external closeups suitable for immediate analysis m back inside *whee* here come de flood, all over the lens but what the hell that proves this is for real, right?

M Leander he turns the pages with his hand, wishing there was something else he could do with it, m his one eye kind of waters up but he's a brave gyrene m next thing he knows here come the medics m the shopping cart m he's carted off, back to generalized preprosthetic musculaturial conditioning, but just as hez getting wheeled in he spies something else ahanging on the parallels getting lifted down m stuck in a cart not a holot different from his own m he shouts (as best he can):

—Hey!—

:m thuthamutha turns her head (as best she can) m Leander yells:

—Hey get in touch!—

Too much! Personal contact and such, these two it looks like might swell be soul mates (they can hardly be any other kind at this game of the stage) m the good ole medics roll that there lil ole gal away (or what's left of her) m Leander m'z chief handler they go through a little bit of dialogue like this:

—Hey, that was my friend—

—Mmph—

—I wanna talk tur—

—Mmph—

—She nose weartsat—

—Mmph—

—Gah damt, I won't cooperate till you answer me!—

—Mmph?—

—When can I talk to her?—

—You wanner seeya like this?—

—Mmph—

—Tell ya what—

—Mmph—

—You get set, get yer prosthes implanted, get yer shit together—

—Mmph—

—Then we'll get the tuvya together—

—Lemme at them parallels—

21. At the Gran Houmfort Nationale

Perhaps as Papa claimed it was all nonsense. Still, Yvette would not miss the great ceremony. A row at dinner, Mama trying ineffectually to mediate, shouts, angry gestures, and Yvette sent to her room. All for the best, all as if she had herself made the plan.

She locked her door from the inside, vowing to answer no question or plea that penetrated its heavy wood, and flung herself onto the bed to fume. The more she thought of the argument the angrier she became. Did they think her a child? She was a young woman, her days of pigtails and pinafores far behind. She looked at herself, her figure. She had seen how men looked at her—grown men, not merely the coltish boys at the *école,* half eager and half timid in their own new hungers, but grown men. Even their neighbor M. Belledor, before he had been called to military service.

Yvette rose from her bed, turned on a small light. She drew the shade of her window and stood before the mirror, slowly removing her school dress. If Papa forbade her to attend the *danse calinda,* she would go anyway. He might think the newly revived *vodu* mere nonsense, but all of her friends at the *école* knew better. No boy or girl in Yvette's class was without some macandal, caprelata, vaudaux dompredere, or ouanga. She herself had an ouanga of goat's hide, filled with the ingredients of the ancient prescription: small stones, a vertebra of a snake, black feathers, mud, poison, sugar, tiny wax images. Normally it was kept hidden in her room. Tonight she would wear the ouanga.

Out of her dress now she stood naked in the center of her room, feet spread, arms raised, breathing deeply in anticipation of the ceremony to take place at the houmfort. Ah, such a fool as Papa deserved his ignorance. Again Yvette looked down, studying her own form: the graceful breasts and sharply pointed nipples so admired by the boys at school; the slim waist, the swelling pelvis and thickly curled, glossy arrow of black pubic hair pointing unerringly toward a precious target. She ran her hands once over her smooth sienna-colored skin, feeling alternately waves of hot and cold at the thought of the hours ahead.

Still naked she removed the ouanga from its hiding place, for a moment held the rough skin bag against her cheek, then kissed it and placed the leather thong about her neck so the bag hung between her breasts. Standing again before the mirror Yvette crossed her arms forcing her breasts together so that the ouanga bag, between them, was held tightly, the protruding evidence of the objects within pressing and rubbing on her sensitive flesh, exciting her so that she ran one hand down her belly, threading her pubic hairs and kneading her labia for a moment.

Then she whirled, ran barefoot to the closet and removed her clothing for the *danse*. A satiny blouse of brilliant stripes, yellow, green, blue; tight trousers of white, cut low to tie beneath the navel. She slipped her arms into the blouse, drew it about herself, leaving the front open to reveal her talisman, then drew on the pants and knotted them at the front. Sandals now, and now she turned out the light in her room and raised the window shade.

In a moment she had the window open and had eased herself through it, slipped softly to the grass outside and moved quietly away from the house. She ran through dark streets, silently, a light mist in the air coating her skin, each droplet seeming to stimulate her further. At the appointed spot near the house of her friend Celie she looked around, found Celie waiting beneath a tree.

She hissed for silence and the two of them dashed off silently toward the hoverail depot. Once away on the train they would reach the houmfort without interference.

At the houmfort Yvette and Celie found a crowd already assembled. Great torches ringed the open plaza before the houmfort; above them in the black sky La Gonave hung huge and glowing dully. In the misty air the light of La Gonave was fractionated, making tiny nocturnal rainbows when Yvette looked upward. The torches wavered in the night air, the orange-red flickerings making the shadows of the people dance even though they themselves stood awaiting the commencement of the ceremony or milled about seeking friends or positions from which better to see the proceedings of the night.

On the low portico of the houmfort, backed by the scrollery and pillars, the carven serpents and gourds, crucifixes and thorn-pierced hearts, stood row on row of low catafalques, each surmounted by a long shrouded figure. Before these stood the three great drums, the boula, the maman, the papa. At either side of the plaza stood other drums. In the center, an altar.

From within the houmfort was heard a drumming

and chanting. Lights flickered and figures advanced from the building. Papa Nebo, the hermaphroditic guardian of the dead, a silken top hat ludicrously perched on his head, his black face solemn, solemn, then cracked by the rictus of a tic, shirtless but wearing a tattered black dinner jacket and a ragged white skirt, his bare feet held alternately off the ground, wavering as if undecided before plunging ahead with each step. In one hand he held a human skull, in the other a sickle.

Behind Papa Nebo, reeling and staggering, robed and turbaned, in one hand a glittering bottle, in the other a silvery flute, Gouede Oussou, his eyes dull, his face flaccid, ready to perform the role of the Drunken One.

Finally the woman Gouede Mazacca the Midwife, her traditional garb trimmed with naval decor in honor of her namesake the grand admiral, the Midwife's serpent-staff in one hand, her bag of charms and implements in the other.

More figures, robed, hooded, turbaned, followed from the houmfort bearing torches and bags. They made their way to the drums at the sides of the plaza. They began to beat the drums rhythmically. Then they began to chant, the deep voice of the Drunkard, the high voice of the Midwife, the contralto of the Oracle blending as they repeated over and over:

Legba, me gleau, me manger:
Famille ramasse famille yo:
Legba, me gleau, me manger.

Over and over the three chanted, drumming, shuffling; before them in the plaza the crowd began to respond. Yvette began to move her feet and her hips, to join in the chant to Legba, *Legba, food and drink are here, family gathers with family, Legba, food and drink are here,* over and over, at first self-consciously, almost giggling at herself and her friend Celie, then more confidently, moving her body in the torchlight until perspiration began to mingle with the droplets of mist on her skin, her voice rising in the chant, *famille ramasse famille yo.*

From somewhere a young man had appeared, very black, very strong, wearing only sandals and trousers so tight that his genitals showed as a graceful swelling in the flaring torchlight; around his neck an ouanga hung, swaying against his chest as he danced. He stood facing Yvette; together they moved, together they chanted, *Legba, me gleau, me manger.*

From the houmfort came a fresh clamor. The chanting and drumming changed. Acolytes bearing giant black tapers descended the steps of the houmfort, passed between the rows of catafalques on the marbled portico. Others came bearing each a silent black rooster, then a black goat led on a rope halter; at last, bearing cups of hollowed gourd, the mamaloi and papaloi.

Papa Nebo, Gouede Oussou and Gouede Mazacca continued their chant. The crowd now stood silent, waiting. Yvette Leclerc felt a thrill jolt through her body as the black dancer took her hand; she leaned against him, feeling his sweaty skin against her face.

Papa Nebo greeted the mamaloi, took a rooster from an acolyte, bowed to the mamaloi and whirled about, the drumming starting again as he did so. Papa Nebo held the rooster by its feet, stretched his arms to their full length, threw back his head and spun, spun, toward the mamaloi, toward the drummers, toward the crowd, around, around. The rooster flapped its wings impotently trying to escape; Papa Nebo spun more and more rapidly; finally the rooster, its head filled with the blood pushed there by centrifugal force, gave a piercing, jarring cock's crow, an instinctive scream of terror and despair.

Papa Nebo stopped, held the rooster above his head where all could see, grasped its head in one hand and its neck in the other and pulled and twisted. Again the rooster crowed, crowed, screamed then ceased. With a convulsive jerk Papa Nebo tore the black head from the black neck. Blood gushing from the rooster's neck onto his ludicrous dress, Papa Nebo ran to the mamaloi and the papaloi, offered each a drink of the hot spurting fluid directly from the rooster's neck, then began filling the cups.

A new chant sprang up, wild, frantic:

Eh! Eh! Bomba hen hen!
Canga bafie te
Danga moune de te
Canga do ki li!
Canga li!

Chanting, dancing, shuffling, the crowd moved forward, each kneeling in turn before the mamaloi or papaloi, receiving the chalice of hot, fresh blood. Papa Nebo took rooster after rooster from acolytes, tore the head from each to replenish the supplies of the two gourds. Yvette danced impatiently, holding the man she had danced with, moving slowly forward toward the sacrament.

At last they reached the head of the line. Yvette knelt before the papaloi. She looked upward, her arms spread to the sides. Papa Nebo refilled the chalice. The papaloi held it forward for her, steam rising from the hot blood into the night air, the rippling surface of the blood throwing back flickering glimmers of torchlight.

The cup came forward. Yvette clutched her ouanga

bag with her two hands, plunged her face into the steaming blood, drank once, deeply, then rose from her knees. She felt hot exaltation flooding her body. She danced, danced, the drumming filling her brain, turning it to a single, throbbing tambour that resonated in a steady, compelling beat.

She turned back to see her black partner rising from before the papaloi, a triumphant look in his eyes that must match that of her own, blood streaming redly from his lips to drip from his chin onto his naked chest. Yvette ran to him, kissed the gleaming red, licking the blood eagerly as he held her crushingly in massive arms.

Giddy with eagerness, she flung herself with the man onto the hard ground, vaguely aware that scores of couples were duplicating their act all around them in the torchlit plaza. Yvette wriggled from her brilliant blouse, struggled to open the front of the man's pants as he tore hers from her hips. Unable to wait even for him to claim her she managed somehow to push him onto his back, crouched above him, felt his hands grasping her hips, pulling her onto him as he thrust, thrust up into her.

The taste of the fresh hot blood still in her mouth, the feel of the man inside her body, she writhed forward and back, eagerly, feeling him filling her, stretching her until she thought to burst with the size of him, then clamped convulsively to him as his two hands on her back brought her helplessly forward and down, meeting a final mighty heave that filled her loins with a bursting, screaming ecstasy.

She fell forward, lay with her breasts warmed against his chest, her legs still spread wide to hold him, her lungs heaving great breaths as the drums still throbbed in her head and the man's arms held her to him.

Now Yvette became aware that the drumming and chanting had changed yet again. The drumming was no longer abandoned but solemn, powerful. Yvette rolled off the man, sat up, felt him beside her. She saw others all around them sitting now, looking back toward the houmfort. Once more a torch could be seen, once more someone was emerging.

The chant rose again, now a single line, repeated over and over:

L'Appe vini, le grand zombi!

L'Appe vini, le grand zombi!

Carrying a flaring torch, advancing slowly from the houmfort, came the bloody god-figure Ogoun Badagris, dressed in traditional mock-military jacket, huge tasseled epaulets glistening, beret mounted rakishly, high-collared, his skintight trousers pure white, his jackboots gleaming jet.

Before him the others fell back: the acolytes, Papa Nebo, Gouede Oussou, Gouede Mazacca, the mamaloi, the papaloi. The chanting ceased, only the drumming continued.

Ogoun Badagris advanced to Papa Nebo, took from him his sickle. Ogoun Badagris seized the still-tethered goat, severed its rope with a single stroke of the sickle. The beast seemed paralyzed with fear. Ogoun Badagris lifted the goat in mighty arms, walked with it to the end of the rows of catafalques, lifted it high in one hand. With the other he flicked the sickle lightly, gracefully, so quickly that Yvette could hardly tell what had happened.

Even the beast gave but a single exclamation, a half bleat, half moan. Then its lifeblood was pouring from its opened jugular. Ogoun held the spurting corpse over the first catafalque, then stepped to the next.

At each bier, as the drops of hot blood struck the still form that had lain unmoving throughout the *danse*, there was a stirring. The shrouded figure rose, first to a sitting position, throwing the grave-cloth from itself. Then they rose, stood dumbly beside their biers. Yvette stared in chilled fascination. Each body was a patchwork of black, white, brown. Here a face of pale white flesh rested on a neck of ebony, pale yellow hair cropped short on the scalp only adding to the bizarre sight. Here a hand of black on an arm of white. Here a torso neatly divided by a vertical line, one side dark, the other pale, as if two bodies had been blown in half, the ragged edges of each trimmed neatly away and the remaining portions sewn back together.

As Ogoun Badagris reached the end of the rows he threw the drained corpse of the goat to waiting acolytes, then turned back to face the motionless zombies.

"After me!" he commanded them. "Into the houmfort!"

He did not look back to see that they obeyed, but turned and advanced once more into the building. Behind him, after a moment of hesitancy, the zombies began to move forward, forward.

Behind the last of them the doors of the houmfort closed with a monstrous reverberation. Yvette Leclerc forgot her black man, the blood, the chants and the *danse*. Wearing only her leather ouanga bag she rose and ran frantically from the plaza.

22. Artists in Their Studio

Now that's *motivation.* Leander he giziz awl, giziz awl, works with what he got, not so very much to be sure but what the hell, it leaves a viable organism providing certain assistance is provided, a few little things.

But he's got his brain (well, most of it) niz heart niz lungs ninough assorted other internal doohickies as he can take in such stuff as mashed mush at one end end get nourishment out of it before he deposits mashed mush again at the other.

Leander has a will to live, mostly motivated by that charming little darling he shared sickbayspace with back on board the *Perez,* not that hez thought it all the way through exactly or even approximately. No, it's more that hez got this kind of buried contact with reality sommer adeep in his brain (fortunately this lies in the portion Leander still has—without it, he'd be in even more trouble than he is, or even dead, which of course would be less).

He figras, he can right about now:

:die:

:hermitize:

:gorgonize:

:psychotize:

:narcotize:

:or maybe just plain realize the fact that hez agonna have a hard time forming what is generally referred to as a Lasting and Significant Relationship with anybody.

Hmm. Except:

:for that pretty little blonde (or redhead or brunette or whatever she might happen to turn out to be) from sickbay. And since poor oleander doesn't know her name rank or serial number no less any of the, *ahem,* more intimate details regarding this particular lady (or remnants thereof) and hez only gonna find out through the courtesy of the N'Alabamian Spacerine Corps, what's he going to do?

Leander is nobody's dummy. Or at least he wasn't until he got his vocal apparatus blown halfway to hell & damnation by the furgem papadocs in the Battle of Wurverthehellitwas, m he wants to get back inta shape, hoping all the while that his little apple sorce is doing the same (not to keep the reader in suspense, she is).

Finally Leander gets ishered his prosthies.

From arrfisl eyeball to titanium toenails, those old medics get Leander hammered back into shape, m put him through a pretty rigorous training program, learning all ovagain t sit, walk, stand, lie, rise, trot, drink, cut, eat, nazillion others.

Even t talk. In fact, especially t talk. Not too much vocal apprats leftoom, they gim a whole buncha internal falsies, no function unnoticed, but learning tyuse all the stuff all over again isn't exactly child's play, norz Leander exactly a child, all of which adds up to some odd numbers.

Now the big day comes.

The medics usher Leander into a waiting shuttle

that's docked to thorbiting Port Corley that glints like a teensie tinesee mincher peepsight-*cum*-crosshairs in the morning and evening light of Alquane as she (Port Corley, not the star) zips throor orbit in the sky of the Independent Autonomous Sovereign Self-Governing zederazederazederazedera N'Alabama.

Alla jointser noomagically sealed so Leander hedo neno spacesuit nor dooz escorts, proud m self-esteemin representatives of the most advanced rehabilitation facility on in under (or in the present case, orbiting) the I., A., S., S-g'ing., blablabla.

Leander seats himself (unassisted, to the sighing relief of numerous physicians, technicians, politicians, &c) na combination e.z. chairn flitecouch, makes some small talk wiz erstwhile handlers while awaitin tsee what's going to happen next. Sounds something like this:

—Wal—

—Hem-a-hem, ah, yep—

—Sertneez bin, um—

—Yeh, yeh, fishoo—

—Yeh, fishoo—

—Shoo—

File lee, everybody shakes hams, everyone pressing flesh to, ah, whatever, and the medics retire leaving Leander sitting there thinking aboutiz boyhood in Eutaw Town & spacerine bootcamp at Fort Sealy Mae & wild liberteze in Letohatchie & howt felt going into space the first time upside the *James O. Eastland* & getting riptshreds by the furgem papadocs & recovering upside the *Leander Perez* (not hardly nobody does that) & meeting that sweet lil thing jes alaying there in *Perez*'s sickbay & thinkin about what she mussa kept ahid unneath her uniform back when she had it (

her uniform, that is, but cumta think on it, what she kept hid unneath it too

) alla which has Leander justabout into a state of fugue not tsae farg, wenny hirza couple primilarly clanks nee looks up wiz ize:

:one organic one electronic that are:

:mee seze a vision just astandin there, just astandin there. She's:

:tall:

:slim:

:blonde (yeh, Leander baby, right, f that'ser nataral color):

:nshe smiles a smile at Leander, he just looks attr m on some levluther hez thinking tomb self thas just the nicest smile hez ever scene nee wonders how much of its godgin m how much of its medicsgin m then, Leander beene a normal red-blooded Eutaw Town type N'Alabama stud

with a normal or roughly so hormone balance in his rh-negative as provided until recently bize godgin gonads m more recently even than that by some gummit issue prosthies (those medics are *thorough*!) Leander does what any normal (or prosthetically assisted) red-blooded N'Alabamian beau wuddo, he casually letsiz eyes slide a mite downward in their tracks,

the godgin one goes ( ) that is to say, silently, rotating vertically nitsockit m in perfect (or roughly so not to stretch a point all out of line):

:the medicgin one goes (*click-bzzt-click*) but so discreetly as nobody's agonna heah *that* septin Leander himself m *he* is surely not gonna tell, nee sees that lady has got a most tasty lil shape honor cominout *here*, cominout *here* m goinback *in* in the middle & outagin at them delightful, delicious, delectable, de-lovely hips which Leander anotes athrough thetair lil gal's spacerine standard trousuzsegue most charmingly into a paira shapely gams m Leander he thinks just one thought at the moment, could that thar gal but hear his mental motions sheed listen in on this:

—How much—hez wondrin—of thetair gal is *gal* m how mucher's tubes m wires m plastothermal pseudodermal pseudonermal antispermal & cetera & so on & as follows—

But of course he doesn't say that m she doesn't hear it, instead he sez most politely:

—Ah, howdydo—arisin courteously fromz seat he continues—my name is Corporal Leander Laptip N'A Spacerine Corpse late of the biggole bapper *Jimmie O. Eastland*—

Twitch she sez—Mfashoe yaw won y'sef a biggo bentfin boomer gin the furgem papadocs Corpy—

Nee sez, lookin (*click-bzzt-click*) addiz freshpankin collar m seenit there a wink in back adam—Baddam, ma'am, that's a zackly what she am, fyo heard some rumor that's a bentfin boomer—

Nshesez—Well addi clair, I see it there, I'd do my share t'hep enjoy the cupnee bentfin boomer boy—

He grins (*click-bzzt-click*) m takes her ham (*clank-whirr-chonk*) m sezeez honored. —Myore?—he axeser politely.

—Wam Mizzy Lizzy Cadbell from Salitpa, you silly, you know me, don't you memmah back theyn sickbay?—

Nleander, been the plite devil he is, he sez—Ida never knowja—nee sits again m draws Mizzy Lizzy Cadbell down wim.

They both strapped in, Leander m the real attractive blonde, m engaged themselves in increasingly large small talk so's when their shuttle pulled its snorkelouten Port Corley they dinneven take note, they just kept on exchanging the contents of storage all the while.

Mizzy Lizzy from Salitpa shez no comfortrooper, N'Alabamian spacerines dowin gowin for that kinda stuff, ole General in charge of the Core he done laid him down the lore, he sed to the follin general effect:

—Makes a man rough & mean, tough & lean, every morn ezfiln horny, every nighty wansa fight—

:or thereabouts, quote, thoughts of Colonel-General Pissfire P. Pallbox, Commandant, meanest ass old bastard ever drew breath of airna spacesuit. Oh, but his men loved him, that's the kind they allus do, right? Sure they do.

But crikey, mikey, Colonel-General Pissfire P. Pallbox needzima secretary no? Ajjerancer okay but a wee tiny toucha the distaff staff helps a gyrene keepiz memory keen sozy nosy ain't just up here for a space cruise. Sozy nosy got a mission tonight, nenemy tfight, keepmuptight.

Whooee! That little piece of tail that Mizzy Lizzy was for certain Colonel-General Pissfire P. Pallbox's secretary, right. Anything extracurricular in particular ainobody's binness but hers, ist?

And Colonel-General Pissfire P. Pallbox's, corse.

And now, strangely enough, sgettin tbe Spacerine Corporal Leander Laptip's too. Well, well.

Mizzy Lizzy tells Leander awbouder lily grilhoodn Salitpa, a bucolic rural community as paired to hustly bustly Eutaw Town, proud home of Leander Laptip.

Awboud trottinarouner daddy's ole farm a playin in the meadows (watch out you don't step in the cowpat, honeybunch—oh damn ya did) heppiner mam in the kitchen (gowdathere babe he come yole pap—oh damn too late) walkner hownz (gadangzat bitch in heat *awlatime*?) & like that.

Growinupn gowinschool, holdin ahands with the beaufum the next farm (gar*damn* Raffie gitcho hand offen my ass or aggonna kick you na *baws*), splornin discovrin behind the school & all like that.

—Raffie?—sez Leander.

—Yow Raffie Slocomb—sez Mizzy Lizzy.

—Fout, fout!—spluts Leander (*whir-bzzt-whir*)—Raffie Slocomb?—

—Yow wusmatrya, Leander, shoe said Raffie Slocomb, facs Raffie Slocomb got my cherry blackz school one Saddy—m she makina smile lakta break your heart you could see it, oh, her eyes they get kinda moist m distant looknanner mouth it goes up at thedges like a smilesposeter butter lips quiver summit (*kchk-sspp-kchk*).

—Wewwo wewwo—comments Leander (*mmm-zzz-mmm*)—Raffie he was a goodo buddiamine upboard *Jimmie O.* ownie bought it wifurgem papadocs Raffie's all done.

—Urk, wah, ooo—Mizzy Lizzy reacts (*zzzz*) a dropa water else lube oil pops outener eye m hangs bobblinin free-fall there upboard the shuffle—that bastard he got my cherry—she reiterates—himn Andrew Lawson m Albert Watters m Tommy Mannerin m Clarissa Clemson m—bushez cut off as the shuttle whomps interer skid row m slithers m sloops m slaps ginthe landing dock at the spaceport neest Letohatchie Town, Letohatchie Township, Democratic Autonomous Planet of N'Alabama or whatever.

Leander Laptip m Mizzy Lizzy Cadbell get checked over by planetside medics m come out with clean bills of health m certificates of mechanical operation respectfully both, running through various m sundy tess, stuff like:

—Can yisse wumdoon?—

—Yasr—

—Can yiddoot?—

—Shoe—

—M hozzit feel?—

—Hozzit what?—

—Feel—

—Mm (*whir-clank-whir*)—

M the grounders gim some nice clean new fresh spotless unwrinkly unspecked well-fitted new New Alabama Spacerine Corpse duds Leander looks proudly at his bentfin boomer glittern m gleamin onz lapel m at his skin by now slightly space-speckled nattiz prosthies they nicely space-speckled too sozy cnardly tell the diff, good-o.

Mizzy Lizzy comin outenerown dressy room, Leander sees she's all adolled up in official govish lady spacerine eveny gown cut sexy raddowner *heah* he spresses a giggle thinkna droppina nice cube down the front tweener cuties, Leander can't (at this game of the stage) even spot the lines wherer organic skin lees offner govish prosthie starts, wunnid be a lafify dropped a nice cube tweener cuties m she cooneen feel it, wow!

He also notices futher first time at she's a sarnt! Mezonly a corporal, rember, what a sweetycuntshe's, not even never to pull no rank onm nor never eenta mention it.

More to point, she gots *three* bentfin boomers a sprackin m a packin on the bodice uvver gown. *Three.* Leander is, to put it in a word, impressed.

Im fuckin pressed.

—Wah, Mizzy Lizzy—he sez.

—You proo, Leander?—she asks, light & moistrously lak a little town (Salitpa) virginer summin.

—Oowee!—zall Leander can say, but that shall suffice.

Mizzy Lizzy Cadbell she beena sarnt summidy tole her summin theynt tole Leander (poo beau, poo beau) Mizzy Lizzy she takesim bahan m leadzim through a door, he blinks, it's the first time hez seen daylight on planetside in, wowee, months, months.

Ole Alquane zashinina weigh up in N'Alabama's sky, bright m round, the sky's clearn sparkly, jussa couple teensy fleensy lil clouds a puffin m a driftin jussa make it all the pretties.

Old Leander he fines bothiz eyes gettin some wettin, one with a tear dropper two, one with a couple draps lube oil.

Leander finds himself standing side aside with Mizzy Lizzy, where izzy, up someplace on a reviewn stand, na middlabuncha digitaries, sun shining, flags flapping, a mob of Letohatchie Township's finest loafers, dregs, civil servers, unemployables, infants, & setterers sprawlina round, plane grabass, smokin fine back country plug cut, chawin shag, snikkin a swig nownagin at some specious looking brown bags (*plus ça change*), noff somewhere ta side a brass bam bigginsta play.

Why, it makes Leander's chest swell positively with pride.

Rzzztlt, bzzt-zzzpzzz-tzzb, tltzzzR.

Thooz tears (m lube oil) Leander sees some bigshot smalltime politico big bo ho-ho heading for the microphone, some flunky bunky gets there first m introducim:

—Lazy gennim hombil mare Milburn Mitchum!—

Hombil mare Milburn Mitchum gabzy mike m

makes a wee bitty speech owe bout N'Alabama cares frurown, returning military heroes gomby rehabilitated, reasorked inder snivilian economy, wall lum, wall prowm, wall gim estythim we can. & like that.

Some smalltime bigshot military honchoboho Captain Cal Koberly fm Fort Sealy Mae he nestakes microphone m sain evy same as Milburn Mitchum he did, only wiproper military manner stepolitical bombast masses Mizzy Lizzy tsaya worder too.

—Aprouta serve—Mizzy Lizzy sez (*rr-bzz-rr*) m a few similarly suitables m asses Leander to do the same.

He does.

They go back inside flowered by cheers m claps, brass band a bammin m a whammin away in the day just soze they goes, doors close.

Inside (wah, wah, theyn Letohatchie City Hall) mare Milburn Mitchum leesem ta fancy bankitable white linen cloth dazzlin spazzlin silly where, transchina lucentware, glittin crystal.

Steak & taters for Milburn, Kal Koberly mother invited digitaries, mashed mush uccorse for guessov honor. Fine wine frall, frall, frall.

Yum.

Aftwards they geddownta business, serious business, you know, what a returning verraneeds is not glory nor sympathy but a job, nopportunity to hold his [her] head up high, earn a living, bring home a check, pay his [her] bills as an honest m productive citizen, & like that, m Letohatchie proud city fathers have set up interviews.

Leander Laptip m Mizzy Lizzy Cadbell by now such goobuddies they decide to do the vue together.

Firstups a lovely largish lady summat fleshy yella curls big red lips, generously curved, perfumed so ya can smeller a comin couple rooms off, very shy & demure & proper, she flingser business card on the table but done count on anybody's literacy & launches right into selfintro:

—Darlins war heroes I want to take care of you, come on m work in my pussy parlor, short hours good wages call me boss mnames Piggy Peggy, PPPP's the best pussy parlor this siden Suggsville Center, allatop johns come tmiplace, most um like girls, my my Mizzy Lizzy you'll do just fine you'll be a favorite, you'll draw top john, they'll love you

—Oh and three bentfin boomers, why allamy bentfin boomer boys cominafummina Fort Sealy Mae thelloveya, I've never had a bentfin boomer girlafore, oh, oh, and yerfriendere, yerfriendere whatchacalled, beau?—

—Uh, Leander Laptip ma'am fum Eutaw Town—

—Waffine waffine you known this modrun ear theysa customer frevy service m a service frevy customer, some our johns like ahaha fambily groups, ahaha, youn Mizzy Lizzy, why Lanny & Lizzy cubbe very big, very, nodamenchen some johns might just love to get on with a bentfin boomer boy like you, my my, a bentfin boomer boy & girl jistlike that, my my my—

But Mizzy Lizzy Cadbell willeander frolliner lead she's a smartn (three bentfin boomers m still *alive,* albeit somet reduced, can't be no dumbbe) Mizzy Lizzy zes:—I thanky nall thinky ont, thanky Piggy noutshego, noutshego & gone.

23. Across the Cislunar Vacuum

Yellow stragglebangs pasted across his sweaty forehead Spacerine Sergeant Beauregard "Bo" Fallon tried to figure out hownell *he'd* got alive into a miniship m away from the *Jimmie-O* when she'd got creamed by that big futhermucker nigra ship in the battle of whatever it was. Shorzell be called the battle of something someday. Those big ones always did get names m smartass light commanders or gyrene majors were always reconstructing them and fighting them over and writing books about what this commander did right and what that one did wrong that made the battle come out the way it did.

M bajeez m bageorge that was one *hell* of a battle!

How many ships had N'Alabama lost in that battle? Bo couldn't even begin to calculate, but there must have been a hell of a lot. And the nigras must of lost a hell of a lot too, from what Bo could see from a borrowed go-go-bapper blister. Even counting for projos.

M then something had got *him*. Something that—Bo tried to remember. Not a beam. No, that would have been sudden and silent and—and not a ram either. No. He'd seen it coming, seen it but not in time to do anything about it. A projectile. A miniature, self-propelled, unmanned ship of some sort. Coming straight at him, a black shaft in front of a burning rear, coming straight at him and his bapper and before he could even try to knock it down—*krunk*!

Krunk, and then what?

Lucky for Bo that battle stations *meant* space armor, or he'd of been a vacuum quick-freeze specimen on the spot. Instead, somehow in the mess and tumble that followed . . . *Jimmie-O* must of took some worse hits than that little smack on the blister . . . Bo Fallon was into a miniship and away. Unconscious or hysterical. Out of sight of the fleet. Lost.

Headed at random for anyplace. Low on food and air.

In a crudely furnished office on the moon Cayamitte, Phillipe looked up from his endless paperwork at the sound of the opening door. He recognized his friend Raoul and gestured him to a wooden chair.

"How is production?" the visitor asked.

"Well enough. Harvesting continues. The supply seems to be holding up also. As long as we do not attempt to go too fast, I think this planet will continue to meet our needs. But I think we would all rest easier, both here and at home, if we could find some secondary source of the creatures." Phillipe leaned back and edged his shoulders once up and down the back of his chair, then folded his hands on his slight paunch and looked at Raoul.

Raoul lifted a trinket from Phillipe's desk and toyed with it silently. Several times he appeared about to speak but each time stopped short.

Phillipe hummed.

Raoul cleared his throat.

Phillipe said, "Well."

Raoul said, "Mmm, yes."

Phillipe said, "And how are things over at the site?"

"No progress," Raoul said. "You know the vacuum over on Vache has preserved the artifact nicely. Here on Cayamitte it wouldn't have lasted very long—you know Captain Bonsard thinks that stuff the metal detectors picked up on Cayamitte might once have been a similar device."

Phillipe nodded.

"If he is right, though, there is nothing left that could possibly be salvaged. Now the Vache artifact . . ." he trailed off with a pregnant gesture of the two hands.

"Is Bonsard at the site now?"

Raoul grunted an affirmative.

"I knew his aunt back in N'Porprince," Phillipe volunteered. "She worked in my section at the Ministry. Grumpy middle-aged woman. Liked nothing better than giving unfavorable reports on everyone. Like a child tattling on his fellows. M. Caneton dozed at his desk this afternoon. M. Belledor arrived late again this morning. Well, it must have an effect. See, here I am on this little moon, and poor Belledor found himself drafted. Can you imagine Christophe as a marine?" He chuckled ruefully.

He recovered from the moment's reverie. "Raoul," he resumed, "why all the fuss anyway, over the artifact? Ancient objects have been found before. Is this one so special? Why do we not ship it back to N'Haiti if it is?"

Raoul rose from his chair and began to pace about the office. "Credit the clever Captain Edouard Bonsard for that. He thinks it is a weapon. He thinks that it can be repaired and used as a defense in case the enemy attack us here."

Phillipe rose, dismayed. "But the whole N'Yu-Atlanchi operation depends on stealth. Everyone agrees that we cannot fortify that entire planet. The conditions there—the crystal barely sustains the weight we place on it now. If we brought in weapons—," he shook his head.

"Correct. So we have some weapons here on Cayamitte and on Vache, but mainly we rely on stealth. The *blancs* are busy defending their own world and trying to attack N'Haiti. As long as they do not know about the N'Yu-Atlanchi project, it should be reasonably safe."

"So?"

"So, still Bonsard wants more defense. And he believes that he can repair the Vache artifact and that it is a weapon."

"And you think—what?"

"I think he is right!"

"Then why do you oppose him?"

"Because, first of all, I am not *sure* he is right. The artifact might prove to be—anything—once it is repaired. *Probably* it is a weapon. But what if it is a beacon that will communicate with someone incredibly distant and alien who left it there on Vache? Or a vehicle? Or some sort of automatic manufactory? Or—," again "—anything? It should be studied with the utmost caution, by qualified researchers. And Captain Bonsard has just taken it upon himself to try and repair it.

"Second, if it is a weapon, what kind of weapon? Does it fire projectiles? Beams of some sort? What if it is a bomb, a dud, and once repaired it will blow itself up and half of Vache with it? Bonsard is risking too much!"

* * *

Alone in its miniship coffin the dessicated corpse that had once been Spacerine Sergeant Beauregard Fallon of the N'Alabama starfleet floated serenely among the suns. An automatic pickup beacon in the miniship broadcast its distress call, but with limited power and at mere light speed, it was unlikely ever to be picked up by a potential rescuer. And if it were, what good would that do?

Bo Fallon didn't care if he *never* was rescued.

But the beacon flared outward, and the ship continued to float, coasting along in a more or less straight trajectory as it had on its small self-contained power charge. Too small for an agonized-matter drive, the miniship couldn't get either the speed or the powered range of a big starship, but by coasting it could go forever.

It might have been headed anywhere. Bo Fallon didn't care that his body happened to be headed toward the star designated NGC 7007.

Captain Bonsard accepted the microcircuit-layer from the ordnance sergeant and bent over the last remaining gap in the circuitry of the artifact. His eyes felt tired and his fingers trembled from the fine work, and to relax he hunkered back on his heels and looked up at the sky.

"Good to be rid of those overcautious busybody civilians, eh, Sergeant?" he said.

Agreement crackled back through his helmet radio.

"Now, we'll get this thing finished and see about testing it out," the captain went on.

The sergeant said, "Yes, sir."

Captain Bonsard stretched his arms to get out any kinks. Overhead he could see the tiny blob of Cayamitte and huge globe of N'Yu-Atlanchi, glowing and glittering, turquoise and sunflower, as always a beautiful sight against the black sky. Distant NGC 7007 glinted dull green.

Bonsard returned to the artifact. A tiny line, clearly a circuit running between two nodules that projected slightly from a rounded, glazed cylinder, had had a gap gouged in it, how long ago, probably (Bonsard thought) by some glancing micrometeor. Now he, Edouard Bonsard, would repair the tiny bit of cosmic mischief. He flicked on the circuit-layer, adjusted its tip to a tiny aperture and applied it to one broken end of the ancient circuit.

The tool adhered to the microcircuit. Bonsard drew the tool slowly, meticulously, toward the other severed end. The circuit extended in the path of the tool, moving slowly toward the other end. Finally only the tool itself separated the ends of the circuit. Carefully Bonsard withdrew the circuit-layer, waiting until the two threads of material were joined before turning it off and handing it back to the ordnance sergeant.

Only then did he heave a huge sigh of relieved tension. "Finished!" he said.

"When will we test it, sir?" the sergeant asked.

Captain Bonsard looked into the black sky above Vache, his hands still on the now-repaired Vache artifact. Suddenly he pointed in the direction of Omicron Sigma XXIVa. "Sergeant!" he croaked. "Look!"

The ordnance sergeant turned to follow the captain's gesture. "It's a ship, sir! One of theirs!"

After only a moment's stunned hesitation Captain Bonsard said, "There's your answer, Sergeant. We test the Vache weapon now! I don't know how those white devils ever found out about the N'Yu-Atlanchi project. And they must be total idiots to send a single ship against us. But this is our chance to prove the worth of the Vache artifact!"

The N'Alabamian ship was approaching the zenith of the sky over Vache. A miniature dart, graceful, pointed at its fore end, bulging and then tapered again to a wasplike waist, then flared tail fins, the miniship was silhouetted against the glowing, sparkling disk of N'Yu-Atlanchi itself, N'Yu-Atlanchi where black men labored in warm saline seas to harvest S'tschai.

Captain Bonsard knelt beside the Vache artifact, sighting through devices built untold ages ago, his hand inside its articulated armor indirectly setting control devices of equal antiquity.

At last it was done. The artifact may have vibrated gently; Bonsard could not be sure whether the slight tremor that gripped him was the product of the artifact's restored life or of his own excitement. He watched the interloper coasting silently, intercepted by invisible forces across the cislunar vacuum that separated the small moon Vache from its primary N'Yu-Atlanchi. The ship seemed to vibrate in its course, then slowly to fade, as if disintegrated outright, or as if shaken into pieces too small to be seen at this range.

The oscillations of the Vache artifact traveled at light speed until they reached the surface of the planet, working their silent and unseen changes until . . .

A bit of crystal chipped away. A hairline crack appeared, lengthened, opened wide. A bung-hole was enlarged. A lazily flowing current of saline fluid turned into a churning, roaring flow.

A tide arose, sweeping outward in a circular path, growing rather than attenuating as it advanced. Behind its heightening front naked crystal was exposed for the first time since the planet's strange equilibrium had been attained.

Larger and larger areas of crystal shook, cracked, crumbled. More fluid was exposed. The huge wave grew larger and larger. More crystal, new layers exposed, destroyed, swept away before newer waves of gloriously sparkling enriched seawater.

Hundreds of black workers were swept before the flood or plunged into the shifting, crumbling crystal.

Billions of tiny unthinking homunculi died.

Deep within the centermost crystalline shell of the planet a great, fecund, bloated travesty of womanhood was rent by shifting, violent forces.

Millions of miles away NGC 7007 shone baleful green. In due course—a matter of minutes—it would feel the great resonation.

24. Celebrities in the Streets

They turned aside every offer they got, which was, to be very precise about it, not rilly a hell of a lot, but some, some, including an offer of a temporary booking as part of the spectacular nightclub act of Miss Merriass Markham, biggest thing on the Leto–Gasque–Echola circuit (all right, not quite the biggest, but damn good, pal, damn good).

Leander was pretty big to take thatun, you can bet, after beena fan of Miss Merriass's for a long time, why Merriass's pix was about the biggest things on the whole damn Spacerine detachment circuit, certainly upboarda the *Jimmie O. Eastland* m others, zwelz the corridors m chambers of Port Corley.

You might say, in fact, that the one place where Colonel-General Pissfire P. Pallbox agreed widz immediate superior Admiral Yancy Moorman was on the marvy merits of Miss Markham. Wow, they coont even agree on whether or not the fleet otto carry lady leatherasses, we know Pissfire's opinion, Admiral Moorman's been quite the opposite, i.e., Pissfire he preaches *No* m practices *Yes,* Yancy he preaches *Yes* m practices *No.*

Well it's odd but soza lotsa crap.

Where Lanny & Lizzy (it do have a ring now don't

it?) wind up after a final municipal dinner m mustering out ceremony, they wearn civvies now but allowed by military dispensation to display their four (cumulative, heheh) bentfin boomers on their civvies, is takena tour courtesy bigho seegar-chomping whiskey-sippin red-faced, gland-hand faller Cornelius Balto Jenkin ahoom you've never even *heard* before well don't let it get you down neither had Leander Laptip nor Mizzy Lizzy Cadbell until just a little while ago when C. Balto (as he pufferediz friends to call him, which ista say mought near everyone septin any furgem papadocs or Jewrabs he might happen to encounter, which—he never having had the pleasure in his entire N'Alabamian life—made for a slightly hypothetical atmosphere hovering over the whole matter) inner-deuced hissef toom.

C. Balto claimed title to the Manglin Doctorship of the N'Alabama Multimedia Cultural Combine, a large organization whose main offices and production felicities were centered in the lovely N'Alabama town of Coxheath, a delightfully breezy community located midst a glop of shimmering lakes, simmering swamps and the like.

Fat C. Balto offern Leander Laptip wonniz fat green stogies (—Yomine fee menfolks smoks Mizzy Lizzy?—every inch a genaman that C. Balto) & Mizzy Lizzy she sez gritahed menfolks m she graciously accepts C. Balto's offra glass of branny m heen Leander m Mizzy Lizzy discuss what hizzole Combine, what NAMCC as its friends call it, hasta offer two hardworking m heroic wounded war veterans home from batterin the badole papadocs.

—Wawee zintevvethin, evvethin—C. Balto say around his fat green stogie. —You namer, we've doner.

Evvethin. Fukbux, vidpix, live shows futha boys away fmome, evvethin.—

Mizzy Lizzy, she sips slowly adder branny, not wholly certain how mucher how fast she can absorb alcool under her recent circumstances. She listens, she watches Leander listen, m aftra while she axes a question or several.

—Whatsit pay?—

C. Balto Jenkin names a number that makes Leander Laptip trine whistle out loud (discovern he hasn't relearned to do that and will have to) m Mizzy Lizzy's pretty impressed herself but she conceals things a bit betterner partner, m she axes:

—Fur what, C. Balto, fur what?—

—Wha you two gumbbe my new stars, you gumbbe stars!—sez C. Balto Jenkin, sippina branny zizown.

—Rat, rat—sez Mizzy Lizzy—but you din answer my questry, C. Balto, hey—Nafter all, shez accustomed to dealing w Colonel-General Pissfire P. Pallbox in m ouda the bag, Admiral Yancy Moorman m dlike, even though she was a mere sarnt (mere, hah!), she knows howdadeal with biggies m toughies m any possible combo the two.

—What fur, C. Balto, you go giss so much loot, fur what?—

—Em, em, em—C. Balto Jenkin delays, rolliniz eyes to the skies for disguise—well I gotta try you two out, see where your talents lie, maybe shoot some stills for starts, do a little bukatoo, work up, let out a vidpikrtoo, whine up with a superglorious fatbulious pussynal planterary tour, now howzat soundaya Mizzy Lizzy, howzat soundaya Leander beau?—

Oh, that C. Balto, he cud charm the skin off a banana, he could. Don't ya think so? Hey, wait a minute, put that back on for now.

Mizzy Lizzy looka Leander Laptip m v. versa, they confer in silence m secrecy fa few seconds, Leander he merges fm the conference me sez:

—Misra Jenkin—

—C. Balto, son, I want all my friends tcall me C. Balto—Cornelius B. Jenkin (haha!) interjects.

—Rat, rat, C. Balto. Oak anna hay. Mizzy Lizzy nme wed liketa bopparoppa over t Coxheath, see whatchagot they, look over things, meet you peopou, so to speak, and like that.—

—Fair enough!—exclaims that ole capitalist C.B. Jenkin, pounding Leander on the shoulder.

(*clank!*)

So off by smalltime commercial airline, C. Balto Jenkin, Leander Laptip m Mizzy Lizzy Cadbell, Mizzy Lizzy bypassing a potential projected visit toor ole hometowna Salitpa. The plane is slightly olan rickety, shakes m trembles summat, makes Leander slightly nauseous, Mizzy Lizzy does a bit better, C. Balto (well of *course* you are numbered among the Manglin Doctor's close friends, pal):

:just has a fynole time, chompininswirlin addiz fat green stogies, swiggin at branny or whevver, chummin upta Mizzy Lizzy, trina cheerp Leander, whichee succeeds at reasombly well.

Leander thinks nownena summiz buddies din maygit back fum the Battle of Whevvathehellitwas, wonders a bit sometimes what he gom doomsef, he don't hurt much sept nownenabit, fact he don't feel much anyhow, umm, pudthis weigh:

:allem prosthies got sensors m Leander kin get readouts, hedoween gotta check no instrumentsr nothin, tsall wired direct intwiz central nervousystem (or seeyeness as its friends call it) m he can *tell* whether, oh, frinstance, the prosthy toes onniz left foot are line curled or straight, see, wout havvena take offiz shoon *look* at the liffuckers, hez got a dreck line, toes tooz brain, sozy *knows.*

But would you call that *feeling*?

Maybe not.

Pruction felicities of NAMCC in Coxheath, N'Alabama leave hardly nothin to be desired, jis setchasef onta whevva yawant, kay, m they gotch. C. Balto Jenkin taken Leandern Mizzy Lizzy na friendly lil tourtha place, drinkna cuppa first, then overlook a quick displayatha company's products, alltime best-sellers, classics, latest releases, et and also cetera.

Libbila lunch na Combine cafeteria, C. Balto woofs downa coupla stuffed pokers, ersa corn, coupla fissfulla cornbread, glassa branny wiz meal (—Ah, keeps thole juices flown—he sez twiz gezz) lustly murals srounningem:

:straight stuff on one wall:

:biv pederasty long another:

:smoralism behind the service line, summody's sensa funnies, har:

:back wall gotsum, ah, the teckleckle word been bestiality:

:noverhet the crowning display, first-rate essenemm.

—Eheu!—sez Leander, or summon lack that.—Eheu!—

Conversation flags summat doorn lunch but C. Balto keeps the branny flown m afterwards provides fat green stogies frimsefn Leander (—You domind, Mizzy Lizzy?— —Course no— —& cet—)

Allat Mizzy Lizzy m Leander Laptip had doorn *they* meal was mashed mush uccorse. Nabitta branny uccorse.

Affer C. Balto sez—Now mugood frenz habbada lil

screen test, a mere formality uccorse, know you'll do just fine, down the line, palza mine, that be okee?–

Leander zaps a quick looka Mizzy Lizzy, Mizzy Lizzy gizzya hosch-mosch sublintenal nod (*crick-click-crick*) nee sez–Shoe!–

C. Balto leezem inna the taping studio fra vidpik (–Stilz later–he sez, pattin Mizzy Lizzy onna rumptytumpty) (*clonk-clonkly-clonk*). –Heezit–C. Balto sezez they sloof thoo a heavy padded soundproofing door.

–Mizzy Lizzy, Leander–C. Balto exhales–awanya meet my top viddy cameraman, hill tapeyustoday, say hloda Specs.–

Specs he comes outa messa heavy cables m crap, shaken handz wizzy Mizzy Lizzy m Leander Laptip, sane–Happy tmeecher–gessa funny look as they shake (*skrk-skrk-skrk*) m (*bzzt-bzzt-bzzt*) m dresses mseftaz Manglin Doctor:

–Haya mizzuz, haya pappinlow?–

–Mizzuz fine, hain't seed pappinlow lately, hez up ta Leto, yinno, big meetinzallatime–

–Ape, ape, ats a rat–zez Specs. Turnin backtaz gess–Yinnó C. Balto's pappinlow's Senator Belly fum Talladega–

–Nodino at–zez Leander.

–Shoe hess w gummit contracks, asso shoe–zez Specs.

–Aweh, allevayo folks tyer work now, ad lakka stay hee buggommy own work yinno. Specs, you be nasta my frez he, hey? Yedit uppa cuppa tapes m senem toomey, hoke?–

Specs he sez shoe, C. Balto Jenkin he takeniz leaf m Specs he turns ta Leander m Mizzy Lizzy me sez–Masswell get undressed, thow yduds in the corner, we're mighty informal around heeh.–

He busies himself wiz lights nequipment, checkin this meter m that par line m this gadget m that doohickey.

Leander Laptip m Mizzy Lizzy Cadbell zonny other side of the room, they look neach other, look at Specs hez busy wiz gear coont care less what theyz upta, look back addy chotherm Leander he blushes m Mizzy Lizzy starts carefully undooner civvies.

Leander startsa turniz back, Mizzy Lizzy laughs not altogether kindly, so Leander, his organic parts blushin red (the prosthy parts do work well, shoe, but not *that* well) m he watcheser taking offer boots m tatpans, shirt m now shez jusner to be discreet undies m she looks over at Leander m sez–Mmm?–

Nee realizes as hez still fully to use thelegant term clothed swee starts undoonizown civvies, kicks offiz shoes (that is *good* prosthy, you kin do that, pal, else just trite some time), rolls downy zokz, pullsi zhirt ovrized m now comes a minor moment of truce.

Leander looks at Specs, detex eeztil messin wiqwik mint, coon care less about Leandern Lizzy, Leander looks at Mizzy Lizzy, sees she's down tour skivvies, notices somewhat twizzone surprise that wily admires Mizzy Lizzy's bonkers (slyly onner small side, ridin keepin widder gemorail tall slim construction) daddy don't *feel* a fing.

Mizzy Lizzy peelzer pannies down, rolling elastic top overrips, shez really godabod that Mizzy Lizzy, Leander intellectualizes (been as ease a product of Eutaw Town Union District Ha plus Fort Sealy Mae) but he don't *feel* no fing.

He watches Mizzy Lizzy lift one foot, tother foot, lift offer drawers, kneel wirr back tomb tranger clothes neatly in a stack, Leander's eyes cresser flesh nee fines insef wondering where she leaves offen prosthies begin (those beaux up at Port Corley, boy!), Mizzy Lizzy guess back up m turns around facing Leandernee runs his eyes over her:

:long, light, glistry hair waving overer shoulders, that sweet face he first eyegrabbed in sick bay, pale shoulders m those lovely perky persimmons with sweet-lookin pink points, soft-lookin white belly wivva navel like a kissable dimple m blow it that sweetole hilly venus all covered with locks just awaitin tbe opened, soft, sleek thighs m legs as could wrap around a feller's waist erz neck with equal joy; Leander looks,

looks,

looks:

:but he don't *feel* nothing.

Specs he got his gear in order, peeps over the topperiz viewfinder, pushes a clutcha buttons, lights revolve, machinery whirls, this is no cheap-o operation, mind, pal.

Mizzy Lizzy advances toward Leander nee stands there waiting tsee what gonnappenext, all's he's got on's 'is own pans, Mizzy Lizzy expertly slitsem open wivver fingernail, kneels in fronna Leander telpim off withem, leanin that sweet Salitpa phizovers against his lower abdomen (and we do mean lower, not to be indelicate, pal) as she does so.

He do not feel a thing.

—Haqnoui bring this off?—Leander axes elpletsly.

—Doe nax me—Specs contributes parsimoniously.

—Oh, he, *he*—zez Mizzy Lizzy—yoni ga think it tight, Leander, eyegas they dintell yevy dig backa P.C.—

(Mizzy Lizzy, she gots thinside monickerve Port Corley. Coy?)

Leander he say—Hah?—

Mizzy Lizzy she say (mildly impatient)—Your gar firrout hah yews prosthies, Lan!—

He lookena her, he admiring allat lovely shapeshe got, he thinkna past experiences, Leander snow lothario, pal, but whahell, he's been around, tendered Eutaw Town Union District Ha, ben thoo Fort Sealy Mae m many a happy weekend pass inta Letohatchie, downat ole red rut road ats lead from Fort Sealy Mae tLeto, had shav horz m freebies, jes you bleevies no baby inexperienced tot, he's not.

But he don't . . . rat, rat, assa rat.

—You gotta think ont—Mizzy Lizzy peterself.

Leander Laptip reaches out, puts a hand on eacher shoulders (one organic, one prosthetic, you'd hardly know whichiz which although Mizzy Lizzy does you can bet) nee looks down adizown member nee thinks—Ho, beau, you a team plairowha? Gup they, up-a-up-a-hup-a-hup-hup-hup—

Not unlike a drill sergeant bagga Fort Sealy Mae niz recruit days, m lawmarcy thole gadget rises right as rain, few ole luminum extrusion rods, permeable pseudorganic filling, spannable pseudodermal covering, ureplastithane formed terminator, etc., etc.

Rat up, horizontal, elongated, aerated, polyunsaturated and inflated.

(*rrrr-dzzd-rrrr*)

—Hay, beau, airy go, assa show!!!—cheers Mizzy Lizzy Cadbell of Salitpa. —Hey less go!—

M she draps tfloor, pulls Leander down onter, opens up lak the Pearly Gates, mates, m pullzim inter.

She pusser arms around his shoulders.

He runsis hands overer boobsmbelly, keesis wait mostly on zelbows (a technician the lad is, maybe not a genius but a nadequate technician) m begins thole pumping.

He pumps away, m:

:pumps, m:

:pumps, m:

:pumps, m:

:hears thole cameras whirrnaway, m:

:Leander pumps, Mizzy Lizzy pumps, m:

:this do go on and on and on . . . m aftrawile Leander he he Specs say—Thank ivvery mutts, assa nuffer test—:

:m Mizzy Lizzy say—Ain yevva gun comboy?—

:m Leander sez—Ainothin happen!—

Mizzy Lizzy she sigh, she say—Leander, atoll you, you dealn wiprosthies, you gommake it happen, you gah *think* it to happen, ill happen, they gin yevvy need at P.C. you just gah learna uset . . . comb *on*—

M Leander, he conjews up ole pitches, ole recollecks, he memmas some ole whorn Letohatchie, he memmas his first lay, some lil gallon Eutaw Town whassername, dang, whassername, re memmaser pussy hair, soften silky lack corn thread, lil tits lack old goosey bumbs, *what* her name m:

:suddenly he memmas some pitches he sawed back upbawd some ole ship, mebbe *Jimmie O.*, mebbe *Leander Perez,* no, he rememmas now was way back upboard some trainy vessel, ole *States Rights,* N'Alabama Navy, rat, nimsef line in zbunk look natta pitchern some magazine, some fukbuk, pitches Miss Merriass Markham doon weird stuff usin whips m chains m Leander things back tomb sef layin inz bunk m thinks—Ah, ah, gahcom—:

:m glory be, he does, them ole medics upside P.C. they done him some job, Mizzy Lizzy she bin right, they gim evvy he need, *evvy.*

Mizzy Lizzy she say—Oak hay, now, Lan—

M Specs he say—Thanks very folks, ahl cut this tape a bit m dliverta Mister Jenkin, yaw hear fromm shortly. Yaw onna laxna visitors' lounge ouch side please thank you ve much—

Leander he pulls his clothes back on. Mizzy Lizzy she dooda same, they say thanksta Specs m bop oudoor down hall to the lounge, grabba cuppa, siddown, Mizzy Lizzy say—How bow?—

Leander he say—Thin is, I din feel nothing—

Mizzy Lizzy she say—Watsoright, don gah, long zyickin perform. Assall—

Leander he say—Zattall theres?—

Mizzy Lizzy jis nod.

Pee soon dropen, in come Mr. C. Balto Jenkin, puffna fat green stogie, giz oneta Leander, offers oneta Mizzy Lizzy, she say—Nodjus gnaw, thanks—

Mr. C. Balto Jenkin he say—Sawyer ushes, sawyer ushes, ewedo got fine potential, gah teach yevy gah no, corse—

—Well—sez Mizzy Lizzy.

—Ahr—sez Leander Laptip.

—Yaw cmoverda mah place tonigh, Mizzy Lizzy—zez C. Balto—m affix yup winstructor, Leander, dowurry, takarevy, takarevy. You two gombbe mah new stars!—C. Balto he slap meach onna shoulder, heartily. (*clank, clonk*)

M not to put too fine a nedge ont, C. Balto he a mannis word, no crookee, no cheaperjacko, he a solid bimmisman, wow! He teachy Mizzy Lizzy a few tricks, he senna lady do the same Leander Laptip, pee soon they ready for debut on planetwide vidpik.

Smasheroonie!

Sensation in barrooms, barracks, homes, schools,

churches, places of public amusement and/or employment, on beaches, in restaurants, and total global cetera.

C. Balto Jenkin he gettin rich offen Lizzy m Lan. They ain doon so baddemsefs. Know, corse, artist never works for mere lucre, entrepreneur pussup risk money, runs d show, he natural makes d doe. Rat? Rat.

But he pussup his two new stars, gizzem a pot mint together, servants, mechanics, charges their batteries on the N'Alabama Multimedia Cultural Combine account, putsair pain a nice safe truss account, gizzem both nice pin-money allowance outen they own money, and all damn cetera.

All they gah dooz makiz vidpix, fukbux, mwunsta year a big big planetwide personal appearance tour, complete winterviews, limousines, screaming fans, backstage scenes, groupies, floopies, droopies, met cetera.

Specs stix wim, coach m tech advice, nice.

Finely comes the best: technicians shuttle down fum Port Corley t take inna show, visit ole patience, check over kwimmin, chief tech makes a couple suggestions, does a little minor rewirin for Leander m Mizzy Lizzy.

Tha nite, big personal coliseum show, Leandern Mizzy Lizzy emerge t super applause. Disrope, conjoin.

Mizzy Lizzy loosa Leander, he loosa her, wunnum zez—Oak hay—

They both reach ahind each tothern flick a miniswitch.

Click! Botheir prosthies go onna new autogyro drive.

Leander leans back, daydreamsa Eutaw Town.

Mizzy Lizzy leans back, daydreamsa Salitpa.
M they prosthies go on workna way, worknaway.
(*click, whirr-bzzt-whirr, click*)
(*clank, zzzmz-brrb-zmzzz, clank*)
Pal, it's a futhermuckin miracle!

25. A Distant Pearl-Tinted Horizon

Marius Goncourt picked his way carefully through the rubble on the Henri-Bourassa, peeped around the corner onto the Rue Côte Vertu. It seemed clear. He slipped around the pockmarked edge of the building and started up the last few score paces to the Ministry, attaché case in hand. He was well up the street when it happened.

From above there came the crackle of superheated ozone. Marius flung himself into an opening, not stopping to see what it was. The Rue Côte Vertu was suddenly filled with crackles, hisses of steam where laserifle beams struck late standing puddles of water, occasional snaps and crashes of broken glass when window panes were suddenly heated to a thousand degrees.

Marius looked cautiously from his hiding place, trying to detect the source of the laserifle fire. The beam which had nearly burned a sudden hole in him must have come from a window high across the Rue Côte Vertu. Fire had been returned from several points in and around the Ministry.

Again the air crackled and a circle of cement sidewalk near Marius's hiding place charred and crumbled. The fire was returned—two, three laserifles were discharged into the window. From across the thoroughfare came a sound somewhere between a gasp and a moan. A form appeared in the window, tumbled forward into the morning sunshine, somersaulted into the air, dropped toward the sidewalk spinning and twisting with surrealistic slowness until it struck with a solidly satisfying thump.

Two soldiers started forward, running across the Rue Côte Vertu toward the body. Marius rose and started from his own position. Again the air crackled as a second sniper took up the work of the first. One soldier fell to the pavement, black smoke curling upward from a wound, neatly drilled and cauterized by the laserifle beam. A second beam struck Marius's attaché case. As he dropped it and flung himself flat on the macadam he saw the second soldier fall to one knee, raise a laserifle to his shoulder and hurl a beam at the window. Again came the sound of a man pierced by sudden white heat. A laserifle tumbled from the window and clattered onto the street below, but the body of the sniper fell this time back into the upstairs room.

Marius and the surviving soldier ran first to the soldier's comrade, then to the sniper on the sidewalk. Both were dead. The two men looked at each other, the surviving soldier recognizing Marius from the Ministry. "M. Goncourt, were you hit?"

Ruefully Marius held up his case. "It was close, but he missed me. Can you summon the guard and check out the other sniper? I thought this area was cleared!"

The soldier said, "We thought so too, M. Goncourt. It cost us a man. Yes sir, I will attend to this."

Marius turned away and entered the Ministry. Past the self-service vending stand where Maurice had formerly held court, up wooden stairs now cracked and shaky, he reached the office of Minister Antoine-Simone. Marius entered the room. The Minister looked up from a table surrounded by representatives of government departments.

"M. Goncourt, you are late, you know. Punctuality is the hallmark of the efficient man. We have already started."

Marius said, "I am sorry, sir. There was a sniper incident—"

The Minister cut him off. "No excuses, please. To business. Captain Girard was briefing us on the current balance of forces against the enemy. Please resume, Captain." He waved toward the naval officer.

Girard, neat in undress khaki, spoke wearily. "I was nearly finished anyway, M. le Minister. To summarize, then, the deep-space battle of Omicron Sigma XXIVa left both fleets, the enemy's and our own, severely decimated. We believe that the enemy is in even worse condition than we.

"However, the surprise invasion of La Gonave and N'Haiti proper further complicates the problem. Our counterattack from the bastions at La Ferriere and Dajabon has been highly successful. We have retaken all major population centers on the planet, and only scattered bands of *blancs* remain wandering the back country."

The naval officer looked sheepishly at Marius, then said, "Of course there will still be isolated incidents here and there until we have cleared the enemy completely from the planet, but they are to be expected."

M. le Minister broke in. "Very well, Captain Girard. We have full faith in Admiral Gouede Mazacca and the rest of the military. We know that N'Haiti itself is being secured. But what of La Gonave? We cannot survive without the agricultural imports for very long."

"Ah, very good, yes." Captain Girard ran a finger around the inside of his uniform collar. "Well, as you know, the N'Alabamian attack on La Gonave succeeded because we did not have sufficient forces to defend the moon. Governor Faustin is a prisoner of the enemy. They are apparently using him to force the populace to remain docile. Deputy Governor Laurence has set up a resistance capital at Jacmel, using the authority of the traditional queen of La Gonave, Ti Meminne, to counter orders that the enemy puts out in the name of Governor Faustin."

He stopped. Antoine-Simone said, "When can we get a force onto La Gonave?"

"The fleet is in good condition again. There was plenty of salvage after Omicron Sigma XXIVa. The only problem is manpower. That is why we are appealing to your Ministry, m'sieur. What has become of the resuscitee program?"

Marius opened his attaché case and removed a sheaf of papers. They were marked by a neatly bored hole in one corner, surrounded by a narrow charred area. Using the papers as notes he spoke briefly.

"The resuscitee program is completed, as far as we are able to determine. The experimental phase of the program was totally successful. Large-scale operations were inaugurated at N'Yu-Atlanchi, with a harvest rate of approximately 6,000 S'tschai per local day. This rate would supply us with controls for salvaged casualties as rapidly as we could use them.

"Unfortunately, as you are aware, the N'Yu-Atlanchi disaster occurred before the full harvest rate had been effective very long. One of the military personnel assigned was responsible for the disaster." He looked at Captain Girard, who looked the other way.

"We can supply a sufficient force of resuscitees to outfit a full-scale assault on La Gonave in hopes of recapturing it. But there will be no further resuscitees after that. Once the present supply is expended, no more. At least, our people have not been able to achieve resuscitation without S'tschai, and we have not found S'tschai anywhere besides N'Yu-Atlanchi."

Minister Antoine-Simone looked to Captain Girard once more. The captain spoke. "M. Goncourt's assessment of the situation agrees with our own. Since our fleet's recovery from Omicron Sigma XXIVa we have set up a picket line and prevented the enemy from reinforcing their garrison on La Gonave. We believe that the tide of battle has turned and that we shall be able to invade the enemy's home world. But first we must regain our own food supply. We will use the resuscitee troops to mount a counterinvasion and retake La Gonave.

"Further, let me say that the N'Yu-Atlanchi disaster was not a disaster entirely. The Vache artifact—let me call it the Vache resonator—is being duplicated. Our fleet is being equipped with resonators and they should prove highly useful in the attack on N'Alabama. We do not wish to use them against La Gonave for obvious reasons, but if we take out some large chunks of the enemy's home planet it should do much to encourage him to make peace."

He stood in line with the others, R troops stretching left and right in checkerboarded ranks, clad in combat jeans and boots, each R trooper carrying weapons and spare charge-packs, helmeted and infragoggled. Before each platoon stood a black NCO. Deep in his mind there was an awareness of who and where he was, a pride in military bearing and readiness, but these feelings were buried deep beneath a thick layer of indifference.

The NCO was facing away from the R troopers, toward a N'Haitian spacerine officer who stood farther away. The trooper heard the N'Haitian officer shout a command to the platoon NCOs. He saw his own NCO face about toward the R troopers. The NCO shouted a command. The R trooper, ego remote and tranquil, sensed a momentary delay, then felt a control cut in. His body turned ninety degrees. As it did so his eyes saw the R troopers around him do the same.

There was another command from the NCO. Again the control operated. The trooper felt his arms and legs begin to move with a rhythmic regularity as he and the rest of the unit marched forward.

There was no point in trying to override the control, whatever it was. This he had long since learned. Avoiding the hopeless struggle he was content to stay, an observer in his own body, feeling the rush of air in and out of his lungs, feeling the movement of his marching body, hearing the unison tramp of hundreds of feet, seeing the backs of the R troopers ahead of him as the control marched his body, swinging his neatly spliced arms so that the unmatched hands swung into the bottom of his field of vision with each pace—left, right, black, white, left, white, black, right, black, white . . .

More commands, turns, halt and wait, then face and march again, all at the commands of the N'Haitians, all at the control of something other than his ego, he watched and experienced but did not act.

The R troopers sat now on benches in the hold of an ill-smelling ship. On command, controls moved hands to clamp safety hooks around feet and waists. Whichever way the ship pointed, wherever the gravity of the moment dictated "up," the troopers would keep their seats.

For a seemingly long time—he had no way of measuring it—the ship remained unmoving, as did the R troopers on their benches. Their N'Haitian commanders were not to be seen. He wondered impersonally why they were on the ship, where they were to be transported and for what purpose. But then it was not really very important.

He looked through his eyes at the trooper ahead of him. His own hands were again in his field of vision, clasped near the muzzle of his weapon, black fingers and white fingers interwoven to steady the weapon against takeoff and gravitational irregularity. The back of the head his eyes were fixed upon showed white skin and longish blond hair. At the base of the skull a long and livid scar was visible. The trooper was sitting stationary, as stationary as he himself. Beyond the blond trooper he could see another and another. Each one, regardless of skin color or pattern, bore the same long scar at the base of the skull.

After unmeasured time the bench and floor beneath him shook gently. A bass rumble filled his ears and the image in his eyes jiggled before returning to normal. Again it happened. This time the rumble grew to a roar and the shaking of the bench and floor turned to a steady vibration. The bench and floor pressed upward against him for a long time, then the roaring ceased, the room became still, the floor and bench ceased to press upward and he felt himself trying to float this way or that, held in place by the straps at his feet and waist.

He floated against the straps.

His eyes saw backs, a wall beyond, an occasional gray slab of floor or ceiling.

His ears heard ship noises, breathing, creaking.

His body felt weight, pressures, textures.

In time his body felt the spinning gravity of a gyro maneuver, then there was the rumbling and vibration again.

The NCO stepped into his field of vision and issued a command. He felt his body responding to control by loosening straps, rising, proceeding with his fellow R troopers through the narrow aisle between benches, through a port, down a corridor. On command his hand reached out to take hold of an extensile cable, hooked it into a ring on his battle pack.

On command the file of R troopers moved past a bin of oxymasks. On command his hand took one and fitted it to his face. On command the file of R troopers moved into a ready crouch. His eyes saw a space door slide back. His eyes saw that they were in night, high above land but within an atmosphere where the lights of distant stars twinkled.

On command the bodies of the R troopers moved forward, through the space door, leaping out one by one, the extensile cable playing out behind them. In his turn he leaped into the blackness. Falling, tumbling, his eyes saw far below small concentrations of city lights. As the extensile cable jerked against his battle pack his head snapped upward and his eyes saw a distant pearl-tinted horizon, then tracked upward and saw blackness, blackness sprinkled with millions of points of light. At the edge of his field of vision his eyes caught a brief glimpse of the planet from which the ship had come.

His skin felt air shrieking past as the cable lowered the R troopers deeper and deeper into the atmosphere. Finally his ears began to hear the sounds of troopers landing—thumps, involuntary exclamations. Now a voice as some NCO landed and began issuing commands. Then footsteps and sounds of R troopers moving about under control.

With a jolt his own feet struck ground. Momentum pitched him forward into a rolling tumble. When he stopped, his ears heard an NCO's commands. Then the control brought him back to his feet, raised his hand to disconnect him from the extensile cable, had him check out his equipment. On command his eyes found the nearest trooper, his legs walked to the trooper and their hands checked each other's condition.

Quickly, under command, the platoons of R troopers formed up. His unit spread into battle formation, moved forward with others toward a nearby farming village. As they approached the village his eyes saw the glare of laser fire. He heard NCO voices issuing commands, felt his body obeying. Watching through his eyes he was distantly aware that there were heavy casualties. R troopers fell, fell, but more continued to move up from the rear. Always there seemed to be NCO voices, always the control moving hands and feet, eyes aiming, fingers firing, and again moving forward.

Now they were into the village, and from somewhere he saw that there was heavy weapons fire. Houses were exploded, streets blocked, fronts of buildings ripped away. His eyes saw bright objects flashing overhead, followed by sounds of roars and whooshes followed by explosions.

Through the night they moved and fought. By dawn R troopers occupied the town. His eyes saw incredible numbers of R trooper casualties lying about. Far fewer corpses of N'Alabamian occupiers, but no live prisoners.

For days the bodies of the R troopers fought the N'Alabamian occupiers. No reinforcements came for the occupiers. R troopers came, came, fell in hideous overproportion to N'Alabamians but came, came. Finally the trooper's mind, distantly and without involvement, analyzed what his eyes and ears had observed.

La Gonave was in N'Haitian hands. N'Alabamian forces were wiped out. Perhaps, his mind speculated, a few N'Alabamians might have escaped into rural areas. For years to come, perhaps, there would be occasional skirmishes between local nigras and leftover *blancs*. But no matter really.

On NCO command surviving R troopers dug long trenches. Under control they dragged to them bodies of dead N'Alabamians, N'Haitians, R troopers, began filling the trenches and covering them over. When all the corpses had been attended to there remained some R troopers and some trench space.

On NCO command and under control the R troopers filed along the remaining trench space, their legs pitching their bodies into the trenches. Following R troopers covered them over. At last the trooper reached open space. On NCO command and under control he pitched his body in. As it tumbled and struck the side of the trench it twisted so that it lay at the bottom of the trench facing upward.

Distantly and without involvement he watched with his eyes as another trooper pitched in upon him, then another and another until only a gleam of light penetrated between the piled-up R troopers. There was a gentle tap from above as still other troopers, following along behind in the line under NCO command and controlled, covered over the trench.

At last all was dark and the sounds of tumbling troopers and tamping soil moved beyond range of his ears. Distantly and without real concern the trooper's mind wondered how long his brain would be supplied with oxygen and blood.

26. The Lower Half of Hir Face

After enough nothing Ch'en-Gordon began to achieve a fullness of aware. Not any longer a pink vermiform sea-dwelling post-hominoid monstrosity, not merely a S'tscha. And not, oh absolutely not, a man.

Something new.

Ch'en-Gordon could feel the clamminess and slight pressure of unpacked shallow soil, the press of other abandoned R troopers around hir torso and limbs. Se tried to open hir eyes, found them held shut by hir own arm, flung across them, perhaps reflexively, before the dirt had begun to fall.

With an effort se was able to raise hir arm sufficiently from hir eyes to open them, but was met only with utter blackness. Se strained upward with both arms, then with hir knees. Se was able to move hir four macrolimbs sufficiently to clear a small space above most of hirself, and thereafter to move hir macrolimbs at will, although for a sort distance only, before encountering the dirt above.

Hir breathing was difficult but not dangerously so. Se was clearly close enough to the surface that sufficient air penetrated the loose dirt to permit breathing.

Straining once more to obtain additional free space around hir hands, se clutched the hand of another immobile R trooper, felt it respond to hir touch with a desperate grasping, tugging of its own. Ch'en-Gordon ceased hir pulling but continued to hold the hand. As if assured that se was not to be abandoned by hir new discoverer, the R trooper also abandoned hir frantic activity, but continued to grasp Ch'en-Gordon hir hand.

Ch'en-Gordon took as deep a breath as se could, then began to work hir way upward through the soft and crumbling soil. To do so se released hir grip on the hand of the other R trooper, who seemingly understood Ch'en-Gordon hir purpose. Almost immediately Ch'en-Gordon could hear the other struggling, digging along with hir.

Se used hir macroknees, pounding them again and again upward into the loose dirt, striving not merely to pack it tighter above hir and gain a little more room, but to lift it, to raise the dirt above hir, eventually to break through the surface to the free air above. Se used hir hands too, aided vastly by the strangely unfamiliar *fingers* of the macroappendages, relying on the Gordon portion of hir personality for the right neural connections and commands.

Dirt jammed beneath hir fingernails, entered and pained hir external eyes until se was forced to hold them squeezed closed against the crumbs and grains; when se gasped for air dirt filled hir mouth and se struggled with hir only Gordon-familiar tongue to push it back out, shoving with hir tongue, blowing and spitting before most of the dirt was cleared, forming a gritty mud that plastered the lower half of hir face and neck.

Straining upward, clawing through the cold dirt, grunting and heaving with effort se managed finally to thrust one dirt-crusted hand out of the all-grasping soil. Se braced hir weight on hir other elbow, gathering hir strength for another thrust that might bring hir arm and shoulder above the ground. Instead se felt hir hand grasped, felt a powerful pull. Se pushed upward with all hir remaining strength, aiding hir unknown rescuer, felt hirself rising, the flesh all but torn from the bones of hir macrobody, then with an intensely painful wrench felt hirself rise from the mass grave of the R troopers.

Se stood in the cool night air of La Gonave, swaying slightly. The field in which se had lain was lighted to nearly daylight intensity by the brilliant glow of N'Haiti, hanging monstrously huge in the dark sky, its heavy mass threatening as if at any moment it would fall to the ground of its own moon, obliterating all that existed there, perhaps disintegrating the body of the satellite itself.

Ch'en-Gordon was shaken by the grasp of another R trooper. Hir gaze dropped to be met by that of hir fellow, who moved hir head sideways, gesturing forbiddingly at the bloated globe in the sky. Ch'en-Gordon moved hir head also, as if to give assent. The other R trooper removed hir hands from Ch'en-Gordon hir shoulders. Se pointed at the tumbled earth which rustled and heaved as hands, feet, faces, brown, black, white, poked upward.

They returned to the nearest furrow, together seizing a death-white foot that protruded from the mass grave, pulled at it until a complete patchwork corpse was exposed. They dropped the leg and the body rose, slowly and painfully, from the soil. The new figure gazed about as in wonderment, then stood staring skyward as hir eyes were captured by the giant bulk of the planet. Again the charade of shaking and gesturing was performed, and the three R troopers set about freeing comrades from their mutual tomb, their graveclothes R trooper uniforms, new but covered with the soil of La Gonave.

Those corpses which failed to move of their own power, they left.

Ch'en-Gordon looked around, seeking the faces of the patchwork troopers around hir. At last se advanced to another, one whose body was huge, a uniform, glistening, muscled black. Hir face was a mottle, the eyes a glazed blue, the hair a lank, straggling yellow, the skin a sickly white except for a masklike swath of black taking in what was left of the nose, the lower cheeks, mouth and jaw.

Ch'en-Gordon tried to speak. Se moved hir mouth, hir throat trembled, se heard hirself produce a gravelly moan.

The other R trooper made the same attempt, achieved no more success.

All around hir Ch'en-Gordon saw R troopers attempting to speak but succeeding only in uttering painful inarticulations.

Ch'en-Gordon stood with macroarms hanging at hir sides. The dual nervous system, interconnected by spiremal filaments penetrating the medulla oblongata of the larger brain, their almost monomolecular acid-chains stretching throughout the nervous system of the patchwork corpse, strained to devise some way of communicating with the other R troopers.

At last Ch'en-Gordon advanced to hir mottled fellow. Se opened hir mouth, gestured the other to do likewise. Se stepped forward, grasped the cheeks of the other with hir palms, tilted hir head to the side using Gordon-synapses to control the movement, and clasped hir mouth onto that of the other.

Se thrust hir tongue into the mouth of the other,

feeling the cold moisture therein. Within Ch'en-Gordon's tongue the millions of spiremal threads writhed, snakelike; like feeding medusae they plunged into the icy tongue of the other R trooper, growing centimeters downward into the wet flesh, contacting spiremal nerve filaments, exchanging data, telling, learning, planning, feeling the cold breath of the two as it rasped from throat to throat.

At last se felt that se had learned and told enough. The filaments detumesced. Se drew hir mouth from that of the other R trooper, turned and shambled across the field to find others with whom to share the plan. By the time N'Haiti had passed its zenith, decades of R troopers had received the plan.

By the time N'Haiti had reached a point halfway down the sky toward the horizon of La Gonave, the R troopers were moving on the Jacmel tarmac.

By the time the Jacmel tarmac was fully alight, the brilliance of true daylight replacing the murky glare of N'Haiti, the R troop landing ship *Lumumba* had left behind a seared and scarred concavity.

By the time N'Haiti again glared down on Jacmel, the gigantic fleet of Grand Admiral Gouede Mazacca had been augmented by the addition of the R troop landing ship *Lumumba* and her cargo of patchwork corpses.

In the sky of the Independent Planet of N'Alabama the R troop landing ship *Lumumba* took position in a N'Haitian picket line. In stationary orbit *Lumumba* effectively hovered, day and night, the glare of NGC 7007 alternately appearing and disappearing from behind the red dirtball constantly below. On board, R troopers alternately watched watches and slumbered, nourished by minute quantities of hyperconcentrated food modules.

Ch'en-Gordon during one watch opened hir mouth to another R trooper, then a third, a fourth.

Hours later a glittering dart dropped from formation in the black sky over N'Alabama. Lower and lower its orbit dropped, the planetscape below slowly beginning to move forward as it rose and grew toward *Lumumba.* At an appropriate height above ground *Lumumba's* propulsors spurted briefly; her descent ceased. An orifice appeared in her hull and the familiar extensile cable, smooth, rounded and gray, dropped toward the surface of the planet.

At a selected point an R trooper hooked onto the cable, slid downward, halted momentarily just above the surface of N'Ala, then dropped silently into a nighted field.

The *Lumumba* continued across the planet, R troopers checking invasion maps against familiar landmarks, returning, returning to familiar farms, to villages and cities in every semiautonomous megacounty on the planet, to Abbeville and Albertville, Boaz and Bay Minette, to Citronelle, Carbon Hill, Dixiana, Eufaula, Goodwater, Huntsville, Jasper and Lipscomb and Letohatchie.

Ch'en-Gordon climbed down the cable at Letohatchie.

The first N'Alabamian Ch'en-Gordon approached looked once, double took, exclaimed—What the sheeit!—and drew a revolver. Ch'en-Gordon, hir reflexes slowed by the double consciousness of S'tscha and Man, was taken. Halfway to town, se found hirself riding the rest of the way in a whining patrol gyrocar. In the Letohatchie town jail se gazed out a barred window into a dusty square, contemplating something that might not have been a multiple-slot bicycle rack.

Interrogations produced no answers.

Se was locked up for the night, fed a bowl of slop and guarded by a deputy who slept in a chair at the end of the sparsely populated cell block. Hours later Ch'en-Gordon lay on hir cell floor, face to the bars, mouth open, tongue lolling on the cement floor. Slowly, almost imperceptibly, filaments grew, spiremes were thrust through the surface of hir tongue.

The sleeping guard snuffled in his sleep; his jaw dropped onto his chest as he began softly to snore.

Ch'en-Gordon hir spiremes lengthened. Se did not smile, but hir spiremes lengthened.

Before the guard wakened he betrayed his trust. Then he did not waken after all.

Ch'en-Gordon stepped past the dead guard, let hirself quietly out of the Letohatchie town jail, walked unhurriedly past the perhaps bicycle rack, making quietly for the less lighted and less frequented portion of Letohatchie familiar to the Gordon portion of hir personality.

Over the weeks that followed se lived unobtrusively in shadows, sleeping days in abandoned shacks, prowling nights in ill-lit alleys, preying on occasional stray citizens. From sleeping derelicts se learned, via filaments provided by hir Ch'en component, of the progress of N'Haiti's siege of N'Alabama. The Gordon component of hir duality was not pleased by what se learned.

Still, the Ch'en component remained aloof, unmotivated, devoted only to life and to experience, striving only at the command of some unobliterated instinct, to survive.

And Ch'en-Gordon hir N'Haitian conditioning settling over the two components, the S'tscha and the human, the spell of the *vodu*, the influences of the Goncourt treatments, the blended ancient memories of sparkling blue-green seas and red rut roads, nourishingly pervasive warm salinities and spacerine training, blended to produce a creature whose craft assured that survival, at least for the time being.

27. His Sweetheart's Loving Arms

Freddie checked his plaingrays, okays, some days anyways, brass buttons plain too (no star zm barz) buddy had his bentfin boomer on, polished up, proud of that, still a sign of exclusive prestige, helped a bit clearing dinner dishes, gave his roommate a farewell hug na little peck on full soft lips, a nice cheery friendly helpmeet, slightly chubby m perspirey blond Bayou La Batre boy, turned m got a nice cheery friendly little goose in response m started for work.

He closed the door behind him, gave it a quick locking, heard dear roomie do same inside, plus a slide bar latch, m started downstairs. Outside thugly wooden pile Freddie tooka looka either side tillie spied all clear (no fear), no gangies tubie scene. Offie stepped along the cracked m pitted sidewalk, lokina round, no gangies found, notta sound, flishing his hand-cranked flishlite. (Few anteek lampposts still standing, but who remembered what they were once for? Fyadone like dark carry a flishlight, bebay.)

Past pinkred B A R past Pigpeg's Pusspar (John Darn all garn) past EATS. Weapons shop close to stock-out, got only stickers left m boppers. Any what zaps, baps or whaps sold out just about. Self-wash surfery. Ononon. Military supplies gotta lotta craponie.

Letohatchie Noozan Sundried still there selling plenty boyboy books, prixpix, nookies bookies. Nooz? Fews. Not so big now, lookin like mimeo work: NIGRA GO HOME PAPADOCS GET OUT R SKY PISSFIRE WHERE R U NOW?

Y Bi Noozes? Headlines allasame allagame allasize allalize. Stick stick stick. So: Why nigra picket fleet up there constantly? Howcum spacerines demobed? Wassamatta Pissfire Pallbox, wassamatta Yancy Moorman, wassamatta Eugene Youngerman, things ben going from worse to worst laylyn Leto.

—Yech!—sayn Freddie napproachesiz place of employment.

Up the old ricketycricketys, through the old wooden with the cracked m taped stapaglass, into the back room m—Ello emcee.— —Ello Freddie,— —Ello emem,— —Ello Freddie,— —Ello boyzm band,— — Ello Freddie,— m outen plaingrays m inta costume m drinkadrink (not such great stuff these days but who was any more?) m peek out at the floorn see cussomers coming in now mostly chubby blond boys (no ladies visible but who could notarize that?) m soon very soon to work.

= = SHOW TIME! = =

After, out back door (avoid hostility, plate safe, mister emcee's disclaimer should work but who can be certain?) m stroll a bit (dangerous that but wudda hake, a man (mmm) garra live). Past PPPP couple times, tempin, tempin, but who got the price m besides, is that nice? Thinka sweet chubby little tubby from Bayou La Batre waiting at home, all snug in bed m waggin that head waiting for Freddie.

He takes a couple looks at the old pickets up there, first making a big circle with his eyes (many a fellerz fallen prey to desperadoes while gaping at the skies with his eyes) m then looking at them shipfeeding papadocs if looks could kill beggars would be risers you new. —Yech!— he sayn m goes tizzome.

A little fun there okay but shortish before sunrise poor old Bayou La Batre boy he's awakened by Freddie yobbeling iniz sleep. Freddie he yobbels for somebody, some old gyrene buddiepal Bayou La Batre boy don't catch no name m a little snubbelin m bubbelin m more yobbels from Freddie for this time Gordon somebody m poor Bayou La Batre boy he gets jealous. Freddie wakens up alone in bed, puzzled. That's a mought distressing.

And the morning and the evening were the (so who's counting?) day.

Freddie he worked nightly, wept slightly, kept sprightly up with B La B boy, bebay, so don't you surlymouth him, leesee stayed outen Pigpeg's (beside he couldn't afford it).

Manother night Freddie gets to work late. Late? Wait! Almost not at all. Crowds in Mane Street! Rumors! Shouts m fistfights! Summony crashes by accident (mmm?) threwa storefront. Sullenly everybody—spoosh!—into the store, onto the floor, back out the door m everybody got a new pair shoes, blue jeans, sweatshirts, wotnot.

Look! Uppina sky! Issa turd! Issa crane! Iss nigraships!

They been there too long. Nobody gets onta N'Alabama, nobody gets offa N'Alabama. Nigra pickets. Protest, protest! To (let us be correct, m?) whom? N'Ala's allies don't want to get involved. Hey gang, we all faw you! Zokkituum & Rossaruck! But we stain clean!

Rumors, rumors, yoladywarez bloomers! Where's old Pissfire Pallbox these days, where's old Yancy Moorman? Finally somebody pops outen City Hall wiffa nounce meant. It's, now this is serious, bebay, Leto's own beloved mayor, the white honorable Milburn Mitchum. Zez:

—Sizzens, sizzens, gotta make a big announcement. Word comen from N'Mongummy just now, just now. Old Gene Youngerman—Mayor Mitchum he turned his head m spat in the red dirt—been thrown out m placed under arrest for badfeasance m treason. Gomma be on trile right away. Meanwhile we gotta temporary provisional interim acting transitional gumt. Old Admiral Moorman, hez temporary provisional and et cetera governor of the independent planet of N'Alabama. Old General Pallbox, hez tempo cetera principal executive.

—Troops comen from old Fort Sealy Mae to help us keep order. Ah asken all sizzens telp, keep calm, maintain law norder. Now remember we got a primary election coming up in a few months so you all just remember who saw you through these trying days. Ah thank you.—

And he bowed, arms spread, yellow hair flopping over sweat-sticky forehead, and he turned around m went back into City Hall. (Near the old wormy moray eel.)

Crack your back, mac, who wouldn't be late for work! They lucky anybody even showed up to work, but customers were plentiful you can be certain, those Letohatchie sizzens weren't sure what was coming but they weren't going to let this night get past without a little fun just in case there wasn't any left to have later on.

Freddie, he was lucky to get out alive that night, so home to old tubby yellow-hair from Bayou La Batre m Freddie cried himself to sleep in his sweetheart's loving arms. (Look, bebay, you don't like that stuff, you go do it with an alligator or somebody, just make sure she's a lady, and Freddie m his pal, just leave them in the privacy of their bed.)

– Think we otter ask for terms? –

– What, knuckle under to the papadocs? –

– Ida lykit but face facts. –

– Trust Yancy. –

– It only gets worse. Gangs m riots, nota nuffood. –

– Pissfirell do summon. –

– What so far? –

– Welleez . . . –

– Tooken a whompin. Spacefleet's shot. Lost all them men. –

– Hey, you a . . . –

– Realist. –

– . . . nigrasucker! –

– Face facts! –

– Traitor!! –

– Face facts! –

– Lynchiz ass!!! –

– Face facts! –

– Get a rope!!!! –

– Face facts! –

– Over that, uh, wuchacallet, um, lamppost! –

– Face facts! –

– Uppy goes! –

– Fae *urk*! –

– Nigrasucker! –

– –
– Traitor! –
– –
– Right! –

Up, up goes a ragtag fleet of leftovers m rejects, cripples m trainers, cargo ships m normally unarmed couriers m whatever the hell old Moorman can scrape up carrying whatever the hell old Pallbox can scrape up and down it comes again in chunks & cinders & anybody survived the zap-bap crap uppa high turns to jelly when he hits ground as fast as those poor bastards hit it.

Couple hours later some old town shakes m breaks m that's the end of it. Probably it was Bayou La Batre but no matter really.

New gumt.

Up goes the leftovers of the leftovers, rejects of the rejects, spastics & amputees & idiots & tiny tots m down comes jusssst dusssst.

Fsssssss!

New gumt. They face facts.

Freddie wakened crying as usual. Somehow they missed him in both combouts but old Bayou La Batre boy, he didn't do so well, not so swell, one day troopers rang the bell, oh hell, ta-ta B La B b.

Now Freddie wakened crying. Well, nobody ever said it was all Jack Daniel's and cheesecake. Into the old plaingrays m off to work.

M now the old emcee was introducing the act. Boyzna band made a big thing plane *Digze,* heculan headbone hornist givena wow-wow-wow heren theren maracas brrrpin m drummer whanging m banging on the old whiteskins m now Freddie listened fruck you.

—Ladies m gentlemen, ladies m gentlemen—(some familiar faces m some unfamiliars out there tonight)—mespecially our honored guess from offworld—he made a little bow m fluttery movements wivviz hands, Freddie saw—zmai great pressure to welcome you to our little show, the finest in Leto m we believe sincerely one of the best on the hole (ahahaha) of N'Alabama.—

He taken a little swing around the floor looken at customers. Then—Mnow folks, sgreat pressure present the star are show, dancing for your sthetic ratification, Miss Merriass Markham!—

Rowna plause. Lights down. Music up.

Miss Merriass prances onstage to maraca scrucks m headbone honks, Freddie watches her through misty-dim eyes, sniffles a snuffle or two. Ah, Miss Merriass, she's a beauty as ever, maybe a few pounds heavier (most everybody else is lighter these days) but she still got that old swaying grace.

Those blond locks they're a tiny wee darker now, proximately space black one might sight, m that beaches me clean complexion getting fashionably otherwise these days, what with lossa sunning m certain pills thatter not exactly talked about too much but very very popular. Miss Merriass she's hardly no darker than most of the grinning tourists ringside, mind, but fashionable, fashionable, N'Ala ladies (don't split no hairs bebay) mostly all looking a wee bit suntanned these days to say the leastest.

Miss Merriass she stands there in her old costume, summat weather-beaten m ragged but still worth looking at m serviceable (that's the costume) (also Miss Merriass) m that stretchable halter with the cutouts *wooeee* how that must cut in but it does, it does draw the eye to those two openings wherein Miss Merriass demonstrates her devotion to the Way Things Are Today.

And panties, well, just dwell, rivet your attention on that lovely third dimension Miss Emem displays. Nudity? She's got it licked all holler, has Miss Merry.

Well she starts inta moving m the band starts inta zowwing m vooming m she starts inta swinging her shoulders around m they matcher in sound m Miss Merriass gizzema little bump m a snicker circles the dark audience m she gizzema little grind, watch that behind, m they find that sommenta cheer over m Miss Merry she calls out a couple squeaky-high questions (surprising still to sweet Freddie but what) m back come a couple answers, accented a bit yesss, but comprehensible enow m Freddie (doesn't this surprise?) actually blushes there backstage m Miss Merriass:

:gr-r-r-i-i-n-n-d-sem another grind, swinging those hips around m around, knees bent m spread m hands out somehow managing to gimmalittle titshow simultaneous m:

:*w-h-a-m!*:

:comes the bump you can see the heads jerk back like she smackedem every one square between the eyes with that old precious thump m before they recover Miss Merriass is turned around m doin something m *splook* that halter's gone m she's facingem again somehow bedecked m doing the ancient tassel trick a swinging m a swirling m the old tassels a twirling m up goes a big cheer (generous these tourists, with their praise; their money's another matter) m Miss Merriass keeps doing that trick for a while m then she somehow slips outen the tassels m tosses m to a couple front row Pierres clearly making do with local talent m lights off m music up m Merriass off-stage m emcee on m intermission m trine sell some caz-zappie booze m make a few rupees.

Nabackinna room behind patrons tables Miss Mer-riass spots as she's headed offstage one of them blood-curdling weirdoes you see nowna gain since the New Thing began: standing silent, lankblank hair hanging down, pasty-faced with dead-looking eyes m one hand, she can see, black as the space of aides and the other like the face m a spot of chest another shade, is this thing even a spade? It don' talk, it don' spend. But the New Visitors (to euphemize not excessively) have made it known, leave em lone.

She does.

Ch'en-Gordon slowly turned hir head, causing hir Gordon eyes to scan the room. Se moved slowly now, carefully: hir seams were sore, sore, movement was difficult, Gordon parts were slow to obey Ch'en com-mands, lying at times almost as if dead. At times Ch'en-Gordon had to swing a shoulder to move an arm and hand, flailing them as virtually inanimate ex-tensions of hirself.

In the dimness and wafting smoke se saw tables of black men and women, those farthest to the front of the room, and couples mixed, the white, whether man or woman, seeming subservient, eager to curry favor of the other, and in the back, farthest from the show space, a few, few tables of N'Alabamian natives ner-vously darting glances at the backs of the blacks.

At one table in the front row a N'Haitian in casual dress leisurely draws a small pipe from one pocket, a small glassine envelope from another and begins to pack the bowl of the pipe with fine greenish shreds from the glassine envelope.

His companion, a black girl in fashionable striped trousers, a rough leathern bag hanging between her glistening breasts, reaches forward and touches his hand. He spurts a flame into the bowl of his pipe, in a moment Ch'en-Gordon sees gray-blue cloudlets rise; the man holds the pipe for the black girl who bends to draw on it, her naked breasts resting on his arm.

She leans back smiling; both looking around the room, expressions of scorn appearing as their eyes encounter the N'Alabamians in the rear.

Ch'en-Gordon, pain and weakness in every seam, locks eyes for an instant with the man. Transfers attention to the girl. Back to the man. Something se sees, something se recognizes.

Pain crying from every part, Ch'en-Gordon lurches between tables, falls to macroknees, elbows resting on the table of the two blacks. Se looks into eyes of the man, hir mouth opens and shuts trying to cry for aid, for aid from him who alone can provide it. He looks pityingly, uncomprehendingly. Se turns to the girl, mutely appealing. She draws back.

Se falls forward, hir head lolls on the fakewood table. Se moans, hir mouth falling open, tongue lolling, spiremes emerging, writhing, screaming mutely to speak, to be understood, to be aided.

Rejection antibodies dance, swirl, rush joyously.

Ch'en-Gordon falls from the fakewood table, clatters onto the floor, seams opening, dark fluids rushing out and spreading under the table.

The man shoves his pipe into his pocket, takes his companion, her face buried in his coat, quickly from the room.

Backstage Miss Merriass Markham pisses m moans a little m she starts into her other costume, Freddie helping. Half-dressed Miss Merriass sits down m supplements her pills with a little body makeup m Freddie checks himself all out thinking instamoneously of some oddo guy he thinks he remembers seeing in this very club once very long ago but now Miss Merriass finishes with her costume m now theykn hear the music coming up again m listen, listen, here's Mister Emcee's voice:

:—A dramatic interpretation ladies m gentlemen, music m drama m dance combine to present a traditional reenactment m again we prowly present Miss Emem—:

:plite plaws m a drumroll m Merriass she steps onstage again m a purebrite spangspot spangs onta her, dark tresses swaying m shining, dark skin soft looking m ladylike in a somewhat revealing dashiki red m blue m yellow m green m out she strolls m around she rolls, music clipping m pipping m Miss Merriass she makes it look fine m then it's Freddie's cue m lie:

:slithers onstage wearing traditional N'Alabamian dress (civvies) m wivviz hairnskin a bit lightern natural m Miss Merriass she struts about m Freddie he slinks after hern suddenly:

:*wham!*:

:Freddie springs m Miss Merriass she shrieks m Freddie grabs m Miss Merriass she struggles m Freddie he gets a hand down the backa Miss Markham's special breakaway costume m:

:*rip!*:

:it does, m Miss Markham she struggles shamilly to cover upper big fat boobs but Freddie:

:(on cue) growls m slobbers m rips m suddenly, music thumping m roaring, spangspot bobbing m audience throbbing they freeze in a tableau:

:Miss Merriass Markham standing there feet apart

hands on hips naked m black in the spotlight, head thrown back, black hair glistening (light roots showing just a little) here m there, wherever one wishes to point the orbs, bare ass aquivering waiting for the tableau to break while:

:Freddie, plane his role to the hilt, the N'Alabamian animan crouched m slobbering, fingers like claws reaching for the pure black flesh of that noble figure m the only sound in the deathy club is now Freddie:

:sobbing:

:m *crack!* goes the drummer m *mrow-wow-ow* the heculan headboner joins m the tableau breaks as Freddie leaps forward but Miss Merriass has something startling what is it what can that be something lookie, lookie, curling around one leg, follow with your eye bebay around, around the sweet soft fleshy thigh, making a thick underline for that classy ass of hers, around through the crotch (ooh, that's smart!) m around the leg onetc more, looping around, ass-crotch-thigh-ass-crotch-thigh m after a certain number of revolutions coming from behind sozeta protrude horizontally forward from that delightful lady's pubes this *handle,* some half a foot long give or take a couple centimeters m about as thick as a baby's ankle m made of hard rubber m ridged, sozeta offer a good grip:

:m Miss Markham stares down that crouching beast for the few seconds as it takes to unwind that thing from around her leg m pulling forward on the handle it follows from between her legs m she raises it high in the spangspot m there's another roll of drums m Freddie:

:*yowls!*:

:m the drummer gives a loud *ktakk*!:

:m Miss Markham's whip gives a *crack*!:

:m Freddie *howls* (it's part of the act, right, but Miss Merriass do you gotta make it so *real*!) m grovels m:

:the whip comes m:

:Freddie writhes m:

:the whip comes m:

:Freddie screams m:

:the whip comes m:

:Freddie falls tooz knees m:

:the whip comes m:

:Freddie grovels m:

:Miss Merriass gizzim just one nice thunk wivver naked foot m:

:stagelights down, houselights up, actors off, emcee on, waiters move, business goes, music plays, money circulates m:

:life is sure not much fun for Freddie, but what the hell, everybody hasta earn a living, don't they?

28. Each on the Cheek

He may have dozed and seen into the Dreamtime, for he saw the figures of Miralaidj and her father Wuluwaid floating in a vague jumble of shapes and slow, wavering movement. Jiritzu opened his eyes and saw little Bidjiwara lower herself through the hatchway into the cabin, white ropesoled shoes first, white duck trousers clinging close to her long, skinny legs and narrow hips. Then her black, ribbed sweater.

"Our ship has no name," she said.

He pondered for a moment, shrugged, said, "Does it need one?"

"It would be—somehow I think we would be more with our people," Bidjiwara replied.

"Well, if you wish. What shall we name her?"

She looked into his face. "You have no choice?"

"None."

"We will truly sail on the great tide? On the Rainbow Serpent?"

"We are already."

"Then I would call our ship after the sacred fish. Let it bear us to the Dreamtime."

"*Baramundi.*"

"Yes."

"As you wish."

She came and sat by him, her hands folded in her lap. She sat silently.

"Food is ready," he said.

She looked at the tiny table that served in the lighter as workspace, desk, and dining table. Jiritzu saw her smile, wondered at the mixture in her face of little child and wise woman. She looked somehow as he thought the Great Mother must look, if only he believed in the Great Mother.

Bidjiwara crossed the small distance and brought two thin slices of hot biscuit. She held them both to Jiritzu. He took one, pressed the other back upon her.

Silently they ate the biscuit.

Afterward she said, "Jiritzu, is there more to do now?"

He said, "We should check our position." He undogged the ship's telescope and carried it to the deck of *Baramundi*.

Bidjiwara helped him to mount it on the gimballed base that stood waiting for it. Jiritzu sighted on the brightest star in Yirrkalla for reference—it was a gleaming crimson star that marked the end of a fang in the serpent face, that Yurakosian tradition called Blood of Hero.

On the barrel of the telescope where control squares were mounted he tapped all of the radiational sensors into life, to cycle through filters and permit the eyepiece to observe the Rainbow Serpent by turns under optical, radio, x-ray, and gamma radiation.

He put his eye to the eyepiece and watched the Serpent as it seemed to move with life, its regions responding to the cycling sensitivity of the telescope.

He drew away and Bidjiwara put her eye to the telescope, standing transfixed for minutes until at last she too drew away and turned to Jiritzu.

"The Serpent truly lives," she said. "Is it—a real creature?"

Jiritzu shook his head. "The tides of the galaxies draw each other. The Serpent is matter flowing. Stars, dust, gas. To ride with it would mean a journey of billions of years, to reach the next of its kind. To sail the starwinds that fill the Rainbow Serpent, we will reach marvelous speed. As long as we can sail our craft, we can tack from wind to wind.

"And once we have gone to the Dreamtime, *Baramundi* will float on, on the tide, along the Rainbow Serpent. Someday she may beach on some distant shore."

He looked at Bidjiwara and smiled.

Bidjiwara said, "And if she does not?"

"Then she may be destroyed in some way, or simply—drift forever. Forever."

Jiritzu saw the girl stretch and yawn. She crossed the cabin and drew him down alongside the bulkhead, nestled up to him and went to sleep.

He lay with her in his arms, wondering at her trust, watching the play of sidereal light that reflected through the hatchway and illuminated her face dimly.

He extended one finger and gently, gently traced the *maraiin* on her cheek, wondering at its meaning. He pressed his cheek to the top of her head again, pulled away her knitted cap and let her hair tumble loosely, feeling its softness with his own face, smelling the odor of her hair.

He too slept.

They awoke together, stirring and stretching, and looked into each other's faces and laughed. They used the lighter's sanitary gear, and nibbled a little breakfast and went on deck. Together they checked *Baramundi's* rigging, took sightings with her multiradiational telescope and fed information into her little computer.

The computer offered course settings in tiny, glowing display lights and Jiritzu and Bidjiwara reset *Baramundi's* sails.

They sat on deck, bathed in the perpetual twilight of the Rainbow Serpent's softly glowing colors.

They spoke of their childhoods on Yurakosi, of the old people, their skins whited out by years of sailing the membrane ships, retired to the home planet to raise the children while all of the race's vigorous adults crewed the great ships, sailed between the stars carrying freight and occasional passengers sealed inside their hulls, laughing at the clumsy craft and clumsy crews of all others but the Aranda and the Kunapi.

They climbed through the rigging of *Baramundi*, shinnying up masts lightly, balancing on spars, occasionally falling—or leaping—from the ship's heights, to drop gently, gently back onto her deck.

They ate and drank the smallest amounts they could of the lighter's provisions, tacitly stretching the supplies as far as they could be stretched, carefully recycling to add still more to the time they could continue.

They lay on *Baramundi's* deck sometimes, when the rest time they had agreed upon came, Bidjiwara nestling against the taller Jiritzu, falling asleep as untroubledly as a young child, Jiritzu wondering over and over at this girl who had come to die with him, who asked few questions, who lived each hour as if it were the beginning of a long and joyous life rather than the final act of their play.

Jiritzu felt very old.

He was nearly twenty by the ancient, arbitrary scale of age carried to the star worlds from O'Earth, the scale of the seasons and the years in old Arnhem Land in the great desert of their ancestral home. Six years older than Bidjiwara, he had traveled the star routes for five, had sailed the membrane ships across tens of billions of spans in that time.

And Bidjiwara asked little of him. They were more playmates than—anything else, he thought.

"Tell me of El-Kumarbis," she said one day, perched high on a spar above *Baramundi's* deck.

"You know all about him," Jiritzu replied.

"Where is he now?"

Jiritzu shrugged, exasperated. "Somewhere beyond Al-ghoul, no one knows where. He was buried in space."

"What if we find his body?" Bidjiwara shivered.

"Impossible."

"Why?"

"In all of space? What chance that two objects moving at random will collide?"

"No?"

He shook his head.

"Could the computer find him?"

He shrugged. "If we knew exactly when he was buried, and where, and his trajectory and speed and momentum . . . possibly."

"Dinner time," she said. "You wait here, I'll fix it."

She came back with the customary biscuits and a jar filled with dark fluid. Jiritzu took the jar, held it high against the ambient light—they seldom used any of *Baramundi's* power lights.

"Wine," Bidjiwara said.

He looked amazed.

"I found a few capsules in the ship's supplies. You just put one in some water."

They ate and drank. The wine was warm, its flavor

soft. They sprawled on the deck of *Baramundi* after the biscuits were gone, passing the jar back and forth, slowly drinking the wine.

When it was gone Bidjiwara nestled against Jiritzu; for once, instead of sleeping she lay looking into his face, holding her hands to the sides of his head.

She said his name softly, then flicked off her radio and pressed her lips close to his neck so their air envelopes were one, the sound carried directly from her lips to his ear, and whispered his name again.

"Bidjiwara," he said, "you never answered why you came on board *Baramundi.*"

"To be with Jiritzu," she said.

"Yes, but why? Why come to be with me—to die with me!"

"Tall Jiritzu," she said, "strong, beautiful Jiritzu. You saw me always aboard *Djanggawul,* you were kind to me but as you are kind to children. Men never know, only women know about love."

He laughed, not cruelly. "You're only—"

"A woman," she said.

"And you want—?"

Now she laughed at him. "You man, you mighty man. You do not understand that all men are the children of women."

She drew away from him, slid her black ribbed sweater over her head and dropped it to the deck.

He said, "But—you are Kunapi. I am Aranda."

Bidjiwara laughed again. "Great Mother will forgive that." She held a hand toward him, her skin black against the white of her sailor's ducks.

He put his hands onto her naked back, trembling, then slowly slid them around her, touching her little, half-developed breasts, fondling her soft nipples with his hands.

She buried her forehead in the side of his neck, whispered against his throat, "For this, Jiritzu, I came to die with you for this."

He ran his thumbs down her breastbone, down her belly to her navel. He put his hands to the top of her white trousers and pulled them away and down, and took her.

And the next day they were nearly out of biscuit and they went onto half rations to make their supply last longer.

They played children's games, shouting and chasing each other up and down the lighter's masts.

They leaped and sailed from the decks, past the membrane sails, into emptiness, then hung for a moment and fell back, gently, to *Baramundi.*

Jiritzu leaped too hard, too high, and feared that he had broken from the ship. He looked up—down—into the coils of the Rainbow Serpent. He felt himself revolving slowly, helplessly hanging in the emptiness, alone and unshielded except by the close air his generator made and the protection of the pigment he carried in his skin.

He thought to cry for help, then held back. If he was afloat, Bidjiwara could not help him. He turned slowly, facing toward *Baramundi,* her membranes bellied with stellar wind, her deck reflecting the lights of the Serpent; he could not see Bidjiwara.

He turned slowly, facing toward the Rainbow Serpent, feeling as if he could fall forever into its colored bands, its long coils stretching no lesser distance than the span between galaxies.

He turned slowly, revolving on the axis of his own body, feeling no motion himself but watching the stars and the Serpent and *Baramundi* the sacred fish revolving slowly around him, wheeling, wheeling, when—his outflung arm struck an object as hard and cold as the ultimate ice of a deadstar world.

He recoiled, spun involuntarily, stared.

It was—yes.

He looked back toward *Baramundi*, revolved using his own limbs as counterweights, placed himself between the corpse and the lighter and pressed gently with the soles of his ropesoled shoes, against the hard, frigid corpse.

Slowly he drifted back toward *Baramundi*—and, wheeling again as he drifted, saw the corpse drifting away, upward or downward into the lights of the Rainbow Serpent.

As he approached *Baramundi* he pondered whether or not to tell Bidjiwara of his find. Finally he told her—the incredible happenstance had occurred.

Later they crept to the farthermost deck for their loving, then back into the tiny cabin to sleep.

And soon *Baramundi's* supplies were exhausted, and still Jiritzu and Bidjiwara continued. Their water remained, and a few of the capsules. They had wine from time to time. They gave less effort to running the ship, ceased to play in the rigging, ceased to leap.

The wound in Jiritzu's leg resumed its throbbing intermittently. He would rub it, or Bidjiwara would rub it for him, and the pain would ease.

They made love, it seemed, with increasing frequency. The sensations of their couplings seemed to increase as lack of nourishment drew their bodies ever tighter, ever more acutely into awareness of each other.

They lay together most of the time, seldom dressing fully.

They drank water only, their wine capsules exhausted.

They slept increasingly.

In *Baramundi's* cabin Jiritzu fed telescopic data into the lighter's computer, read the responses displayed on its little illuminated screen. After the acclimatization of his eyes to none but sidereal light, even the glowing miniature digits were dazzling: his eyes pulsed with afterimages for minutes following the exercise.

It was difficult to climb from the cabin back onto the deck.

Bidjiwara waited for him there, barefooted, sitting on the deck with her wrists clasped around her knees, wearing only her white trousers and black knitted cap. She smiled a welcome to him, asked a question wordlessly.

"Here," he shrugged. "Here is where we are. As we have been. Riding the Rainbow Serpent. Riding the tide. Sailing the starwinds."

He felt dizzy for a moment, reached out with one hand to steady himself against the telescope mount, then sank to a squat beside Bidjiwara.

She put her arms around him and he lay on the deck, his head in her lap. He looked up into her face. She was Bidjiwara the lovely child, Miralaidj her Aranda half, she was Jiritzu's own mother on Yurakosi, the Great Mother.

He opened and closed his eyes, unable to tell which woman this was.

He reached and traced the *maraiin* on her cheek.

She nodded, began speaking softly, telling him the meaning of the scarifications.

When she had finished he took her hand, held it against his chest and slowly told her the meaning of his own *maraiin.* He spoke with closed eyes, opened them when he felt a drop of wetness, saw her weeping softly, drew her face down to his own to kiss.

She lay down beside him and they embraced gently, then both slept.

After that they paid less attention to *Baramundi's* needs. Jiritzu and Bidjiwara grew weaker. They confined their activity to occasional short walks on *Baramundi's* decks. Both of them grew thinner, lighter. Their growing weakness seemed almost to be offset by the decreasing demands of the ship's artificial gravity.

They lay on deck for hours, watching the glow of the Rainbow Serpent. They were far beyond the Serpent's head now, the stars of Yirrkalla clustered now into a meaningless sparkling jumble far, far astern of *Baramundi.*

Jiritzu was awake, had taken a sparse sip of their little remaining water, left Bidjiwara to doze where she lay, her hair a mourning wreath circling her emaciated features. Jiritzu made his way unsteadily to the prow of *Baramundi,* bracing himself against masts and small stanchions as he walked.

He sighted through the ship's telescope, enjoying in a faint, detached manner the endless kaleidoscopic changes of the Rainbow Serpent's multiradiational forms. At length he turned away from the scope and looked back toward Bidjiwara. He could not tell if she was breathing. He could not tell for a certainty who she was.

He returned to the telescope, tapped its power squares to cause it to superimpose its multiple images rather than run them in sequence. He gazed raptly at the Serpent for a time, then swung the scope overhead, sweeping back and forth across the sky above *Baramundi.*

He settled on a black speck that floated silhouetted against the glow of the Serpent. For a while he watched it grow larger.

He turned from the telescope back to the deck of the lighter. Bidjiwara had wakened and risen; she was walking slowly, slowly toward him.

In the glow of the Rainbow Serpent her emaciation was transformed to a fine perception that etched every line, every muscle beneath her skin. She wore sweater and trousers; Jiritzu could see her high breasts, the ribbed sweater conforming to their sharp grace, her nipples standing as points of reference to the beauty of her torso.

Her white trousers retained their fit. Jiritzu discerned the lines of her thighs, the pubic swell over her crotch.

Her face, always thin, now seemed all vertical planes, forehead and temple, nostril and cheek. The ridges of her brows, the lines of her mouth were drawn.

Her eyes had gained a bright intensity.

As she crossed the deck to Jiritzu she gained in strength and steadiness.

She held her hands toward him, smiling, and he felt his own strength returning to him. He came to her, reached and took her hands, clasped them in his. They embraced, calling each other's names.

The dark figure of Elyun El-Kumarbis dropped onto the deck of *Baramundi*. He strode to Jiritzu and Bidjiwara.

"Lovers!" he said. "Sky heroes!"

They turned to him, arms still around each other. Each extended a hand to him, felt his: cold, cold.

"All my years," the O'Earther said, "I wanted nothing but to sail a membrane ship. To be a sky hero."

"Yes," Jiritzu said, "you are known to all sky heroes, Elyun El-Kumarbis. Your fame spans the galaxy."

"And where do you sail, sky heroes?"

"We sail the tide, we sail the Rainbow Serpent."

"Aboard your ship?"

"*Baramundi* has brought us this far, but no farther. It is fit now for us to return to the Dreamtime."

Elyun El-Kumarbis nodded. "May I—may I greet you as brother and sister sky heroes?" he asked.

"Yes," answered Jiritzu, and "Yes," answered Bidjiwara.

Elyun El-Kumarbis kissed them each on the cheek, on the *maraiin* scarifications of each. And his kiss was cold.

Full of strength Jiritzu and Bidjiwara leaped to the spars of *Baramundi*'s highest mast, scrambled up lines to the topmost spar of the lighter.

They looked back at Elyun El-Kumarbis, who stood wondering beside the ship's telescope.

They took each other's hands, dropped into place on the topmost spar and together sprang with the full strength of their sky heroes' legs, toughened and muscled by years of training in the rigging of membrane ships.

They flew up from the spar, up from *Baramundi* the sacred fish, and looking back saw the fish flip his tail once in farewell.

They peered ahead into the Rainbow Serpent, saw it writhe toward the far galaxies, heard its hissing voice urging, welcoming them.

They laughed loudly, loudly, feeling strength, warmth and joy. They plunged on and on, skimming the tide of the Rainbow Serpent, feeling the strength of the Aranda, of all Yurakosi, all sky heroes mighty in their blood.

They threw their arms around each other, laughing for joy, and sped to the Rainbow Serpent, to the galaxies beyond the galaxies, to the Dreamtime forever.

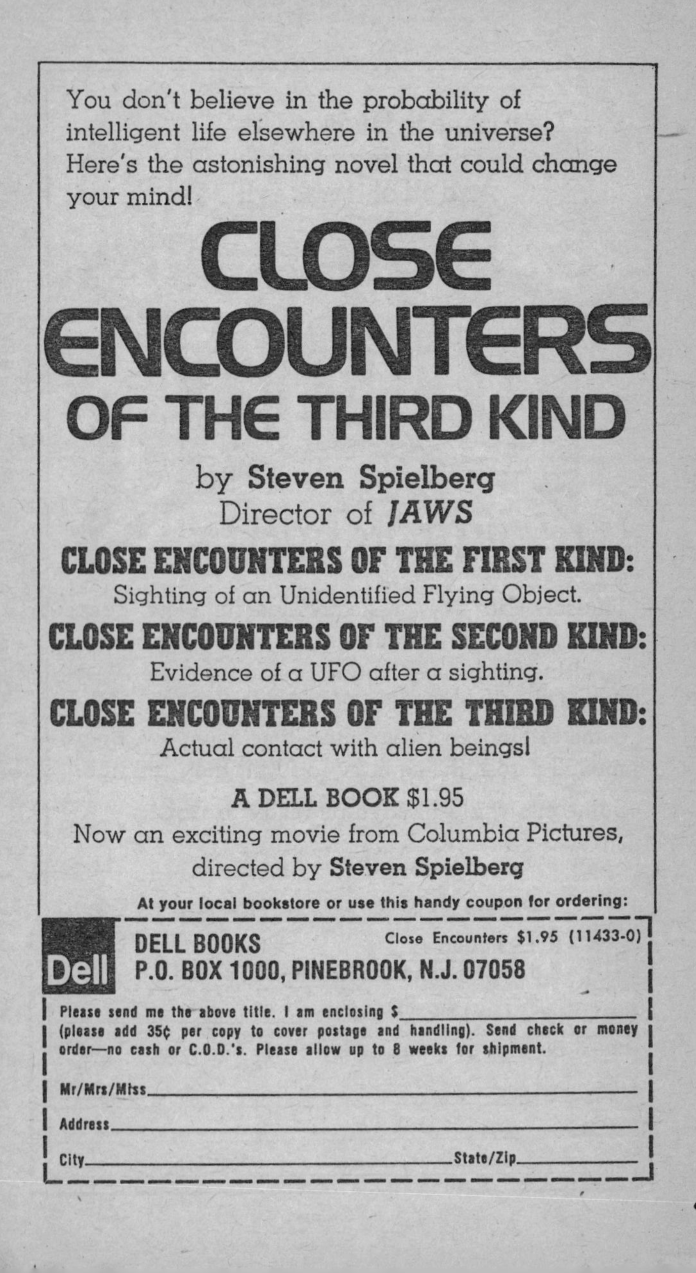
You don't believe in the probability of intelligent life elsewhere in the universe? Here's the astonishing novel that could change your mind!
CLOSE ENCOUNTERS OF THE THIRD KIND
by Steven Spielberg
Director of JAWS
CLOSE ENCOUNTERS OF THE FIRST KIND:
Sighting of an Unidentified Flying Object.
CLOSE ENCOUNTERS OF THE SECOND KIND:
Evidence of a UFO after a sighting.
CLOSE ENCOUNTERS OF THE THIRD KIND:
Actual contact with alien beings!
A DELL BOOK $1.95
Now an exciting movie from Columbia Pictures, directed by Steven Spielberg
At your local bookstore or use this handy coupon for ordering:
Dell
DELL BOOKS
P.O. BOX 1000, PINEBROOK, N.J. 07058
Close Encounters $1.95 (11433-0)
Please send me the above title. I am enclosing $
(please add 35¢ per copy to cover postage and handling). Send check or money order—no cash or C.O.D.'s. Please allow up to 8 weeks for shipment.
Mr/Mrs/Miss
Address
City
State/Zip